She's the Girl

Susan M. Brooks

small dogs

press

A Small Dogs Press book
Seal Beach, California

She's the Girl. Copyright © 2004 by Susan M. Brooks. All rights reserved. No part of this publication may be used or reproduced in any manner whatsoever without written permission, except in the case of brief quotations embodied in critical articles and reviews. For further information, please contact the publisher.

Published by Small Dogs Press,
P.O. Box 4127, Seal Beach, CA 90740.

www.smalldogspress.com
info@smalldogspress.com

LCCN: 2003104746

ISBN 0-9729329-2-5

This book is dedicated to everyone who's ever taught me anything about love.

Acknowledgements

Special thanks to Jenna, John, and Amanda for their support; and to Liz Burton, for her editing expertise.

Special acknowledgements go to all the artists whose music and lyrics inspired me and kept me going when I had so many more interesting things to do than sit down and write. Their words and music provided the soundtrack to the ideas in my head, and without that inspiration, it would have been much harder (and taken much longer) to get to where I wanted to go. My favorites for this book include: Mel Carter, Leonard Cohen, Bob Dylan, Billie Holliday, k.d. lang, Van Morrison, Sade, Sixpence None the Richer, Wings, Stevie Wonder, and to all the others who helped put me in the right mood at the right time.

Hey to my constant companions: Gracie, Buzz and Lola. And love always to Stiggy, my best bud.

She's the Girl

Though she's the girl, I am the one who's shy;

And though she walks with heavy hips, it's I

Who cannot move for heaviness, and she

Who is the woman: but the coward, me.

She is the one with high and swelling breast,

But I the one with weariness oppressed.

Clearly, in her casual factors lie,

But the effects in me. I wonder why!

--Amaru (5th century)
Translated by John Brough

one

Natalie loved love, and would have rather found herself in love than in a relationship.

It wasn't that relationships were really terrible things; it was just that Nat's were really terrible things. The shift from love to relationship—from *these are my possibilities* to *this is my reality*—came abruptly and irrevocably. Usually while watching him dress, or eat, or sleep, or doing any of the other things one could expect to watch him do the same way for the next fifty-plus years.

Love has definite rules: If you love me you do these things.

Relationships have no rules. In fact, they discourage rules; what succeeds one week will fail miserably the next.

And so it became the anticipation of love's arrival, like a fix, in which she found her thrill. In Nat's experience, possibility held more promise than reality, that sad moment when two, expecting to find themselves blissfully conjoined in love, discover themselves instead in relationship.

It was for Possibility alone that Nat set out one morning to Ruune, North Dakota, two thousand miles northeast of Los Angeles, where a high school sweetheart was now living. Once there, on his doorstep, once in his arms, she would recapture the romance, the love, out of which she had spent the whole of her adult life feeling gypped.

A sudden decision, some friends would say; others, a gamble. It came less than a month after her thirty-fifth birthday, the evening spent with Paul, the man she thought she might love. Somewhere between her making a wish and blowing out the candles, he had gazed at her soulfully across the Black Forest birthday cake and announced, like a dare, "You know, my therapist thinks I'm in love with you."

With that statement was pissed away the latest in a string of disappointing relationships, all of them having at one time or another disguised themselves as love. It was a turning point in Nat's life, aside from the thirty-five candles.

Nat's earliest exposure to and infatuation with love came at an early age, listening to her parents in the kitchen, in the living room, in the market—fighting, arguing, having a relationship. As often as possible, she would escape to her grandparents' rambling, romantic Craftsman, where she would sit in their living room, nestled in the comfy chair opposite the sofa, and watch her grandparents...in love. Both of them at least eighty, they had been together forever, and that is how she heard them jealously described by aunts, uncles, and others: "Christ, those two have been together forever!" While drama and dysfunction, while relationships plagued the rest of the neighborhood, including her parents, Nat would enjoy the sight of these relics—cuddling on the sofa, holding hands that were wrinkled and flecked with liver spots but remained supple and moist. The living room, normally subdued by the company of family came alive when inhabited by these two ancient things. Their coos,

(I love you sugar)

an enduring allegiance that somehow never lost its meaning, falling into nearly deaf ears. Tender kisses blown with cool, limp lips while the rest of the family complained, "Jesus, in front of the children?"

Ahh, love.

When Nat was eleven, her parents divorced, her father having taken up with some bleached blonde in a tatty apartment on the far side of the San Gabriel Valley. Nat, her brothers and mother sold their family home and went to live with her grandparents in the rambling Craftsman to which Nat had escaped so many Sunday afternoons from the relationship that ultimately destroyed her faith.

The summer of her twelfth year, accompanying her eldest brother, then sixteen, as he messengered threats between her mother and father, Nat spent most of her time dreaming of ponies in a pasture and basking vicariously in the love of her grandparents. She loved the smell of mentholated balm that wafted through the house and settled onto her shoulders and in her hair, the smell that never did wash out.

She loitered in the wide hallway outside their bedroom, sliding her bare feet over the cool floors and leaning back against the wall, where her bony elbows knocked against the polished woodwork. She would, when the door was left ajar, peek into the privacy of their room, that mysterious place to which they retired every night.

They would nap in the afternoon, and Nat would spy on them while they slept. Her grandfather in a thin white undershirt and baggy trousers, suspenders loosened and strung limply across his hips. Her grandmother—so fragile, in a thin cotton housedress that she never wore outside of her own room—spooned against her husband's massive chest as she slept through the afternoon. Nat would watch them until it was time to deliver another message or note or demand for payment of some kind. Money, attention, apologies—always something was needed, always something was missing.

The next summer came her own first real taste of love, the one that all girls wait for, the one to whom every boy afterward will be compared. Crouched in the hot, breezeless shack nestled between the garage on the left and a cinderblock wall on the right, bordered in back by a narrow, dangerous alley and in front by a tidy vegetable garden her grandmother had nurtured. There, where the lawnmower lay still and insect poison was kept in Mason jars, a neighbor boy's hand up her shirt, her first real boyfriend, a boy with blond wavy hair and lazy eyes. He was nearly sixteen and would have been beaten back to twelve had Nat's brothers discovered what they'd been doing. What a glorious introduction to love—hearing the workbench rattle beneath their weight as he deftly introduced her to Possibility.

That day, as the hour grew late and the scent of jasmine came through on a warm Santa Ana, Nat heard her mother's voice, distant and surreal, calling her home. Against the wall, beside the smudged window and out of sight should anyone peek in, they kissed with tight, pressed lips and grappled in the diminishing light; and Nat found the glory of love amongst the hedge clippers and a family of daddy-long-legs. They stayed till way after dark, enjoying what she knew even then to be love at its most potent, its most persuasive.

He told her good-bye, and she watched him disappear down the alley. She spent the next two weeks in giddy, frightful anticipation of what he might ask her to do the next time; but he quickly forgot about their afternoon of love and moved on to an older, more sophisticated girl of fifteen who was rumored to be getting a car for her next birthday. He was gone for good, and she was left with not the slightest inkling this tender introduction would become just another nostalgic bit to tell other lovers.

That summer, while playing baseball on her grandparents' street with her brothers and her only friends, boys from the neighborhood they knew, Nat looked up to see her grandmother wander out onto the porch in her housedress.

Nat dropped the pop fly that should have been a cinch to catch, and dropped her glove as well.

Her grandmother teetered down the front steps and wove her way across the lawn toward Nat, mouthing her name softly.

("Natty ... Natty ...")

As the other kids instinctively backed away, Nat moved toward her grandmother; and as she wrapped her arms around her tiny frame she caught sight of the gaping front door, beyond which she was sure was some very bad news.

"Grandpa," Nat whispered as her brothers ran up the front steps, two at a time, and her grandmother collapsed into her arms.

In the house, her grandfather lay still, like he was napping, on the chenille bedspread; and when the ambulance came, the family crowded the widow into the center cushion of the sofa, as if trying to squeeze into a family portrait. It was the end of Nat's summer of love, and she wouldn't even know it for decades to come.

Autumn came; and the long evenings were spent at home, watching television and struggling with algebra. There were more boys, more clandestine meetings that eventually became real dates. She was a prolific dater in junior high, where in eighth grade she racked up a total of nine boyfriends. None of them was as memorable as her geography teacher, a dreamy man with a bushy brown moustache and feathered hair she simply could not keep her eyes off of.

It didn't take Nat long to learn that boys her age were not interested in love, but only in girls who knew how to French kiss and who were not so attached to their tight white panties. Anticipation, however, always proved to be the real thrill, and each failed experience was felt more acutely than the last. Inheriting a girl's love legacy—one of self-doubt and self-recrimination—she tried desperately to grasp wisps of sense from the mysteries of a boy's mind.

Nothing could ever compare to hiding out in the hallway and knowing the smell of balm that wafted in from her grandparents' bedroom. Nothing like the smell of pesticides and the feel of a spider on the back of her neck to remind her of the time when she had not yet learned love's limitations. Nearly twenty years later—twenty years comprising seven boyfriends, one premature identity crisis, no children, and total estrangement from her mother—Nat would, upon hearing that voice on her answering machine

(Hello, Nat! It's Guy...)

recall the details of her last, best love and allow herself to fall foolishly, madly, and completely in love. All over again.

＊   ＊   ＊

Heading north on Interstate 15, just past the interchange where the 10 splits off and disappears into the low desert, Nat caught sight of a cute red convertible as it passed her on the right. She'd first noticed it approaching too fast in her rearview mirror; but before she could move out of the way, it swerved sharply into the number-two lane, the driver flipping her the bird out the window as he sped away.

Just two weeks had passed since her thirty-fifth birthday—the first spent in that miserable after-love stupor that usually resulted in an expensive variation on some celebrity haircut and a temporary vow of celibacy. During the second she reorganized closets, cupboards, shelves, and drawers, as if the elusive answers to all of love's toughest questions were hidden there behind the eyelash curlers that were never used, perhaps, or the shoes that never did wear in. She made a donation of four bulging bags of old clothing to the Salvation Army but no new discoveries about the meaning of life.

It was at the end of the second week things took an abrupt turn for the better, when she received the phone call that would change everything, that would set her on the path to love-success. That would set her on the road to Ruune.

Ruune, North Dakota, where her last, best love

(Hello, Nat! It's Guy...)

had been keeping himself all these years since high school.

Guy: The one who got away. Technically, the one who was put away. He was a year ahead of her in high school. He was a god. Loved and admired by everyone, he dated the kind of girls who could only be described as "fresh." The kind who always smelled like they'd just showered, whose hair was never frizzy or flat. Unlike Nat and her friends, mere mortals bound by the laws of adolescence, Fresh Girls could wear white jeans and never walk down the hall to whispered giggles and smirks behind their backs because they had sat in some goo.

Nat had watched in abject envy as the Fresh Girls got

better grades, better boys, better seats in the lunch area. Fresh Girls got Guy.

At least, they did until the day when the world stopped making sense, the day that Guy asked Nat if she'd like to go out sometime. She did, and they did, and they fell in love...sort of.

Never really in any danger of becoming a Fresh Girl herself—her close-cropped, unruly red hair exactly the sort that might entangle a boy's stubby, inexperienced fingers; her bony, boyish figure not the right shape; and her awkward, self-conscious small talk having nothing to do with what shoes go with that bag—Nat nonetheless raised the bar in her crowd by dating Guy for three torrid weeks.

To the student body, to her friends and brothers, but most of all, to the Fresh Girls, the pairing of Guy and Nat was stupefying. It was like the lines in the sand had been redrawn when nobody was looking, like years of high school Darwinian dating politics were suddenly being challenged by this strange new monkey. But to Nat it didn't have to make sense. It was simply meant to be, and that was good enough for her.

All that ended less than a month later, when Guy tried to kill himself by jumping out of a speeding car. What made this feat so magnificent and so enduring in the legend of their youth was that he had been driving the car himself, and in one grand gesture opened the door and leapt to the pavement. The California Highway Patrol estimated his car had been traveling at least eighty miles an hour.

There was some debate afterward as to whether a suicide attempt, by definition intentional, could be described as "freak," but those were the words people used when telling the story

(That boy had gone off and tried to kill himself in a freak suicide)

She never could imagine how someone could do such a thing, and prompted by crisis counselors and freaked-out parents who met in the evenings and demanded answers from administrators, that was all anybody wanted to talk about. They'd stop her in the cafeteria...

("*How* could he do such a thing?")

and in the gym...

("How *could* he do such a thing?")

and sometimes, driving down the street, she would be at a stoplight and see beside her a car full of frightened sophomores staring like they were gazing at the goddamned Medusa. Like she'd put the stink-eye on the poor fucker. Like it was because he dated out of his fucking species or something.

After Guy tried to kill himself, Fresh Girls ruled for good.

Nearly twenty years later, Nat still couldn't grasp the logistics of such an incredible feat; and it occurred to her nobody really wanted to know why he'd done it—they weren't especially interested in what secret could torment him to such lengths—but, literally, *how*. She had speculated as much as anyone. Was it the crushing pressure of being a star athlete? Were his parents divorcing? Was he involved in a gay love affair with a kid from another school? But such speculation was never made in front of anyone else, and never with any success.

Nat squinted as another pair of bright headlights suddenly appeared too close behind, and she instinctively gripped the wheel tighter. That was his car, in her mind, going eighty down the freeway, its driver's-side door flapping open like a pair of big, tattling lips, veering off to the right side of the road to career off the highway and spill into the ditch that ran alongside. Where it would not be found till morning, when commuters saw it overturned like a fat turtle, its wheels no longer spinning, having hours ago given up their futile attempt to grab a piece of the road and hold on tight.

"What the fuck?" the highway patrolmen would say to one another, and it had taken a few more hours for Guy's broken body to be found.

After that, Nat's parents forbade her to see him again, as if the message sent by his attempted suicide were not clear enough. He spent the rest of his senior year in the hospital, and after that a special school where he was able to get his GED. Between his daily therapy sessions and Nat's busy senior schedule, and with all the machinations of the meddling mothers, they lost touch. Only through fate—in which Nat knew she should have held her faith all along— had they connected again. That wonderful, promising evening she came home and heard his voice on her answering machine: "Hello, Nat! It's Guy!"

Guy.

The sky was clear when she left the Westside, but by the time she approached the Inland Empire it had started to cloud. On the 15, heading toward the high desert, it started to drizzle. She slowed and moved out of the number-one lane, finding herself just two carlengths behind the red convertible that had passed her a few miles back.

Guy.

He had never tried to feel her up in some dirty, dusty shack. He never said he'd call and then didn't. Of all the boys—and men!—Nat had known, Guy was the only one who ever seemed able to grasp the simple physical fact that her brain was actually, yes, attached to her vagina and wasn't just some homely stepsister that couldn't get its own dates and must be humored at all costs.

They'd talked at least three times a week since she received his first call. He left messages for her while she was at work, sent her cards with nothing in them except for his own handwritten confessions: "Thinking of you." They reminisced about high school, people they'd known, and remembered together what it felt like to have their whole lives ahead of them. He hadn't married, had no children, and remembered their time spent together as the most peaceful of his high school years.

These were the signals that Nat understood. The methods of others—discussion, negotiation, compromise, and ultimately, change, the methods of her parents and others—she could no more fathom than black holes or a dog's intuition. It was much more interesting to think of the shine in his eyes than to argue over who'd had a worse day at the office. Likewise for pondering the level of relationship and are everyone's needs being met?

Nat's new strategy was of a more visceral kind: as love lay unaware in the night, steal into the room under a cloak of darkness—hidden in the fog of their new, consuming lust; safe within the depths of their untried admiration. Tell him, take his love, while he sleeps. Give reason no time; logic, no importance. *Do these things,* she thought, *and you will never find in the morning a relationship where love lay the night before.*

After just a month, Nat had decided to seize the second chance she'd been given. Taking two weeks off from work, she planned a road trip from Los Angeles to Ruune, North Dakota, to get to Guy before the whole thing was revealed as one of those nostalgic relapses men are prone to as they grow older. Traveling on nearly two thousand miles of interstate highway, the drive would take three to five days, depending on the weather and how often she stopped. The whole thing could be accomplished in just a few hours by air, but that plan held none of the romanticism she craved. It was not a story the grandchildren would want to hear again and again.

He could meet someone else, she thought while packing. He'll get bored, or depressed, or... Each potential outcome—save hers—was too terrible to contemplate; and so, on a sunny, mild day in April, Nat loaded up her wagon with CDs, maps, and a suitcase of new clothes and headed north to surprise Guy.

The clouds started to gather beyond the rocky mountaintops on both sides of the highway, but the sun still shone through in spots. The roads were slick from drizzle, but traffic was light; and she made good time over the winding, sometimes treacherous two-lane road. Just past Victorville she spotted the red convertible again, this time rushing down the onramp from an exit populated by two fast food restaurants and a gas station. It was the kind of car Nat had always wished for, not like the boxy, fuel-efficient wagon she'd been sold by a smarmy salesperson who'd convinced her reliability was sexy.

A few car lengths ahead, the chrome-bumpered MG settled into a comfortable lead, a distance Nat subconsciously began to maintain. She fantasized about the occupants of the little sports car. Who were they? Where were they going? Were they dating, married, having an affair? Were they headed out to some dusty motel in the desert for an afternoon of tender, illicit sex? Did they sleep on a mattress on the floor and did she toss scarves over the lampshades to give their place a sexy, bohemian feel?

She wondered if they'd bought the car together, and did they spend their entire savings on it? Did she find it one day while he was at work and call him, breathless and excited, and did they make love with their fingers while sitting parked in the carport that first night they brought it home? Like their first loves, was it something they'd both remember for the rest of their lives?

The rain picked up and the temperature dropped the further north she drove. It had been an early spring, and she'd counted on mild weather most of the way there. It would be a long drive through fog, rain, or, worse, snow. She hit the wipers and peered through the sports car's torn convertible top; it was probably soaking wet inside. Not that they would notice, the two of them. Not that they could know anything outside of their moment.

Nat tried to make out their silhouettes through the open space in the back where the chipped and clouded window, stained to a dirty rust color in spots, was torn from the seam. The man slouched in the driver's seat; and a shorthaired girl lounged next to him, bobbing her head back and forth, nearer, nearer still as they shared a private joke and then back again.

Nat eased up on the accelerator, trying to maintain her anonymous POV, when she drew too close. The drizzle turned to a sprinkle, giving the air that came in through the vents a musty, oily smell. Fat drops hit her windshield with a splat and then streamed downward; their path was at first fluid and graceful and then, diverted by scabs of bird poop and minute, dried-out carcasses of mosquitoes and other bugs, became erratic and unpredictable. She hit the wand with her thumb, and the blades skipped across the windshield, right to left. Thump-thump. Thump-thump. Like the heavy heartbeat of some big mammal.

Even through the streaks on her windshield, Nat could see the girl in the MG loving her man, the way she longed to love Guy. The girl traced her fingers along the contour of her companion's right ear, tickled the lobe and tugged on it gently. Nat tried to remember if she had ever touched any man like that.

"Oh, Guy," she said out loud.

Love. It was something they shared—her and Guy, the girl and her man—and Nat knew that if there were anything more lovely than love it was showing it to others.

She tilted her head and dropped her gaze and imagined herself up there in the sports car, Guy driving while she sat cross-legged beside him, laughing and loving the feel of the breeze blowing up her skirt. There would be a big red dog, happy and panting, sitting in the back where a bottle of Beaujolais and a picnic basket were stowed. Love songs would be on the radio, something she couldn't bear when not in love, something soft and 70s. Guy's right hand would rest on her thigh, the hem of her skirt between his thumb and forefinger, tickling the pudgy spot above her knee.

Oh, Guy...

On that rainy morning on Highway 15 just outside of Los Angeles, Nat's love fantasy oozed up like crude oil from the deep cracks in the pavement. Every sight, every sound and smell stirred her anticipation in a way that only those conjoined in love could know. But none of it—not the memory of Guy, the fantasy of what waited for her in North Dakota, not even the CDs that would provide the soundtrack to this, her most carefully orchestrated attempt ever—would affect her more profoundly than the couple in the little red sports car, now four or five car-lengths ahead and to the right. She watched, disbelieving

(like an episode of World's Worst Ironies)

as the car hit a slick patch of road and suddenly hydroplaned into a 360-degree spin.

It was Big Bad déjà vu, like watching for real something that had, up till now, played only in her mind while she busied her body doing other things—flossing her teeth, painting her toenails, sitting on the toilet. She contemplated the accident unfolding abruptly before her and the others on the highway just like she sometimes contemplated the memory of Guy: like watching your winning lotto ticket blow into the sewer.

The MG pirouetted across two lanes of traffic and slammed the center divider—not in slow motion as witnesses would later be tempted to describe it, but going as fast as physics would allow—then leapt back to the right again before flinging itself over the embankment and disappearing into the scratchy weeds that crowded the shoulder.

Nat braked and swerved to the right shoulder, narrowly missing a compact that had come to a nearly complete stop in the middle of the road to avoid a collision with the MG. She spun around in her seat and watched in amazement as this fresh fantasy took on a jarring, blunt twist. A hundred yards back, motorists stopped their cars in the middle of the highway and rushed to the rescue of the young pair

(in love?)

who had not yet emerged from the crumpled sports car.

What the fuck?

None of her lovely what-ifs included bad brakes or a trip to the emergency room.

Traffic behind the accident had come to a complete stop. A chaotic assemblage of cars, trucks, and people blocked all lanes of traffic, and curious, concerned citizens—as well as those with a taste for the macabre—abandoned their vehicles and crowded the road in the aftermath of the most amazing thing they had ever seen.

Nat covered her mouth with her fingers and could only gasp in wonder as her radio offered the melodic reassurance that "At last, my love has come along..."

Storm clouds, which had been wandering in from the east, were now directly overhead; and although it was not yet noon, it had become difficult to see anything not directly in the path of someone's headlights. Nat pulled a sweatshirt from the backseat and, in the cramped, dim car, put it on backwards, inside out. Leaving her belongings, the motor running, and headlights on, she popped the glove box and pulled out a small first-aid kit before she pushed her door open and stepped into a rushing cascade of icy water.

Not knowing CPR and having no stomach for the sight of blood, she couldn't know why she was drawn to see what the others could not wait to witness. But more than curious, and not like those who would relish the retelling of this at dinnertime, she approached the unfolding scene with trepidation. Passing uniformed highway patrolmen as she neared the outer circle of onlookers, she nursed the feeble hope that what she would actually find would be a cleverly concealed off-ramp, upon which the MG and its occupants had made a breathtaking, narrow escape from injury.

She pressed through the crowd, wrenching her arm from the grasp of a cop who was trying to shepherd everyone back into cars and on their way. But their efforts were futile; and their flashing red lights only added to the urgency of getting out and seeing for oneself what the fuck had happened.

Nat remembered from junior high science lab that solid matter could never disappear completely, but only shift in form. You burn wood down to nothing, her teacher had explained, but it doesn't really disappear; it turns to ash. Organic materials decompose but may be eaten by bugs or animals or be absorbed into the ground another way. Something like that. Seeing what remained of the MG, now bunched up in the wet grass at the bottom of the embankment, she could not imagine what form the sports car had now taken, and to where the rest of it had disappeared.

With palm outstretched, she wondered. Gas, like the vapors that rose from the heat of the now-quiet engine? Liquid, like the sludge beneath the car that seemed to want to swallow it whole? Surely not solid, for there were no signs of what the rest of the car might have morphed into during the time it took Nat and the others to reach it.

What the earth did not absorb in the force of the impact lay before them like a science experiment gone bad, like an entity interrupted in the middle of a transformation too hideous for others to witness. Most of the car simply was no more. The people previously inside, Nat thought as she turned and made her way back up the slippery embankment, seemed to have completely disappeared. Whether their matter had transformed into something else or they had simply been tossed from the vehicle and lay in the tall grass, helplessly waiting for their rescuers, she didn't know and didn't wait to find out.

Nauseated by the smell of gasoline and burning rubber, by the lack of oxygen in the middle of the crowd, she gingerly set the first-aid kit on the roof of the nearest patrol car and headed back up the highway to where her vehicle sat, engine still running, heater still warming the chilly inside, and stereo still crooning with thoughts of new love and unrequited desire. Badly shaken, Nat sat for a few minutes fingering the steering wheel cover, contemplating her next move as if it were of such importance it could not be taken lightly. She struggled to remove her sweatshirt in the confines of the front seat and took care to fold it up before tossing it into the backseat, where her bag lay opened. Arranging the CDs she'd brought along —first alphabetically by artist, then by genre—she busied herself with make-work that was designed only to keep her mind busy while her body gathered the strength to get the fuck far and away from there as soon as possible. She was afraid to look back, or forward; her lovely purpose had jumped track and lay like a fatally wounded beast on the side of the road.

She's the Girl

Less than two hours from home, the trip's first lesson—*love is never what it appears to be*—came and went unnoticed, unlearned.

two

Before any subtext—real or imagined—of the probable fatalities on Highway 15 could be gleaned, Natalie came upon Trina, a hitchhiker, and P, her dog, and, in that mindful way those with a calling often follow, simply shifted her reality from one circumstance to the next.

She found them in Barstow, a rocky, high-desert town whose residents suffered ungodly heat in the summer and snow nearly every winter. It was a place where motorists stopped only on the way to someplace else—usually Las Vegas or other points east—for which it provided easy access to hot coffee and a wide variety of fast food.

It was P she saw first. He wasn't a big dog; he was brown and stout and small and out of the corner of Natalie's eye could have easily been mistaken for a tumbleweed or maybe some road trash that someone had tossed out of an RV. What she noticed about the dog was not his size or his canine-like manner—for he had none of that—but the way in which he positioned himself on the shoulder of the road, bravely blocking the tiny bits of gravel that splashed out from the wheels of the big rigs as they took the last curve going twenty-five miles an hour too fast.

The rain had eased to a light drizzle farther up the road from the accident, and narrow beams of sunshine pierced the rain clouds in all directions, casting an ethereal glow upon the scene and creating a brilliant glare on the surface of the highway. This, combined with Nat's temporarily stalled enthusiasm, prompted her to reduce her speed by at least twenty miles an hour; and that's how she saw first the dog, and then the girl.

The pair stood passively aside while respectable folk drove past with no notice. The tops of their heads were dusted with a silvery coating of light rain, and waves of gritty road sludge sprayed them each time a big rig rumbled past. At first sight, the girl's appearance belied the fact she was a girl at all—her baggy pants and heavy jacket bulked her up beyond any recognizably female form. She slouched, huddled against herself, and posed a fearsome sight for a woman driving alone.

When Nat spotted them, however sorrowful a sight they were, her first instinct was to keep on driving, like someone who actually knew what was good for her. Weren't there all kinds of stories on reality TV about hitchhikers and the misery they visit upon their victims, bilking unsuspecting Samaritans out of their vacation savings and mutual fund accounts? From what Nat knew about such criminals, she could be tasty prey.

But as she slowed and eased her car onto the exit ramp that led to the last McDonald's for at least an hour's drive, the wind from a passing truck pushed the hood off the girl's head and revealed a bright blue bandana that covered it like a babushka. Patiently, she stood two steps behind the dog, almost as if it were he who would ultimately give the nod to whoever stopped to offer a ride. The girl's right arm hung straight at her side, her thumb lazily pointed toward the ground and her elbow pressed into her side. Her left hand clasped the front of her bulky jacket in a vain attempt to keep the wet out.

Her legs were crossed at the knees and pressed tightly together, and her pants were soaked up to her kneecaps. Over her right shoulder was hung an olive-green backpack, without the weight of which she looked light enough to be sucked into the backdraft of the next passing eighteen-wheeler and blown over all lanes of traffic, like an empty chips bag on a strong breeze.

Nat thought of the Catholic girls who hitchhiked home after school, and how much she'd envied their nerve. They could kill an entire afternoon hitching rides up and down Burbank Boulevard, just for kicks. She, suffering her Middle-Class Valley Existence in the back of her mother's boxy minivan, would gaze longingly out the back window as the Catholic girls strolled in twos or threes, walking backwards, their thumbs pointing backwards as they delighted in carefully choosing their lucky rides like the bouncers at exclusive dance clubs might allow the most elite to pass and leave the pathetic wannabe's to hungrily circle the scene. This one's too weird, they might have deemed—too poor, too old, too creepy, too this, or that. What freedom those girls enjoyed, Nat imagined, between the hours of three and four p.m. The Catholic girls were an impossible variation of The Fresh Girl, and she was glad they didn't go to her school.

No, picking up hitchhikers was something that Nat was not likely to do under usual circumstances. Picking up a man was out of the question because of the inherent danger in doing nice things for strange men. Picking up a woman was barely more imaginable, not because she was afraid physically of women, but because she wasn't entirely comfortable with them. "Not good with girls" is how she'd explain her lack of female friends.

Over years, Nat's lack of close female friendships had left her convinced she was unable to connect with other women even on the most superficial level. All of her close friends were men; she'd grown up in a house of boys, and times spent with her mother—a built-in best friend for most girls—were infrequent and memorable only in their lingering wretchedness. She had simply grown unaccustomed to talking with women, to knowing how they thought and what they wanted, what they liked to do. Nat never considered herself an accurate barometer of What Girls Like; and truthfully, aside from dating men and possessing all the components that make up a female, she had never thought of herself as a girl.

There were times when she was younger that she longed to just pick up the phone, dial a friend's number, and ask, "Should I cut my bangs?" The men didn't care one way or the other, and she had never developed a talent for developing the kinds of friendships that could take that topic and run with it. As Natalie grew older, she cared less about such superficial bonds but longed increasingly for the shared perspective of another person who had lived their life on the X side of the chromosome fence.

On those rare occasions she found herself attempting small talk with a woman she'd just met at the store, or at the park, she could rarely get past the initial introductions before being overcome by the awkward pauses that usually precipitated one or the other's exit.

As she eyed the girl and the dog on the side of the road, Natalie weighed the pros and cons of such a selfless act as stopping to offer them a lift. The girl looked young and in sore need of a break. On the other hand, the possibility of spending two hundred miles or more of awkward silence with another woman would definitely put a damper on any deed, no matter how well-intentioned.

But that afternoon, Nat felt rise within her that glorious magnanimity that comes from believing yourself to be on the brink of love. A temporary kind of altruism that prompts one to give away one's possessions but refuse the tax credit.

Impulsively, she pulled over to the side of the exit ramp and tapped the horn twice. She stretched over the console and pushed the passenger side door open, exposing the interior of the car to the freezing rain and tiny pebbles that had been blown upward in the vacuum. The girl made a run for the car and got in quickly, without even a cursory inspection of Nat or the backseat for whatever weird contents may be hidden back there.

"Hey," she said breathlessly as she tossed her bag into the backseat and lifted the shivering, wet dog onto her lap. "You are so great, really," she said and smiled at Nat.

No visible bruises, no sullen moodiness. So far, nothing to indicate a possibly risky encounter.

"My car blew up back there at the Burger King," the girl offered. "Just died on me." She grinned at Nat, who for a moment wondered if this was going to turn out to be some cleverly disguised Fresh Girl beside her. "You wouldn't believe how hard it is to get a ride with a normal person," she added, emphasizing normal.

"No problem," Nat said, trying to sound casual, nonchalant. "Looks wet out there."

No fucking duh

"Looks wet...*is* wet," the girl confirmed, and to illustrate her point peeled the bandana off her head, waved it like a beauty queen would and let go a spray of that cold rain over the front seats and dash.

Nat watched in mute fascination the girl sitting beside her, who was unlike anyone she had ever known. Her hair was platinum blond and stick-straight, parted on one side and combed straight across so as to obscure her right eye. All the while she spoke, she absentmindedly pushed it back with her fingertips in a futile attempt to tuck it behind her right ear. But it had not yet grown long enough to do anything but simply lie flat, so it just continued to fall against her narrow, black-framed glasses, wetting the lenses with tiny droplets and distracting Nat.

Just above her ears, on both sides of her head and along the nape of her neck, her hair was nothing more than stubble, as if it had recently been shaved. Placed on her left temple, and not obscured at all by the light fuzz of her hair, was the distinct, graceful outline of an orange-and-black tiger poised on its haunches, ready to leap forward at any moment and devour whatever it was it had been stalking.

Although Nat was initially startled and unsettled by the girl's appearance, she also admired the nerve it took to achieve it—both the tattoo and the shaved head. Neither was something she would ever have the nerve to do, even drunk, so she imagined both acts to be the sign of a brave, independent person.

Although from a distance the girl's posture and physical mannerisms were decidedly masculine, up close her features were delicate and refined. All girl. Her almond-shaped eyes were black with flecks of yellow that were magnified by her eyeglasses, which she occasionally removed to wipe clean. Her eyelids were completely nude; she wore no mascara and not a hint of shadow. Her cheeks exuded a pinkish glow, probably from the cold, with olive undertones elsewhere in her face and neck. Her lips were thick, pale bands of flesh that could barely contain her wide pirate grin, and her flat, wide nose was bent slightly to the right—the result of a blow,

Nat would later learn, suffered in a girl fight.

Her clothes were soaked completely through, the thick, faded denim of her jeans stuck to her flesh like a cold compress. Nat turned the heater up, and the girl sighed with appreciation as she rubbed her stubby, frozen fingers in front of the open vents. Her nails were bitten down to the quick; and she wore a variety of silver rings—some plain, some inset with deep, murky stones.

She struggled to remove her only wrap, an air force flight jacket that was green on the outside and bright orange inside, with a worn, fur-trimmed hood that dangled behind her back. The jacket's zipper and snaps were useless; they had been ruined long ago by thick, coarse rust.

She looked nothing like the girls Nat had known in the Valley, but she could have passed for one of those scary punk girls that came up from Hollywood once in awhile trolling for fights and scaring the sophomores. She was definitely not of the Fresh variety, and for this observation Nat felt a guilty pleasure.

"I'm Trina," the girl said as removed her jacket and heaved it into the backseat. "Stands for Katrina, but I don't like that. I don't like being called Kat, either," she added, as if to say *so don't do that.* She stroked the dog's wet ears and pulled his face close enough to hers that her breath warmed the poor thing's frozen face. She nuzzled him, rubbing his icy black nose over hers and talking a baby talk that Nat would have normally found utterly repulsive but which, coming from this girl, was imbued with a strange, irresistible charm.

"P wouldn't like that, either, would you?" Trina cooed. "No, you wouldn't want to be seen with some dirty old Kat."

Before Nat could even offer her own name, the girl said she'd been named by her father, a Guatemalan immigrant who owned a transmission shop in Barstow. Her mother, the daughter of a Native American princess—four generations back—liked the name and didn't learn till Trina was eight that her only daughter had been named for a stripper her husband had known in the early years of their marriage.

Trina wiped her glasses on the hem of her sweatshirt while she talked. She formally introduced the dog comfortably nestled between her legs and already fast asleep. P, upon hearing his own name, briefly raised his head. Trina told him to lie back down and he did, glad to be out of range of the sharp pebbles that had assaulted him roadside. P was nearly five—which made him what in dog years? Nat wanted to know. Trina shrugged and said I dunno. She'd been P's surrogate mother since the day she found him in the back of the closet at a home that had been used as a part-time trash dump, part-time dog kennel. She discovered him curled up in a cardboard box, nestled like a newborn baby between empty aluminum cans and a solitary high heel. Named for the stink it took weeks to rid him of, P was near death when Trina brought him home but was soon nursed to perfect health.

"You're a lifesaver, really," Trina said again. "If you hadn't have come along when you did...I don't know, I probably would have just gone back home and forgotten the whole thing."

"The Whole Thing," Nat learned, being the long trip out to the Southern Desert Correctional Complex for Men in Indian Springs, Nevada, where Trina was to be wed at five o'clock sharp to Arizona Tyler, a man who, by decree of the state of Nevada, would not likely consummate his marriage for another forty years. The Reverend and the others would be waiting, Trina said, and she had to get there by four or she wouldn't be let in and there was no burden on Earth like the paperwork of a girl trying to marry a man in lockup.

That Trina was in love and on her way to wed began to make up for the debacle of the sports car some miles back on the highway. It was a love link between the two of them—both on their way to find true love—and bound them as nothing less than kindred spirits. It was fate that Nat should find Trina on the highway, on the way to Arizona. Not fate in the way that reunited her with Guy or placed her on the road to Ruune; but more like twins who, when reunited after thirty years, discover they both like baseball and own a cocker spaniel named Bob. She wondered what else they might have in common.

So, relieved to put all that business of the wreck behind her and get back down to some serious love business, Nat nearly missed the part about the prison. Not in a church or even a civil servant's office, Trina's wedding was to take place behind bars and under maximum security.

Nat remembered a stark documentary she'd once seen on women who pursue the men of Death Row. Throughout their long, strange courtships—punctuated by censored letters and the occasional phone call—they carried a resolute faith in their man's good heart, while victim advocacy groups counted the days till the state was ready to throw the switch.

"Armed robbery," Trina suddenly blurted out.

Spoken matter-of-fact, the comment unnerved Nat.

"It's okay," Trina reassured her. "I mean, you were wondering, right? I would be...it was a liquor store," she added, as if to suggest what else?

Thinking herself a pretty good judge of character, Nat had guessed, when she first spied Trina alongside the road, the girl was running from—not to—some bad thing. Ditching her minimum-wage job in food service and leaving all her stuff behind, save for her dog and whatever she could fit into her backpack. Nat had been happy to help her escape an abusive husband, a molesting stepfather—whatever it was back there she had finally taken a stand against. But with this confession about Arizona—where she was going and what she was doing—she had in a way dared Nat to put her out on the road again.

The sun had disappeared; and the straight, flat road was slippery, especially near the shoulder, where puddles formed to create treacherous conditions at high speeds. Nat stayed in the number-two lane and let the trucks pass her one by one. Aside from the few big rigs that blew past them, she and Trina were the only ones on the road.

Did this girl have a knife hidden in her boot, and was she really on the way to break her sweetheart out of prison? Was she also wanted by the law; and would she make Nat drive her to Canada, or would she just kill her and take the car? And what about Guy? Would he be overcome with guilt when the reporters came to his door and spilled the story he didn't even know? Would he remember her forever? Christ, would they ever get together?

The Volvo's interior had darkened, illuminated only by the faint ambient light of a far-off daytime storm and the dim amber glow of the instrument panel. It cast an eerie, surreal mood on the scene that was nothing like Nat had pictured for herself on this, her first-ever road trip and her last, best chance for love.

Hitching a ride to marry your sweetheart would make a lovely, offbeat story. But hitching a ride to a maximum security facility to do so was an act Nat couldn't reconcile. There would be no RSVPs for this girl and her groom. No matchbooks upon which would be printed "Trina and Arizona, Till Death Do Us Part." There would be little, if anything, to put in the scrapbook of their anniversaries and other times spent together; and while the story of getting married in prison was one people would like to hear, it was one your children wouldn't know and in-laws and other relatives would never let you forget.

It wasn't the way love was supposed to be, but in a way, all the more reason to support her. That she undertook the trip alone—in an ice storm, no less—that she had to hitch a ride in the first place illustrated, in Nat's mind, a magnificent intent that she had always found missing in herself, until now.

Bet on the long shot, back the underdog, because you never know when the loser will be you.

Nat was suddenly jealous of Arizona Tyler and Trina. It was serious business, this love of theirs. The way love should be. Instinctive. Visceral. Innate. Nat had never loved like that, and this thought brought regret first, and then hope for the trip north.

"So," Trina asked, "what's your story?"

"Oh, you know..." She started to stay "the usual" but caught herself and instead just said, "...road trip," as if that phrase, out of context, actually meant something.

"Uh-huh." Trina smiled and nodded. "Where you goin'?"

"North Dakota," Nat replied.

Trina gaped at her. "On purpose?"

Nat knew, on some level, that this was a question she would have done well to ask herself some time ago. She'd read once in a self-help book that the way to turn around a bad situation was to learn how to ask oneself the right questions. When faced with some calamity, one does not beg to know "Why me?" but rather "How can I fix this?" For Natalie, and Guy, the question asked could not be "Why am I doing this?" but must be "What's the best way of doing this?"

"I know, it sounds kind of...lame," she replied. "But, hey...Mt. Rushmore!" she said in that damned, disjointed way again, and she feared Trina was probably wondering if she could string together a proper sentence.

"That's South Dakota," Trina corrected her.

"Oh, yeah, you're right," Nat said. "I forgot that."

A lie. Even at the apex of her junior high career, Natalie did not know in which Dakota Mt. Rushmore was located.

"What's in North Dakota?" Trina asked.

"Guy," Nat replied.

"Oh...well, there you go." Trina said, as if to confirm for Nat that she had made the right decision. "I guess a guy's as good a reason as any to go someplace." She looked Nat up and down in that sly, knowing way girls sometimes do and clicked her tongue twice, like giddyup!

"No," Nat corrected her. "Not a Guy. The Guy...I mean, Guy. Just...Guy."

"That's his name?"

"Yeah."

"How...descriptive," Trina deadpanned. "So, this Guy...I mean, Guy...he's obviously your boyfriend or something?"

Sensing a perfect moment to share her love story out loud, Nat laid the groundwork by proudly declaring, "High school sweethearts. We haven't seen each other since senior year."

Trina pulled a pack of cigarettes from her jeans pocket and offered one to Nat, who declined.

"I quit years ago," she said.

"Yeah, I'm trying," Trina said, "but I'm kind of edgy today."

Nat pressed a small rectangular button on the console and Trina's window was lowered five or six inches.

Trina pulled a smoke from the pack and lit it, inhaling deeply. "Go on," she said.

What to tell, where to begin? That this time next week she hoped to be madly, foolishly in love? Better yet, engaged? Or voice the embarrassing admission that part of her felt a little bit like a loser? That she really wasn't someone who perused decades-old yearbooks as if they were this forgotten reservoir of potential dates and looked up old exes on the Internet in her spare time.

Unspoken, her trip north made perfect sense. From the moment the idea took root there was a never a doubt it was the correct, the true thing to do. Like Adam and Eve and Easter Sunday, the theory of Guy and Nat required faith, not understanding. Reason, logic, proof: these were the tools of someone working a relationship, and that's not what Nat and Guy were all about.

But out loud, and especially for the first time, Nat feared her story could sound contrived or false. Emotional reasoning was as good as any other—even better, in her opinion—but usually worked best in the heart of a true believer, not someone who sat waiting to be convinced. How to express the perfect sense in what she was doing? How could she make Trina realize the fantastic possibilities that lay in someone from so long ago? Long enough to ensure that most events, however awkward or plain at their moment, had over time taken on the patina of nostalgia, creating emotions that would never again be matched in their depth, their genuineness. Was it just the passing of twenty years that had imbued those times with such vivid emotion? Would she, in twenty years, be yearning for the silly things Paul used to say? Would anything, given enough time, be remembered more fondly than it deserved to be?

Trina took a deep drag off her cigarette. Holding her breath, she pursed her pale lips into a tight O and turned her head toward the opening in the window. Nat watched as she exhaled softly, sending a sinuous trail of white smoke out of her mouth. Nothing resembling a smoke ring, which she was obviously attempting. Trina sighed with disgust and flexed her lips a few times before taking another drag.

"I have a very good reason for going. I..." Nat struggled to maintain her train of thought. "We know that...it's not going to be, that..." She kept her eyes on the road and stole glimpses of Trina out of the corner of her eye. "Guy's a very complicated...guy," Nat said, for the first time realizing the absurdity of naming your boy child "Guy."

Trina's cigarette was nearly down to the butt, and she had not yet been able to form anything even remotely circular.

"Oh, here," Nat said, reaching for the cigarettes where they lay between them on the seat. "You'll never get it that way, you're doing it all wrong!" She lit her cigarette and took a couple of deep drags. "Ahh," she sighed. "How is it that science can clone a human being but can't make a cigarette that won't kill you?"

Trina shrugged and grinned. "You keep 'em, I need to cut back."

"Okay, now, watch this..." Nat said. "You have to relax your jaw and your mouth." She formed a loose O with her lips. "Like this."

She took a deep drag. "Now, Guy, he's a great... a great...man," Nat said, but started to laugh and coughed all the smoke out. "Sounds like Abraham Lincoln, doesn't he?" They giggled at the imagery.

"I get the idea," Trina said. "He's a great guy."

"Exactly!" Nat replied. "We were very close in high school. We haven't seen each other in a long time, but I feel really good about seeing him again." She looked at Trina and reminded herself more than anyone, "I think this is going to be really good for me."

"So, let me get this straight," Trina said. "You're driving all the way to North Dakota to see this guy... this man you used to date in high school. You haven't seen him since high school?"

"Yeah."

"Wow," Trina said, shaking her head. "That's a whole lotta faith you got there."

"He doesn't know I'm coming. It's a surprise."

Trina was silent for a moment and just watched as Nat took another drag. Momentarily, a perfectly shaped circle of smoke emerged and floated through the front of the car like a tiny oval angel. They both watched in awe as the ring caught a slight gust from the vent and started to waft gracefully around and around, until it eventually lost its delicate shape and began its transformation into just another cloud of secondhand smoke. Eventually, it floated too near the open window and dissipated. Nat smiled proudly at Trina.

"Not so lucky with the whole romance thing, huh?" Trina said.

This was an ironic statement from a girl on her way to wed a convicted felon, is what Nat thought.

"Okay, here's the thing..." Nat said as she straightened in her seat, determined to say exactly the right things, in exactly the right order. She told Trina about the phone call that came out of the blue and how it had come exactly when she needed it. She told her about Paul, and the therapist, whom she had never met. And she told her about the half-dozen or so other men in her past and the relationships that always ended because they had, in fact, started out as something else. She did not tell her about the car going eighty miles an hour and the way they found Guy in the morning.

"I know I'm not exactly a Capulet," Natalie said, "but I never got over the feeling that we were...you know, interrupted."

Guy worked for a major retailer of outdoor clothing, which was based in North Dakota. He had earned not only a GED but also a BA in marketing and had moved shortly afterward out of California. A charismatic people person, as Nat described him, Guy had done well in his career and was living this fantastic athletic outdoor existence—skiing, hiking, ice fishing—all at a forty-percent employee discount.

Coincidentally, only two years earlier Nat had purchased a pair of waterproof hiking boots to wear on a three-day weekend up the coast.

"What a coincidence," Trina commented dryly, not entirely impressed with the behind-the-scenes maneuvering the gods had supposedly undertaken on Nat's behalf.

"Well, when I bought these boots, my name goes into their customer database, right? And I get on their mailing list. Turns out that it's Guy who's, you know, the mail order guy that sends out all these catalogs and things. One day when he's sitting in his office he's looking at some report or something like that, and—bam!—whose name just jumps right out at him? Mine! Natalie Dresden. Me. Imagine that."

"Imagine," Trina concurred.

"And he's thinking to himself, 'I used to know a Natalie Dresden,' and so on and so on. He gets my number, makes the call, hears my voice on the answering machine, and there you have it. A month later, I'm taking two weeks off and heading up to North Dakota to surprise him."

"And you're wearing your hiking boots," Trina observes.

"Aren't they awesome?" Nat exclaimed.

Nat was glad she'd picked up Trina and P, prison wedding and life sentence aside. The two girls sat contentedly for five minutes or so, enjoying the warmth of the heater and one another's company. The silence that had fallen on the car was filled with the rhythmic hum of the tires on road; it was a sound that felt like home, like going home.

"Hey!" Trina's face suddenly brightened at the thought of some fantastic secret she had stashed away in her backpack. "I've got a dress!" She pushed P onto the floor between her feet and reached into the backseat. "Oh, good God! You've got to see this!"

"It doesn't bother you that he's in jail?" Nat asked suddenly.

"Jail," Trina corrected, "is where they put you when you get drunk and throw up in the bowling alley. Oz is not in jail, a fact I have to keep reminding his sister of. Arizona is in prison."

"Still..." Nat continued.

"Yeah, it bothers me," she replied honestly. "It bothers me for his sake, you know what I mean? Does it bother me in the way that I don't want to be associated with someone in prison? No."

She pulled herself back over the seat and turned toward Nat. "Look...at...this," she said each word singly, as if it were its own sentence, and held her dress up for Nat's disbelieving eyes to behold. It was a short, white, spandex dress with spaghetti straps and a slit up the left side. The back was low—it would reach almost to the base of Trina's spine, where the straps crisscrossed in a funky spider web pattern. It was truly awful.

"Now, I know what you're thinking," Trina said. "You're thinking it's the tackiest thing you've ever seen..."

"No—" Nat started to say.

"It is, it is! I'd just as soon do it in these," she indicated her jeans. "Believe it or not, it gets worse..."

"How?" Nat laughed, disbelieving.

"This," Trina said, holding the dress up for emphasis, "is Arizona's mother's wedding dress."

The two of them howled with laughter. Trina tossed the dress back into the backseat and said, "That, Natalie Dresden, is what passes in the Tyler family for an heirloom." She shook her head, as if to say can you believe that? "Says it all, don't it?"

"But still you love him," Nat said, spoken not like a question but as a statement of admiration and envy.

"Oh, he's the best," Trina said with affection. "We've been best friends ever since I can remember. I don't think I could ever know anyone as well as I know Oz." She thought about this statement for a moment and then added, "Course, I didn't know anything about his plan to rob the Quickie-Shop, did I? Didn't you ever do anything bad for love, Nat?"

To Nat, it wouldn't make sense that anything for love could be bad, not truly bad. The only bad things she did, she did for lack of love. "No...have you?"

The rain had slowed to a drizzle; and off to the northeast, where Vegas lay behind the hills, the clouds had parted in places to reveal a bright blue sky. Nat slowed the car as they came upon a sign by the side of the road: SOUTHERN DESERT CORRECTIONAL CENTER FOR MEN, EXIT HERE

and they did.

"No...but, hey!" Trina said with a wink and a grin. "We're still young!"

three

The prison and its occupants, enclosed in a chain link-and-razor wire perimeter, lay at the end of a newly paved two-lane road that shot perpendicular off Highway 15, which continued into the horizon toward Las Vegas. The narrow road stretched directly east for about a quarter of a mile then came to a sudden stop in front of a massive gate at least fifteen feet high and fortified at the top by more razor wire. Through it all, Nat imagined, probably ran an electrical current strong enough to fry any living thing. On a trip that was supposed be about Possibility, Nat and Trina's immediate destination held none.

As they slowly approached what to many could appear to be a mirage, a figment of a guilty imagination or the final scene in a bad, recurring dream, Nat scanned the openings that passed in this place for windows, behind one of which might be sitting the groom, fumbling with his shoelaces and smoothing his hair back with gel to keep it in place.

"Pull over here, would you?" Trina asked about a quarter of a mile from the gate. Above, the fat, dark clouds refused to give way to the late-afternoon sun, which had already started its slow, steady descent behind the mountains that lay westward.

Nat pulled off the narrow road and parked among some wet, frantic tumbleweeds that littered the shoulder. She lowered her window halfway and breathed deeply. The desert had fallen still after the rains, and a chilly dampness had descended upon the car. The windows were cold to the touch, and she wondered how much worse the trip could have been for Trina had she not stopped to pick them up. The dog's thick coat had not yet dried completely, and his wet fur stank up the car like an old rug that'd been left out in the rain. Trina seemed not to notice at all.

Trina hoisted P over her shoulder, cupping his wide butt in her hands and deftly balancing him midair as she lifted him over her seat and gently set him down in the back, where he prompted rooted himself a nice dry bed out of Nat's jacket and a bulky, flannel-lined sleeping bag she had bought on impulse just before leaving.

"Why are we stopping here?" Nat asked. The car idled softly beneath them, and without the ambient road noise it seemed strangely still.

Trina reached for her bag and pulled out the dress she had promised Arizona's sister she would wear. "Gotta change," she said, and then added, "Can't do it in there." She indicated the prison with a nod. "They've got cameras everywhere, you know. You can't even take a pee without wondering if you're going to end up on the video that night."

Nat sat a little uncomfortably in her seat as Trina grasped the hem of her sweatshirt and started to lift it over her head, exposing her belly and breasts as it started to take her t-shirt along with. In her bulky, shapeless outerwear, Trina's true figure was hidden from Nat, whose body image was unable to spike even when "waif" was in. But close up, and without all the extra weight of the rain-soaked layers, Trina was revealed to possess the sort of soft, rounded shape that only the young and impossibly vain could not appreciate as fully female. Worse still, she appeared not at all self-conscious when her left nipple popped out of her bra as if to give Nat a sly wink.

"Oops," Trina laughed, pressing her flesh back into its protective cotton pocket.

The last time Nat had disrobed in front of another woman—or witnessed another woman undressing—had been eighth grade gym class, when, for fifty minutes each day, she would spend the entire period devising new and creative ways to avoid the communal shower and cursing those damned, doorless changing cubicles. Girls like Nat would cower with their backs to the others, desperately hiding their plain bodies, while Fresh Girls and others who developed earlier than the rest paraded about in matching bra and panty sets, sporting the precise combination of flat and round that was irresistible to boys that age. The most valuable lesson learned from that experience was how to talk to a girl without looking at her, because if your gaze had happened to land, even accidentally, on another girl's body—especially a Fresh Girl—you were sure to find "lesbo" written on your locker by the end of the day.

"I was wondering..." Nat began, as her gaze self-consciously wandered about the inside of the car, finally to notice the width and depth of the built-in cup holders with much interest.

"Ask away," Trina replied as she unbuttoned her damp jeans and struggled to shimmy her wide hips out of them. Her openness made it easy for Nat to talk to her. The conversations had so far been deceptively easy, but it would be only a matter of minutes before Trina was sure to notice that Nat wouldn't—couldn't—look back in her direction, and then the quiet would come.

Arrrgghh. Emergency topics were dredged up from the back of her mind: weather was good, interesting facts about dogs would fly well. Hard-earned experienced told Nat not to reveal anything too personal—or too embarrassing—too soon. Nothing would induce a hasty retreat in a new friend like prematurely sharing some weird physical anomaly.

(Hey, here's something interesting for ya: I've got three labia...)

Even Natalie—who had recently been going out of her way to make new female friends—was likely to immediately excuse herself from that conversation.

"So, what do others have to say about you getting married?" she asked, as she forced herself to turn and face Trina, who was now clothed in nothing more than a thin cotton bra and a pair of panties that had embroidered upon them in pink script "Sunday."

"Others?" Trina's clothes lay in a cold, damp heap on the floor between her feet. She was in no rush to get dressed, a fact made obvious when she kicked off her boots and socks, reached for a cigarette from the pack that lay in the center console and sat back in her seat. She held it in her left hand and laid her right on her bare pouch of a belly, where her splayed fingers traced over the gold hoop that had been threaded through her navel. Her full, pale breasts rose and fell rhythmically with each deep inhale—and then release—of tobacco. Like some sensuous metronome, hypnotizing the pianist even at the slowest of speeds.

"This is my last cigarette," she said firmly.

Good God, is this what girlfriends do? Nat wondered.

Knowing it was a rare man who could acknowledge

another male's beauty, as a sometimes-self-confident female, Nat took pride in being able to look at another woman and think, *She's pretty* or *I wish I had hair like that.* Such praise was never spoken out loud and, therefore, never really parted with. But learning to not feel threatened by another woman's beauty—even if the assurance was only temporary and only in one's head—was compulsory in achieving true self-esteem.

Sitting beside this girl—this live, nearly nude girl—a girl who could never by any stretch of the imagination be described as Fresh, Nat felt envy. Not just at her physical beauty or the voluptuousness of a figure that would never be mistaken for a boy's (as Nat's had often been), but at her spirit as well. Nat wanted to be her friend, she wanted to know that someone like Trina could look at someone like her and find something to admire, and envy.

Natalie reluctantly removed a cigarette from the pack and lit it, inhaling deeply and turning her head to exhale out her half-open window. Even while not looking directly at Trina, she could sense coming from the girl a wonderful sense of self she wished she could own. The praise she had for Trina was true, but she could not express it.

Is there a place on Earth where I am the cool one? Nat wondered.

"You know...friends, for example," Nat said, trying to squash her discomfort at being in such warm, close quarters with a partially clothed girl. "What do they think about you guys getting married?"

Trina laughed, as if sharing some private joke with herself, and responded in kind. "What do your friends say about what you're doing?"

Nat knew it was probably a rhetorical question but answered it anyway. "Well, my guy friends think it's pretty frightening..."

Trina grinned, as if to say *Well, sure they do.*
"Yeah...what do the women think? They probably love
it, right?" She nodded, as if to answer her own question.
"Women eat that shit up."

"Well," Nat confessed, "I don't really do girls, you
know?"

"You don't do girls?" Trina arched her eyebrows.
"Shame," Trina smiled broadly at Nat. "Kidding," she
added with a grin. "I'm kidding."

Nat was becoming increasingly aware of a private
joke, or shared experience, that was going on between
the two of them but from which she felt conspicuously
absent. Trina was telling her things but not *saying* them.
It was a flawless execution of that elusive girl/girl transmission—some unspoken female language—which Trina apparently did not yet realize Nat lacked facility for.
To Trina, it might have been a moment that deepened
their connection, but for Nat its fluid simplicity was
overshadowed by the dialogue in her head and continu-
ally posed questions to which she did not have the answer: what did she mean by that, what clever way can I
reply? "Not good with girls" was never truer than when
one was called upon to respond in kind to some innate
girl awareness.

Trina sighed heavily, as if she were finally undertaking some chore she had been putting off for a long time.
As she struggled to fit her head through the impossibly
narrow opening of the dress, she offered, "Too bad my
folks could not be here. He's gonna be sorry they missed
it."

"Your parents...so they approve?"

Trina laughed out loud. "Ha! That's an understatement!"

This, Nat found to be remarkable. She couldn't
imagine what parent would be happy to see their daughter marry a felon and spend the rest of her life making

the laborious biweekly trip out to the middle of the desert just to say Hello, how are you doing.

"Maybe they figure he's better than nothing," Trina said, "you know?"

Natalie nodded, though not really sure what she meant.

"They like to visit when they can," Trina said. "They would have come this trip, too, 'cept my mom's been sick. She can't travel." Trina struggled to squeeze her breasts into the tight fabric as Nat waited, filled with anxiety, to be called upon for help.

"I know Arizona's mother thinks he could do much better," Trina continued as she rolled the hem of the dress down her waist and hips. "Really," she said. "Can you imagine how much I must be despised if she actually believes he could do better? I mean, does that woman even realize where he is?"

The girls laughed. It was the sort of thing any girl who's ever had to meet her boyfriend's mother could relate to.

Arizona's mother's dislike of Trina had little to do with her losing her little man to another woman, Nat learned, but was really about blaming Trina for his circumstances.

"Not that she misses him in any way," Trina explained. "The only thing she misses is the paycheck she used to take from him. She's mad 'cause he's not around to support her and now she's gonna have to get off her ass and get a job."

Arizona's ill luck didn't start with the sentencing, or even the robbery itself. According to Trina, his bad streak started the moment he was born to Wilhelmina Tyler—her fifth and last child, her only son. His life story read like soap opera: broken home(s), abusive stepfather(s), a string of foster homes, and ultimately, enough early brushes with the law to designate him as "high-risk"—a label that brought with it admittance to special after-school programs and classes designed to turn his life around.

Trina was sure that, aside from Wilhelmina, Arizona's most obvious problem was simply his name. The name might be great for a state but bad for a boy. "A man could never grow to be President with a name like Arizona," she guffawed, "any more than he could with a name like Patricia."

She speculated that the name had some unsavory origin in the place where Arizona may have been conceived, and remarked that they should all be glad the woman had never been to Virginia.

Arizona and Trina met and became best friends in the second grade. They played soccer together until Arizona's mother could no longer afford the uniform fees and then both quit. In sixth grade they were rumored to have had sex together—years ahead of their classmates—but rather than deny the stories they played them up and enjoyed an undeserved reputation as a bad influence on the others.

Creative and shy, Arizona never really developed a taste for the criminal life, despite the path his life eventually took. As a teenager, cutting school and getting into fights—usually after a bellyful of insults hurled at either Trina or him by the rest of the school—were the worst of his crimes. Counselors and other sympathetic adults diagnosed it as "acting out," trying to find a way to get some attention in a household of four sisters and no father.

But his mother's solution to every bad event in her life—Arizona included—was to beat on his ass for a good long time.

Arizona came to live, unofficially, with Trina and her parents in the ninth grade, having developed a strong mutual affection for the whole family.

"They'd always wanted a son," Trina said, "but I think I sort of pushed that envelope too far, you know what I mean?" She looked at Nat in that knowing way again; and Nat was beginning to think *Yes, I think I know,* but just nodded. "We got an apartment after high school, hung around doing crappy jobs for awhile. A few years ago we went to work for county animal control."

Rescuing treed cats and scraping up road kill wasn't the worst way to make a living, Trina told Nat, and it allowed them to work together, unsupervised, until a carjacker stole their truck—and eight dogs inside—one day when they were having lunch at the BurgerBarn.

"After that we both got put on desk jobs," she continued. "Took all the fun out of that."

It was Trina's idea for the two of them to move someplace else, maybe New York or Miami or some other big city. They'd had enough of the rural life, and LA just wasn't far enough. It was Arizona's idea to get there by robbing the Quickie-Shop; and one day while Trina was at work, he borrowed a friend's .38—no bullets, Trina was quick to point out—and chose a place on the edge of town where there wasn't much drive-by traffic.

"It went badly," Trina told Nat in a tone that implied "of course." The events, as Trina explained them, came across as true tragedy. Not just something bad that happened to someone nice, but one of those incredible, freak chains of events that not even the most diligent planning, taking into consideration any possible outcome, could have anticipated.

"When all was said and done," Trina said sadly, "one man was dead and another might as well have been." The person working the counter at the store that day—just a kid, according to Trina, not even old enough to buy the liquor he was selling—became flustered when Arizona showed his gun. Believing he would be fired or, worse, docked for the cash Arizona was going to take, the kid reached for a heavy iron bar from which the bathroom key was suspended by a thin chain. His plan, the police could only imagine, was to beat the shit out of Arizona for trying to rob the store and endangering this, his first full-time position.

What followed could never be fully known, being that the only witness was dead. The kid accidentally knocked over a football-shaped cooler full of ice and soda bottles, dousing his bare feet in a wave of ice water and flooding the floor behind the cash register up to an inch and a half in some places.

"No offense to the dead," Trina said, "but if you dumped a cooler full of ice water over your feet in the middle of defending yourself against an armed robber, would your first thought be to take off your socks and shoes?"

After narrowly escaping an iron pipe to the temple, Arizona bolted and was not even present when the next swing caught the electronic cash register. The bar punched through the plastic cover and hit some wires, and the next person to come into the store found the clerk dead behind the counter, having been rightly fried by the current conducted through the icy puddle in which he stood.

Although Arizona was not directly responsible for the boy's death—and, as his public defender attempted in vain to point out several times during sentencing, was not even on the premises—the state found the case to have "special circumstances" that tripled Arizona's sentence.

It could happen only in a town like Barstow, Trina said, and only to a sad fuck like Arizona Tyler.

Now fully dressed in the form-fitting wedding dress, Trina woke P and hoisted him back up onto her lap. The dog whined restlessly and rubbed his wet nose all over the inside of the window until Trina lowered it to give him a breath of wet desert air. P caught a bug in his mouth and ate it.

"How do I look?" she asked.

"Great," Nat replied, and meant it.

"All right then," she said firmly. "Let's do this."

Nat started the car and headed toward the gate. Soon, they approached a large speed bump, and the whole car shook as the front wheels, then the rear, climbed the foot-high mound and fell to the asphalt with a thud. They hit two more, each placed less than twenty feet apart.

"They sure don't make it easy for you—coming or going—do they?" Trina said.

Despite all the trappings of razor wire and armed guards, the buildings themselves didn't look especially confining. Disciplinarian, but in a trendy way, like the minimalist architecture that was sprouting up all over the East Valley and going for a small fortune. Nat wanted to wish Trina well but, in the shadow of the prison, in the stark surroundings of the moon-like landscape that surrounded them on all four sides, was afraid her words would sound more like a hurtful prank. They fell silent as they approached the gate.

"Hey, it would be cool if you could stand witness," Trina said suddenly. "If you want."

Nat's first impulse was to say yes, but she hesitated. In the back of her mind was the terrifying possibility that a sight such as a prison wedding would spoil her appetite for the whole rest of the trip, upsetting her system like tainted tuna fish. Trina was persuasive, told her it would be fun and would give her something to remember the trip by.

"It'll make a great story one day," she grinned at Nat in that pirate way, and added, "Don't ya think?"

And so Nat, with her own love-skew on things, a

take she was wont to inflict on others' lives as well, instead of taking pity on the girl who was marrying a felon chose to believe that running concurrent to any degree of suffering in Trina's life, no matter how extreme, was an equal if not higher ratio of romance. As with stressed-out executives who envy the freedom of homelessness, Nat's imaginings became just another romantic, unfulfilled *what if?*

They stopped at the gate, where the guard met them with a typewritten list of expected visitors. Trina leaned over the console and spoke her name out Nat's window then nodded at Nat and told the guard, "Her, too," and Nat enjoyed a growing anticipation of seeing love in action. Trina and Arizona Tyler. Forever devoted, forever committed. The whole Nevada State Penal System couldn't keep them apart. Nor could hundreds of miles of desert sand, nor the love-starved judiciaries who could simply not see what this man had done in the name of love.

They should give this guy his own holiday, Nat thought. They should throw a tickertape parade down the strip in Vegas, put him on a float with a big-breasted Kiwanis girl and a painted sign that reads GOING THE DISTANCE FOR LOVE.

She inched the car forward, gripping the wheel tightly and nervously eyeing the towers where men sat with scoped rifles and waited for the impatient ones. She found a parking space near the entrance, pulled in and cut the engine.

"The best advice I can give is don't make a sudden rush for the gate," Trina deadpanned.

After an elaborate, exhaustive check-in, they were led into a small waiting room, where they joined a group of others who had come to see their own loved ones. The room's occupants sat uncomfortably on stiff orange vinyl and avoided one another's eyes by moving their gaze continuously over the tops of lamps and underneath the low tables. On a mental roller coaster, they reeled and spun around and did everything they could to keep their focus from landing smack in the center of that awful room.

There was an old man wearing a cowboy hat, and several young women who looked like they'd been baked to a hundred years old in the desert sun. Small children with round, happy faces—wearing none of their mothers' weary boredom—played obliviously on the floor with empty soda cans and metal cars with no wheels.

Nat took a vacant seat in the corner and nodded to Trina, who sat beside her.

"Now what?" she asked.

"We wait," Trina replied. "They'll come when they're ready."

On a small laminated table was a stack of fashion magazines and others that featured grocery coupons and casserole recipes. Nat grabbed one off the bottom of the stack; the cover was torn off and some of the pages had been colored with orange crayon and hurried, frantic streaks of yellow marker. She perched on the edge of the stiff vinyl and wondered if P would mess up the car.

The first thing she came upon was a full-page ad for Human Restraint, Inc. It showed an illustration of a man in a strait jacket, and another of a man's legs booted in leather and steel. "To stand the test of time," boasted the copy. At the bottom was a toll-free number for a full-color brochure and a promise that no salesman would call.

A young girl cried softly on the other side of the room while an older woman beside her applied a fresh coat of lipstick and then blotted it with a tissue she had pulled from inside the sleeve of her sweater.

Nat tossed her magazine back onto the table and crossed her legs tightly. She smiled nervously and nodded at anyone who looked her way, though most ignored her with a practiced skill. She tried to muster the excitement she imagined a bridesmaid should bring to such an occasion; but she'd never been one and wasn't sure at all how one would work a prison instead of a wedding hall, so she sat stiffly and waited to be called.

Although Arizona would not be put to death by the State of Nevada (not actively, anyway) he and Trina might never know one another as man and wife. It was not just sex they would be denied; more, the simple, shared, day-to-day experiences that Nat imagined married couples treasure: cooking dinner for one another, raising a family, planning a second honeymoon or golden anniversary.

"All of this probably seems kind of weird to you, doesn't it?" Trina asked.

"What do you mean?"

"Well, I mean, here you are, on this kind of beginning... and then you meet me, and...well, it is kind of weird, if you think about it."

"Yeah." Nat preferred her own angle on things—the one where their love was better because they'd never know what it was like to catch your spouse in bed with your best friend. Where he would never look up from the table and say that, while he loved you, he was no longer in love with you. Where she did not have to lie awake at night and grow to hate his still, sleeping silhouette. It was a testament to something that such cynical thoughts could come as comfort, but Nat kept them to herself because she didn't know for what.

The small room had poor lighting and even worse ventilation. The recycled air was thin and hot; and Nat wondered if, during the summer, friends and relatives could at least wait in air-conditioned comfort. Along one wall was a collection of bad paintings—bright, breezy landscapes hung in subliminal denial: a green meadow with happy yellow flowers; a red-and-white barn, leaning slightly to the left and situated on a rolling hill under a baby-blue sky. The last, a seascape with white and blue spray coming off the rocks, did little to refresh the stale air.

A pay phone stood in one corner, its chrome sides plastered over with little rubber magnets shaped like gavels—like plastic broccolis that you hang on the fridge—that advertised a bail bondsman just off the highway. A phone book hung below on a cord, its pages torn and dog-eared. One small boy made regular wide sweeps of the claustrophobic room, thrusting his chubby, sticky fingers into the coin return slot on each pass, searching for nickels and pennies that might come divinely to him from the phone company. This annoyed everyone in the room—except his mother, who seemed not to hear it at all.

"What about you?" Nat asked.

"What about me?"

"Well, this must be kind of hard on you, too."

"How so?"

"What if you meet someone else?"

"What if I do?"

"Well, you know...what if you fall in love?"

"Oh, I plan on it...as soon as possible." She grinned like a pirate.

"Seriously."

"What's to stop me from falling in love?" She shrugged indifferently.

"What if you want to get married again...you know, for real?"

Trina laughed with genuine surprise and eyed Nat; and when she finally spoke, it was not to answer Nat's question directly. "Somehow, I don't think that will be a problem."

Suddenly, a set of wide double doors to the right

opened, and a guard stepped into the room. Reading from a clipboard, she announced, "Arizona Tyler."

Trina rose and motioned for Nat to come. "Her, too," she said to the guard, and added, "Bridesmaid."

They were led down a long, wide hallway by a female prison guard whose uniform was stretched too tightly across her broad behind. The guard moved slowly in front of them, like there was nothing but time on her mind; and Nat fought the urge to keep from overtaking her on the left.

Nat observed that from the moment they entered the prison she had the sensation of living underwater. Even though voices are muffled, one hears things coming through on the current that normally would be missed, and vibrational changes in the environment can be easily detected. In this strange, protracted state, every movement, however slight, every word spoken, is experienced to the fullest—not, Nat imagined, so as to enjoy it more fully but rather to stretch it out and fill up the days that were relentless in their monotony.

Trina was silent, her head was bent to her chest, and she seemed to be concentrating on her feet and how they fell on the black-and-white linoleum squares—the left falling only in white; the right, in black. Nat wondered if she was doing that on purpose or if she had found within herself some internal rhythm, some peaceful cadence that would lead her to Arizona and where he waited patiently behind a locked door and under the watchful eye of a security camera. She wondered if she were praying, if she were full of regret, or just trying to remember if she'd unplugged the coffeemaker that morning before leaving home.

"Hey," she suddenly murmured to Nat. "You're driving through Vegas, right?"

"Mm-hmm."

"Mind if I tag along?"

Nat's first impulse was to say *No, please come.* She was enjoying Trina's company; and the more time they spent together, the more surprised she was to realize how effortless being with a girl could seem. But with such a simple request must come more, Nat worried, and part of her was sure the experience could end up costing her.

"No, I don't mind," she said, half-truthfully. "I mean, it's your wedding day, I'll buy you dinner."

"Sounds good," Trina said and smiled.

"Yeah."

The hallway was lined with heavy steel doors, each outfitted with a tiny, square reinforced window. Even though Nat could occasionally catch glimpses of people on the other side, she could hear only the muffled, indistinct sounds of human voices.

Nat played the music in her mind, the march that virgins and others walk to; and she wondered who was going to walk her down the aisle when her turn came. Trina clasped her hands, interlocking her fingers where a bouquet should have been. Nat wished she'd picked some of those flowers that grew in bright, hectic clumps along the freeway; and when she mentioned this to Trina she was told there weren't any flowers out there, just dirt.

Passing the infirmary on the right, Nat peered through the window to see two men on cots, one with a thermometer under his tongue and the other lying supine on a gurney. Both were laughing, and it sounded like contentment. It reminded her of sitting on the back porch and having a wine cooler, knowing everyone on the block and everybody's kids mixing it up on the lawn. It sounded like home, except for the occasional slamming of a metal door and high-security lock.

The muted sounds of a television emanated throughout the hallways, accompanying Nat and Trina around a series of sharp, ninety-degree turns that seemed to place them exactly where they had started. The disembodied voices followed them the whole way, their source mysterious and divine.

At the end of the last hallway was the office where the ceremony was to take place. A small plastic marker on the wall, just to the right of the open door, indicated *Rev. William Sorenson, Chapel, Room No. 6.* Somebody had gotten hold of a thick black marker and drawn a nine next to the six, a hopeful consequence of what was to take place inside.

Behind the narrow door, standing out of the way and positioned like an observer, Trina's groom, Arizona Tyler, waited. Two bulky male guards flanked him, each standing at least a foot taller than Arizona. Behind the desk sat the Reverend, for whom Trina was holding a check.

Arizona Tyler wore gray. His clothes were faded but clean and pressed. Except for his forearms, which were covered in a fine coating of blond hairs highlighted by a deep tan, his skin was pale. It had long ago gone sallow under the fluorescent light—only eighteen months' worth so far—and the way he squinted his eyes even when not in direct light indicated he didn't often look into the sun. The way his hands and feet were bound with thin plastic strips said it would be some time still before he would get another chance.

The ties, the guards told Trina, were on account of Arizona's over enthusiasm about his upcoming marriage, an eagerness that had caused him—and a few unlucky others—more upset than was allowed by the rules of the prison. During lunch he had stabbed another inmate with his fork after the man was overheard to have made a crude speculation about what color Trina's wedding dress would be. It was a very un-Oz act, Trina assured the guards, who nodded sympathetically like those who really had seen, and heard, it all before.

The sight of them marrying was exhilarating. It was terribly disheartening. Simply, it screwed with Nat's mind—the same way the MG had but much, much worse. It left her a little jealous and reminded her of some old saying—living on your knees, dying on your feet...something like that—but she couldn't remember the whole text. The two of them stood like some conservative politician's wet dream—the poster couple for good grades and perfect attendance, but in Nat the sight of them being wed left only an insatiable lust for love, a longing for Guy.

Tyler was just as tall as Trina and standing toe-to-toe they seemed to fit together perfectly. His hair was long and brown and was tucked behind his ears, not slicked back like Nat had pictured it. The tips were blond for about three inches and then abruptly turned brown again.

Was Nat the only one thinking of making love, or did anyone else realize that Tyler would not know his wife for years to come—if at all?

"Oz," Trina said to the groom, "this is my friend Natalie. She's going to be my bridesmaid...you don't mind, do you?" Nat smiled at Arizona and extended her hand, grasping all ten of his fingers when he offered up his bound wrists. He smiled warmly, looking her up and down while Trina talked about the trip and how they had come to meet on the highway.

The only word Arizona had spoken so far was a loving, happy "Hey!" when Trina entered the room. When he finally spoke again, it was to ask Trina why she was wearing that awful dress and then to tease her for a few minutes about what a sight she was in it. After those few minutes of small talk, the Reverend asked everyone to take their places, and they began.

In five minutes, it was done.

After Arizona and Trina were pronounced man and wife, they kissed one another's cheeks. Trina's hands locked tenderly around Arizona's neck as he stood with his hands, like a paraplegic's useless limbs, dangling limply between their bodies. Nat said congratulations and that they made a nice-looking couple. She wished them both the best of luck and told Tyler he was a lucky man, a comment filled with such obvious irony that even the guards seemed to take pity on the pair.

The Reverend busied himself in the corner with paperwork for Trina while the newlyweds stood together, their heads bent in collusion, whispering as if they were making their getaway plans and arranging to meet in the limo. She cupped her hands over his, not minding the plastic ties that bound his wrists. She murmured something, and Nat was sure it was sweet but would be little consolation for what would come missing that night. The guards, having already been through two ceremonies that day, popped their gum loudly.

"Gotta go," one of them said sympathetically to Arizona, punctuating the remark with firm hand on his shoulder. "Places to go, people to meet."

Nat and Trina were led back to the waiting room, where they were again separated. Nat read stories about how to drive a man wild in bed and how to pack for a weekend away with your boss, and waited for Trina to come back from the bathroom, where she was changing back into her street clothes.

The clank of locks disengaging echoed through the hallways, and Nat had the sense that Trina was very far away.

She took her seat again, growing anxious for the rest of her trip to begin so she could get back on track. Checking her watch, she calculated that Guy was probably home from work, making dinner for one and hopefully thinking about her. Before leaving LA she had vowed not to call him, partly for fear she might accidentally spill her guts and ruin the surprise, partly for fear that if she did tell him what she was up to the whole thing might blow up in her face. Now, in that place, she felt the need to realign herself with the purpose that had set her out on the road in the first place.

"I ain't never seen you here before," a raspy, crackling voice came from above.

Startled, Nat looked upward to see an old, sunburned man staring down her blouse. His thin lips were drawn over the fleshy gap where his teeth used to be, and the tip of his tongue dangled in one corner of his mouth, from where saliva pooled and poised to drip down onto Nat's face at any moment. He looked like a carnival snake-man, like some kind of desert mutant that tourists on their way to the Grand Canyon would pay fifty cents to see.

Nat quickly slid into the next seat, motioning for the old man to sit in the one she had just vacated.

He stank of oil and burned rubber.

"I said, you ain't never been here before, have ya?"

Nat shook her head.

"I knew it," he said, wheezing and wiping his mouth with a yellowed handkerchief. "I know ever'body here. I knew I ain't seen you before."

A woman sitting two seats down suddenly cursed loudly and started rooting through her handbag, searching desperately for whatever it was that had so far eluded the pinch of her long, red fingernails. Nat patted her hip pocket absentmindedly, and seeing this out of the corner of her eye, the woman asked her in a thin, anxious voice, "Got a light?"

Before she could answer, an opaque window, like the doctor's receptionist hides behind, slid open and a rude voice barked, "No smoking!" The window closed just as suddenly, sliding effortlessly along on its tracks.

Nat shrugged apologetically; and the woman nodded and flipped the finger to the occupant behind the frosted glass, turning her attention back again to her handbag, where she was sure she had a book of matches stashed somewhere.

Just to the right a baby choked and threw up on the seat.

The young woman who had been sobbing quietly suddenly shouted something in Spanish and pounded her small fist to her chest in futile protest.

Nat had never before felt so much love in one room.

She stepped to the pay phone, happy to see the little boy was now gone, and contemplated phoning north. *It would be good to hear his voice,* she thought. *It would help a lot.*

"Natalie," she hoped to hear him sigh happily into the phone. "I was thinking about you today."

"Me, too!" she would coo through pursed lips.

She dropped some coins into the slot and punched in his number. The simple ring on the other end tripped inside of Nat some swelling, desperate need to bare her soul not only about her plan to reignite their love but about anything else she'd been too ashamed to speak out loud. With the kind of repentance that comes from some close call, confessions of all kinds were now begging to be spoken out loud—ignorance of love, of life, and herself. Self-doubt and the fear of being alone. Failure.

The phone rang eight times.

Would he still be there in three days? In the time it took to reach North Dakota, would he move? Would he fall in love with someone else? Would the crazy fucker up and try to kill himself again?

In the waiting room of the Southern Desert Correctional Complex for Men, Natalie wanted to tell him everything; there, enveloped in the anonymous comfort of other's loved ones, she wanted to let go of herself and cry into the phone *I need you.*

It could have been the prison, a temporary need for redemption brought on by the razor wire and the endless linoleum hallways down which armed guards trolled for someone smaller and weaker to pick on. It could have been the electronic locks and the reinforced windows and the whole concept of imprisonment. In less than an hour at the Southern Desert Correctional Complex for Men—and even then only as a visitor—Nat had experienced an intensity of remorse that such a place could only hope to inspire in the guilty hearts of its lawless inhabitants.

He picked up on the tenth ring; but she didn't hear him. She had already set the receiver back into its cradle.

Trina was standing less than a foot behind when Nat turned around. She appeared suddenly and without warning, like when Nat had found her in Barstow. She was dressed in her jeans and tight T-shirt, the white wedding dress having been rolled and tucked into her gym bag.

"Let's get out of here," she said hurriedly.

A guard released the big electronic lock at the main doors and let them out. The heavy door slammed behind them as they pushed the double glass doors open and saw the first hint of sunlight in the skies above Vegas. The last sound they heard from inside the prison was the echo of aluminum.

P was sleeping peacefully in the backseat, having made himself a fresh bed in the washed and pressed clothes he had skillfully dug out of Nat's overnight bag. They let him out to pee on someone's tire; and then Nat pulled back toward Highway 15, toward Vegas, where she'd planned to treat Trina to a nice dinner before saying goodbye and heading out the rest of the way alone. Her original plan was to spend the first night in Utah;

and although the prison wedding had definitely put her behind schedule, it was time she could easily make up, and it was worth it, anyway.

The landscape swallowed the prison whole as they drove away, Nat gazing at the horizon and Trina concentrating on the desert floor, where the sand blew and collected in small dunes at the foot of the prison walls. No smell of magnolias, just hot grease and the faint rumbling of a big rig pounding grooves into the highway on its way to somewhere else. Not as romantic this time, not like the whoosh of cars that could easily lull them to sleep. Now more like escape.

Natalie tried to calm her anxiety by imagining the love in Arizona's and Trina's eyes as they said their vows, but it was a weak, temporary fix. What must she be feeling, Nat wondered. The longing shared for decades to come, aggravated all the more on those two days out of every month separated by bulletproof glass and endless miles of scenic landscape.

But the day—*God, has it not even been a day since I left?* she thought—had been a long one, and in just these few hours on the road she couldn't help but feel she'd been the butt of some macabre love prank. Something was fucking with her head, for sure, starting with the couple in the sports car and ending in a maximum-security facility for hardened criminals. Like Ebenezer Scrooge, she could feel forces at work behind the scenes, screwing with her sensibilities and testing her limits of what is real and what is not, of what is true and what is not. Even an Elvis wedding would help, she thought. Tossing rice and wearing white—for real—organ music and witnesses: these were the landmarks upon which she would plot the rest of her life.

So far, none had been spotted from the road on which she traveled, and the signals that were there were simply unrecognizable.

four

They came upon Las Vegas abruptly, as if the horizon they had been nearing for the last hour, like so many other desert illusions, simply ceased to be. It wasn't like being at the prison, where they anticipated the razor wire and armed guards from nearly a quarter of a mile away. Cresting the last hill before the descent into Sin City, Nat and Trina awoke from their preoccupations with wedding nights and premature deaths and looked up to suddenly see a million watts of power.

Nat had planned to buy Trina a nice dinner, wish her well, and say goodbye before continuing on to Utah, where she'd stop for a few hours sleep before hitting the road north again. But when she glimpsed the first portent of Vegas, an enormous neon sign at The Lucky Seven Motel that shone like a beacon, it felt like she was on the brink of another of those blessings in disguise, or one of those mysterious, tragic things that people often describe as "God's way."

The Lucky Seven Motel came in the first real block

of McCarran Boulevard, a vast span of hotel casinos, wedding chapels, coffee shops with two-dollar steaks, and gift emporiums. The motel that accompanied the sign was itself not nearly so breathtaking—in mint green stucco, it was just a faded pastel playground for retro freaks on weekend from LA and hardcore gamblers who had pegged their savings for blackjack, not luxury accommodations. There were twelve bungalows in all—offering what was termed "The Ultimate in Privacy"—arranged in a shabby semicircle fronted by a lanky, rusted-out jungle gym perched on a bed of sparkling white gravel, like a fossilized spider frozen in time.

On the marquee out front, in big, broken-down letters and with two giant threes positioned to make one big eight, guests were promised eight-dollar rooms, per person, double occupancy. But that's not what attracted customers and made them slow their cars. Nor was it the moss-sheathed swimming pool or free cable TV in every room. It was the incredible neon sign itself, a fifteen-foot pair of tumbling dice that, because of their size and the menacing way in which they were positioned above the boulevard, gave the illusion of being rolled straight from the heavens. This was entirely possible, as each time the huge blocks rolled streetward, their bright white borders gelling into a frenetic neon orchestration, they revealed seemingly random combinations (a three and a five; two ones) until a five and a two—a lucky seven—was rolled.

Trina showed no interest in the dice, and Nat was unnerved by the very sight of it. P, however, was spellbound, unable to take his tiny eyes off the way the electric cubes followed their precise, illuminated journey and began, every thirty seconds, a brand-new, complex, and utterly fascinating lifecycle.

The dog studied the lights intently, as if stalking a

fallen baby bird in the low grass. A thousand blinking bulbs reduced to black for one moment and then, in less time that it took for his heart to skip a beat, flashed brightly again, hanging a quarter of the way down and showing a three and a five. This, P found terrifying. He barked ferociously, his stale bug-breath gusting like a hot desert wind against the glass.

Trina raised her window to keep the dog from leaping out in attack. She smoothed P's ears back and tried whispering that it was all right; but when the dice came still closer, blinking off and then exploding again in bright white light to reveal the dreaded snake eyes, P lost all composure. He scrambled for the backseat, digging his nails into Nat's forearm, and began to howl.

The sign's fantastic design could be seen from the street as Nat slowed to see what all the fuss was about. The tubing, a nearly transparent maze of glass and metal, intricately wound its way through the night sky in a random, frantic fashion, like a bumblebee's flight path. Unlit and empty, the tubes were nothing more than a mess of glass humming softly in spent energy—no reason, no pattern. But once lighted, even a small portion would reveal a true technological wonder.

"Lucky Seven Motel," Trina read aloud, as if to say to the dog See, there's nothing to be scared of.

Next, massive gold script emblazoned across the darkness, revealing that it was, indeed, The Lucky Seven Motel. The snake eyes disappeared into the anonymous maze of tubing; and less than a moment later, a five and two blazed gloriously, accompanied by the invasive buzz of electric energy that could be felt even inside the wagon, even with all the windows up. The light bathed the interior of the car like a hundred flashbulbs going off at once and, in just another second, was gone.

If a dog could gasp in wonder, that is what P did next. His lips trembled and his nose twitched and he paced worriedly, and Nat wondered if it were true that animals can sense impending disasters like earthquakes and floods. She and Trina sat silently, suspended in the half-blue, half-black light of the spent neon, waiting for the ringing in their ears to die. Nat's heart pounded in anticipation of what would happen when the white light would again explode overhead like fireworks, and somewhere next to her Trina whispered "Come on, come on, let's get out of here before this dog goes completely wacko."

Before she could punch the accelerator, though, the huge dice appeared again, this time fifteen feet up and perched to begin their happy assault on the next car back. P curled his lip and spit through a crack in the window even after they were blocks past and, finally, the gigantic quasi-cubes had been swallowed up in the resplendent sea of electric light that lined the strip.

"Whoo-hoo!" Trina howled as she lowered her window and shouted out to the crowd. "Welcome to Vegas, bay-bee!"

Starting in Barstow, the trip had taken a decidedly weird turn, and it seemed that the harder Nat tried to stay the course the more likely it was she would be unable to. She had enjoyed a brief respite in the short jog from the prison to the perimeter of Vegas—a time during which she had again happily succumbed to the dull purity of her quest. But the resolve she had felt before leaving home—before the accident and before Arizona Tyler—like the sterile silence of the prison that was shattered by automatic aluminum locks would someday be remembered as just a faint ringing in her ears that nothing, not popping gum or forcing air through her eardrums, would rid her of.

The prison wedding, spider webs, and the smell of burning oil haunted her heart. Dirty wildflowers and razor wire. They were random, disconnected images,

coming slowly, like looking at a stack of vacation snap-
shots, waiting impatiently for them to be passed along
one at a time

(and this is us at Hoover Dam.)

Come on, come on, already... she thought impatiently. *Let's see how this is going to end.*

Vegas: one minute just a sign along the side of the
freeway, the next an epiphanic roll of the die that would
knock her right on her ass.

As they made their way slowly down the strip, crawl-
ing through the thick of traffic, Trina pointed out places
of interest she had known on other trips, some with Arizona, some not.

"That's a great restaurant," she'd say excitedly,
or "That place is dirt cheap!" Passing the lumbering,
graceless cityscape that was fashioned to look like the
New York City skyline, she squealed with delight, "I
won two hundred bucks last time I was there!"

Driving slowly past the five thousand-room hotel
casinos that crowded the line of sight on both sides
of the strip, past the lots where, with your winnings,
you could rent a luxury sports car or Rolls limo for the
night, Nat and Trina felt the heat of neon on their faces
and the backs of their hands. All-you-can-eat filet mi-
gnon or the Folies Bergere at the Tropicana; maybe a
magic show at the Sands or some 70s TV star in a one-
man revue. One need only imagine something fantastic
in Vegas before finding in on the menu at one hotel or
another.

Inside, behind the automatic sliding glass doors that
led to the cool, carpeted casinos, children fell asleep
under the inattentive eye of the security cameras while
their parents made short order of losing whatever meager savings had been set aside for college.

Irony: The Sequel is how the night would play on
the marquee if someone were to document it on film.

But trying to remember, much less record, anything that happened in Vegas—weddings, winnings, losses—was futile, because whatever happened there happened fast, and mostly when one wasn't looking.

Nat followed Trina's directions off the strip and headed down a wide, dark boulevard that was sparsely populated by large economy hotels and supermarkets with slot machines. As they drove further from the main drag, the sounds of civilization quieted; and they could hear the wind for the first time. They lowered their windows, and let the night blow through the car; their faces and hands cooled without the sun-like rays of electric light that seemed to follow everywhere one went in Vegas.

Trina watched the dark landscape out the window and, with her left arm slung over the backseat, rubbed P's head as he quieted and eventually fell asleep. She told Nat to slow the car in front of a cluster of small businesses about two miles south of the main drag. There, they spotted the address they were looking for in front of a place named The Star-Struck Room. Placed precariously over the parking lot was a bright-blue neon sign with pink comets and trails of stardust in lemon yellow. Nat observed that, in Vegas, almost everything was spelled out in neon. Beauty parlors, Chinese restaurants, even the key shop next door. WE NEVER CLOSE, it said, even though it was dark inside and no signs of life came from within.

The parking lot smelled of dried beer and cigarette butts. Nat coughed the smell back up and pointed to a tattered sign above the doorway, ENTER AT YOUR OWN RISK; but Trina just shrugged and stepped inside, disappearing behind the ninety-degree angle of a faux wood-paneled entryway. Nat lowered the windows a few inches for P to get some fresh air, locked the car, and tentatively followed her inside.

The first thing Nat noticed about the inside, the first thing anyone could notice about The Star-Struck Room, was its homemade outer space motif. This consisted mostly of Day-glo Styrofoam planets and a Milky Way mobile dangling off some metal clothes hangers stuck into the ceiling. Several black lights, placed strategically around the room and hung close to the ceiling, gave the room a deep-space glow, casting a brilliant purple shine on even the dingiest white t-shirts and lighting up everyone's teeth nice and gruesome. The bar—a massive, graceless semicircle made of fake bamboo—was inconsistent with the spatial feel of the rest of the club, and Nat guessed that after spending all that money on a new neon sign not much had been left over for interior decorating.

She had never felt comfortable with the club scene in LA. Not a joiner by any stretch of the imagination, she did not believe herself to possess that girl vibe that incited men to send drinks to her table or come and introduce themselves. It wasn't her looks that kept men from approaching—she'd been described as cute, even beautiful, by lots of them. More, it was some endogenous discomfort, expertly albeit unintentionally transmitted through a subtle and complex combination of body language and avoidance of eye contact. On the infrequent occasions when she would join some women from the office for Ladies Nite, she would sit with wretched anticipation while each girl in turn was eventually asked to dance, leaving Nat alone to watch the purses and make sure their drinks were not spiked.

Even more infrequently, there had been times when one of those men would ask Nat for a dance. She was convinced it was not due to any real attraction on his part but instead a compliance with some twisted "must-play" rule, that unspoken pact among some singles that stipulates all girls at the table dance, or none do.

It was of little consequence either way. How could anyone find love, Nat thought, in a place where female bartenders specialized in something called a Blowjob? (It was always a pretty clear indication that the evening was going to tank if the man you were with got an inordinate amount of pleasure from ordering a Blowjob in such a place.)

The Star-Struck Room was as far as one could get from the clubs of Wilshire Boulevard.

The dance floor was strewn with a dozen or so tables—some square like card tables, some round that would fit only two people—laid out in no particular design. The stage, at the far end of the room, was nothing more than a wooden platform set a couple of feet above floor level, with a curtain of sparkly tinsel behind. One yellow spotlight hung above; but as the light was dim, the room was hard to maneuver.

A massive Wurlitzer jukebox sat silent in the corner while customers were treated to the melodic crooning of an all-girl band playing a wistful cover of "To Sir With Love."

"I hope we didn't miss anything," Trina whispered excitedly as she took Natalie's hand and led her through a maze of splayed legs and feet that blocked their path in nearly every direction.

They found a small, private table against the back wall, next to the restroom and with a good view of the stage. It was cluttered with a few empty drink glasses and bottles, some smeared with lipstick, some stuffed with doused cigarettes, bloated with stale crémè de menthe. The tabletop was sticky with spilled drinks so Nat let her arms fall limply to her sides, tapping her fingertips against her thighs and trying to find someplace clean to lay her hands.

"Isn't this great?" Trina asked excitedly, waving her arm to get the waitress's attention.

"What is this place?" Natalie asked.

A brassy young waitress arrived and eyed Nat with suspicion. She was tall and thin and dressed in an outfit that looked like something out of a Flash Gordon serial. A short, silver skirt sat low on her hips, exposing a gold navel ring and a colorful tattoo of a popular cartoon character. She wore white ski boots, which made it nearly impossible for her to walk, and a silver bra over which someone had pinned two hand-formed foil cones that covered her small breasts.

Trina ordered a plain tomato juice.

"Diet Coke," Nat said, and when the waitress rolled her eyes, Trina changed Nat's order to a Kamikaze.

"Relax," Trina told her. "You know, if you're not careful, you may even have some fun."

"Could you clear our table?" Nat asked the waitress before she could skulk away, and then immediately wished she had not. Glowering at Nat between admiring looks in Trina's direction, the space girl emptied the table top with one wide sweep of her bony forearm. Empties and wadded up napkins landed with a crash into a brown plastic tub she struggled to keep from dropping. She dragged a wet rust-colored cloth over the table, leaving on the surface wide circular streaks of whatever goo had previously been wiped up from somewhere else.

As the young waitress awkwardly made her way back to the bar, Nat noticed a silver tail had been pinned to the back of her skirt. She tapped her elbows on the still-sticky tabletop a few times, looking for a not-so-gummy spot in which to place them.

"This used to be the Wanna-Lei-a-Girl Bar," Trina said, looking around and taking in the new decor, "but I guess they went outta business."

"I guess," Nat replied, pushing sticky bits of stuff left over from the table onto the floor with the edge of a folded-up napkin.

"This is way better," Trina said, a statement that gave Nat cause to wonder what it could have looked like before.

The band, which had broken into a soulful, melodic ballad that sounded something like a cross between New Age and Country, was comprised of four twenty-something girls. The guitarist and lead singer, a short-haired blonde with no visible tattoos or piercings, maintained eye contact with the audience and eventually came to lock eyes with Nat, who looked away with embarrassment.

"Check it out," Trina teased. "You're getting some action over there, girl."

The Star-Struck Room was a place Nat would never have found by herself and, if she had, would never have had the nerve to go into, not even to get change for the phone or to ask directions. She was a little intimidated and out of her element, but had to admit enjoying a certain degree of cool at being in a gay bar with someone like Trina. Even knowing this, on some level, and now admitting it—Trina's gay?—brought Nat into a kind of unspoken, imagined accord with the others in the place. Commonality was something she did not find easily; and even though she knew things might turn a dime if one of the women were to actually approach her, she felt, for the moment, content to sit in the back with Trina, checking out the crowd and waiting, like the others, for the show to begin.

There were less than two dozen people in the whole place, but the purple walls and tight floor arrangement made it seem much more crowded. An odd assortment of couples and singles sat at the tables laid out in front of the stage. Talking amongst themselves, tapping their feet and singing along with the girl band that was clearly a favorite, they gelled with a cohesiveness that wasn't often felt in a gathering place of total strangers.

Most women were in pairs, or threesomes; there were two good-looking men sitting off by themselves, nearly hidden in the back, and an assortment of young women occupied two small tables near the front of the stage. Groupies, maybe, Nat thought. Two slightly older women, the sole occupants of the dance floor, clung to one another and dragged their feet across a surface that stuck to the bottom of their shoes.

Those who sat at the bar, with their backs to the rest of the club, aligned themselves in an upright position, waiting for either a refill or for last call, prepared to blithely accept whichever would be suggested first.

The room seemed to spin a bit, probably owing to the twirling planets overhead that banged into the waitress's forehead every time she approached the bar. Venus was plastic and hollow like a whiffle ball, and it bonked the back of her head like one of those 70's desk accessories with the chrome balls on string. Thump, thump, thump, thump—the rhythmic hits coming closer together but softer as their energy was spent on that waitress's fuzzy red hairdo and mangled foil antennae that had been fitted to a headband.

The bartender was a gorgeous, muscular guy with beautiful feathered hair and a thick mustache. He reminded Nat of her junior high science teacher, Mr. Poquette, for whom she had harbored a powerful crush all through the eighth grade. She received a week without TV when her mother was told a student had been calling Mr. Poquette's home and accusing him of being "adorable" but "a tease," and that Mr. Poquette thought it was Nat's voice. Of course, that was never proven, and it still angered her that he had allowed her beautiful, innocent crush to end so badly.

Trina was giddy with excitement; but as intriguing as it felt to sit in such a place, with such a person as Trina, Nat feared her trip was in danger of going abysmally awry. She feared the whole thing might end there in Vegas; and even worse, that the others—the guys who told her not to go—might have been right all along when they told her "just because you believe it doesn't make it so."

In the dimly lit, purple gay bar, Natalie clung to her naiveté like the ladies on the dance floor clung to one another; but reality has a pull like quicksand, and she mostly felt that she never should have stopped on the highway. She started to feel rise within her a panic that she'd just gone too far this time, and she had to admit it, even if just to herself.

As Nat's fear was about to overtake her and send her running for the parking lot, for the highway and all points north, the drummer onstage broke into a drum roll, indicating something momentous was about to occur. Unfortunately, it looked at first like the long wait for the big show had built much more anticipation than could be satisfied by the entertainer hired to "thrill and chill" audience members: Psychic Madame Silvia, a woman whose entire career had been built on a unique gift she called "Face Reading," which was the ability to decode a person's romantic aura based on the lines in their face and the shape of their features.

"Not exactly bending spoons by the sheer will of your mind," Nat whispered to Trina, who shushed her and fidgeted in her seat, hoping, no, *willing* Silvia to come and read her face.

The act had potential in a freaky, exhibitionist way. But as Silvia moved from one audience member to another, revealing such secrets as "You've had a painful breakup" and "You're looking for your soul mate," Nat was disappointed to realize the show might be just plain bad. Not a cool, campy sort of bad that would make for a hilarious story one day, and not even the kind of bad you'd find in some offbeat dive in Hollywood where only the coolest people knew to go. No, this was Valley Bad, a term coined long ago by Nat and her friends that meant bland, ordinary, unable to excel even at stink.

Trina vibrated with anticipation as Madame Silvia stumbled toward the back of the room where she and Nat sat obscured by the purple shadows of the black light.

"Aha," Silvia drooled and pointed a crooked finger toward the dark corner where Nat tried to blend into the background. "I'm getting something here..." Nat watched in abject horror as the buxom, elderly psychic shuffled toward their table. She was tanned like leather, and the surface of her skin was covered in ripples of loose, spotted flesh. She wore dozens of jangly bracelets that clanked together like trash can lids when she raised her arms, and her transparent chiffon costume was marred by runs in the delicate fabric and small, neat craters most likely caused by a dropped lighted cigarette.

Nat could feel the entire world's gaze upon the back of her neck.

"Oh, yes, I'm getting something here," Madame Silvia cooed in a throaty, raspy voice.

"Oooh, do me, do me," Trina squealed, unable to conceal her excitement any longer.

Madame Silvia eyed first Trina, then Nat, then remarked coyly, "I think I speak for all of us, dear," she said to Trina, "when I say nothing would delight me more." She laughed lewdly and licked the corner of her mouth, and Trina just howled. Nothing seemed to please this girl more than the chance to laugh at herself.

The audience whooped their approval, and Nat gripped the edge of her chair with her fingers and prayed that Madame would keep on walking.

Encouraged by the cheers and shouts of the audience, Madame Silvia placed her fingers under Trina's chin and lifted her face into the eerie, otherworldly light. With one hand she removed Trina's eyeglasses and set them on the table. With her other, she waved at the audience behind her back, indicating her desire for complete silence. A hush fell upon the room, and Nat half-expected Trina to levitate right out of her chair and up to the moon that was stapled overhead.

"You are in love, my dear," Madame Silvia said as she touched Trina's eyelids, and the crowd gave a short burst of quiet applause and then fell silent again. She looked sideways at Nat and added, "And who can blame you?"

The psychic moved her long, leathery fingers over Trina's nose and cheeks, feeling the few wrinkles that had started to form around her eyes, tracing the path of her dark, thin eyebrows as she read Trina's love aura.

"You have seen heartbreak," Madame Silvia said. "You have experienced a loss..." Trina nodded in agreement. "But you are embarking on a new beginning," the Madame said with firm optimism. "You are starting over. You have made a great change in your life."

"Oh...my...God!" Trina gasped, looking deep into Madame Silvia's creviced black eye sockets.

Nat rolled her eyes and thought of the palm readers on Venice Beach who would titillate tourists with their lame predictions of change, growth, and loss. Like the anonymous horoscopes you could find in any magazine on the newsstand, Madame Silvia might as well predict that the sun would rise tomorrow.

"But you..." Madame Silvia's tone changed as she slowly turned to face Nat, a flurry of jangly bracelets and torn chiffon billowing over them like fairy dust. Her voice was questioning, unsure. "You..." she said as she looked deeply into Nat's face, her fingers reaching out but not touching, indicating with a small gesture the distinct outline of Nat's square, set jaw. She regarded

Nat silently for a moment, and then declared, "You are not in love..."

Trina gasped; Nat sat dumbly, waiting to be revealed for the high-school-sweetheart-chasing, man-losing, girlfriend-lacking non-Fresh girl that she was.

"You were married once," Madame Silvia continued softly. "...but not anymore..."

Nat's gaze dropped, and with her left arm, she gently pushed Madame Silvia's hand away. The whole world was watching. The room had fallen silent except for the rustling of shoes on the sticky floor and the occasional soft swoosh of someone exhaling a deep drag off a cigarette.

"The path you have recently chosen is wrong for you..." Madame Silvia warned. Nat coughed and reached for the pack of cigarettes, but Madame Silvia's cool, leathery came hand to rest softly on hers, covering her fingers. "...but you will correct this." Then, with a sly smile she added, "And you will find what you are seeking."

As if on cue, the girl drummer hit the snare and burst the stupor that all had fallen into watching Madame Silvia read Nat's face.

Ba-da-bing.

Madame Silvia turned to face the audience, who burst into applause. She waved her arms over her head as she shuffled back to the stage, where the yellow spotlight was now joined by an orange one of equal dimness. She bowed deeply. Once, twice, again as she backed into the glittering tinsel that hung from a dowel overhead then disappeared backstage.

"That was kinda fun, but sort of a gyp, huh?" Trina said sourly, as Nat lit her cigarette and the girl band broke into a funky version of Roy Orbison's "Pretty Woman." The lights came on behind the bar, and the crowd got up to pee or order another drink or just stretch their legs. "And here I thought she was dead-on."

Nat tapped the tip of her cigarette nervously against the ashtray. She sat in silence, feeling like Cinderella at 12:01. It wasn't just being unmasked in front of the whole kingdom that was so hard. More, it was the rude awakening of finding out she really might not be whom she says, or thinks, she is. Like rifling through the memory box in her grandmother's attic, coming across a letter or a card that sparked a bad memory, leaving her to sit there and say, "Oh, yeah, I had completely forgotten about that."

Nat's marriage had, until that night, been stowed safely with lots of other remembrances she just didn't care to own—just another event from the past one could almost erase from history simply by remembering around it. Not denial, really, because to deny would be to acknowledge the existence, and that alone could give the memory form. Nat's method, the method of those who truly mean to rewrite history, was a blunt, skillful delusion. To ask whether Nat had ever been married might as well be to ask if the sky held two moons. Such a question could not be given so much merit as to even ponder, even for the briefest of moments.

That night, though, two big fat moons sat high in the sky, and Nat was left to wonder what to do with the warning that had been dumped in her lap by professional psychic Madame Silvia.

"Oh...my...God," Trina said. "She was right, wasn't she?"

"Ugh, could you not do that?" Nat said.

Their surly, spacey waitress had returned, this time with another round, on the house. "From Madeline," she said in her best churlish manner.

"*Madeline?* Oh, God, where is she?" Trina squealed with delight. "Nat, you have to meet Madeline, you have to!"

Suddenly, a shrill scream pealed through the club. It was a sturdy but high-pitched squeal like the Fresh Girls would make upon seeing each other in the halls on Monday morning, greeting one another in an way that would make you think they hadn't seen one another in years and, at the same time, inflicting upon everyone else the reminder of an unbridled, unknowable bliss that came from belonging to a clique they would never be invited to join.

"Aaaaaaaaaaaahhh!" Nat winced when the second scream came, this time from Trina. "There you are!"

Trina jumped up from her seat and flew into the open arms of the very tall, very broad-shouldered woman whom Nat presumed to be Madeline.

"You bitch!" Madeline laughed as she wrapped her muscular arms around Trina's body and lifted her off the ground. "You were in town and you didn't even tell me?" She effortlessly twirled Trina like just another bright, random star in the murky Milky Way above their heads.

"We just got into town, I swear!" Trina gasped breathlessly. They kissed hard, with tight-pressed lips, like a girly version of the serious business handshake. "Oh, God, it's good to see you!"

"I know." Madeline released her bear hug grip on Trina, and they looked into one another's faces. She towered at least eight inches over Trina, who strained on tiptoes to keep her nose from crashing into Madeline's gigantic bosom. She kissed Trina and hugged her close again, tossing her like a rag doll from left to right as she spoke, accenting each word with a flail in the other direction. "I...missed...you..."

"Ugh!" Trina laughed. "You're crushing me!"

They sat across from one another and giggled like children, brushing one another's arms and faces with their fingertips, as if touching a beautiful apparition they were afraid would, at any moment, turn out to be nothing more than a fond, vaporous memory.

"Oh, baby," Madeline said warmly, squeezing Trina's hand. "It seems like forever since you were here."

"I know." Trina smiled and touched her hand to Madeline's cheek. "I missed you, too." Madeline nodded. "Oz says hello, says to give you a big ole kiss!"

Madeline laughed. "Ha! That little SOB would send you with his kiss! Do you think if he were standing right here he would give it to me himself?" For the first time, she looked straight at Nat, as if expecting her to supply the most obvious answer. "Of course, he wouldn't," Madeline said. "Chickenshit," she added and then laughed.

"Madeline," Trina said, taking Nat's hand, "this is my friend Natalie. Nat, this is Madeline."

Madeline looked warmly into Nat eyes and took her hand. She shook it gently but firmly and held on for almost a full minute. "Of course, it is," she said to Trina without taking her eyes from Nat. "Welcome, Natalie. Consider yourself at home."

"Speaking of home, what happened?" Trina asked.

"Do you like it?" Madeline asked. "I don't know what came over me, I guess I just burned out on that whole Hawaiian thing. Everything in Vegas is so Elvis, isn't it? Well, one night I was having a night of passion with my new love...oh, my God, Trina, I've fallen in love!" she said with surprise, as if having just realized she'd lost ten pounds or found a pair of lost earrings or discovered some other wonderful hidden thing. "His name is Bob," she said to Trina. "Mexican Bob."

Trina pressed her hands together like in prayer and touched them to her lips. "Mexican Bob," she repeated with awe. "That is so great!"

"More later," Madeline said with a wink, and then

"...we were together one night and it just came to me... rockets! And spaceships! Star Struck! It's perfect for Vegas, don't you think?"

Trina and Nat both nodded in agreement.

"On Sundays we have celebrity look-alikes," Madeline said. "We've got a mean Dionne Warwick comes around every week and wins hands-down. She is not to be missed."

Nat watched Trina and Madeline reminisce and talk about the things they had missed most about one another. They laughed and squeezed one another's hands and sat knee-to-knee like best friends, and a large part of Nat was jealous. They didn't look, physically, like they would fit together at all, even as casual acquaintances. Trina was natural, tomboyish, and had a funky, urban style that made you think of words like "unemployed" and "alternative." Madeline looked like the trophy wife of some aristocratic jetsetter, every inch of her body, from the part of her jet-black hair to the tips of her painted toenails, prepped to perfection. She could have been Miss Texas, sitting there on that crappy plastic chair like it was a custom-built divan.

She wore a black sequined floor-length gown that highlighted the smooth, pale skin of her neck and bare shoulders. Her lashes were long and delicate, like the feathers of a peacock; and she deftly batted them at just the right moments in conversation so as to captivate the listener and require their full attention. Her figure was perfect, her breasts big but not in that too-big Vegas-y style that looked so fake. Her long legs crossed at the ankles, her narrow, delicate feet fit into her high heels perfectly. She had rosy, full lips, natural shadow; and just the hint of color on high, sculpted cheekbones made her look like the Freshest of girls. It was hard not to stare; it was hard not to be a little bitter that the awkward bunch of chromosomes in Nat could shape in someone else such a flawless example of a girl.

Madeline wore little jewelry—no earrings at all and just a few rings on the slender fingers that were each capped with perfectly manicured nails, buffed to a satin shine. She wore diamonds—set in platinum probably, not just white gold—two on her left hand and one on her right. She was an anomaly in The Star Struck Room, instead looking like she belonged on a poster in the lobby of the MGM—anywhere but there, in deep space.

Yet even in the dingy club she evoked a confidence that, whether she were sitting atop a solid gold throne or on a pile of dirt and rocks, let you believe she was precisely where she should be.

"What'd you think about the Madame?" Madeline said then, turning to Nat, "So, did she get you?"

"She got me," Nat said with a reluctant grin.

"I had no idea…" Trina said, mouth agape. "I had no idea Nat had been married!"

"Well, I can't wait to find out what other secrets are hidden inside of Natalie—if that is your real name…" Madeline said dramatically and with an exaggerated wink." She waved to the dreamy bartender, whose sudden presence beside Nat made her blush. "Whatever it is they're drinking," she told him, "more please…and bring it upstairs. We've got girl business."

Nat took in that simple phrase. She suddenly realized that she'd never been properly taught how to conduct Girl Business; and that if she had, she would likely be much further along than she was at that moment—in life, in love, on the highway, on the way to getting drunk. The things that make up a girl's business were to her, at thirty-five, still about love and finding the right one. Like a needle stuck in a never-ending groove, she could hear her own business resounding in her head, above the girl band, above the voices of Madeline and Trina and above the pounding of her own heart: I can't get it right I can't get it right I can't get it right I can't get it right.

Girl Business. It was time she got it right.

Nat had over fifteen hundred miles still to go and was already way behind schedule. In less than ten hours, she'd witnessed a fatal car crash, made friends with an actual girl, acted as bridesmaid in a prison wedding, and had her deepest secret revealed to a crowd of lesbians and others. She knew that any decision other than the one to get up and leave—now!—surely meant nothing but trouble, on so many levels, but after just two Kamikazes decided to allow one more detour.

It was her burning bush, that night of Girl Business, though this would not be known to her for several more weeks.

"Girl business," the dreamy bartender laughed. "No men? Shame." He eyed Nat and winked.

"Oh, he's harmless," Madeline said to Nat as the girls gathered their things and headed up a dark, narrow staircase. "He woos widows and takes their money. Oh...your ex isn't dead, is he?"

Nat shook her head.

"Are you loaded?"

Nat shrugged.

"Money, not liquor," Trina laughed.

Nat shook her head again.

"Well, then, consider yourself out of harm's way," Madeline reassured Nat, who took no comfort but great delight in knowing that to not be true at all, at least for the time being.

five

The happy sounds of Abba played from a compact portable record player in a pink vinyl case, the kind Nat had used to play her favorite records over and over until one of her brothers would storm in and yank the cord from the wall, shouting "That's not rock and roll, Nat!"

Waterloo, promised you'd love me forever more...

"What the hell happened to the 70s? Can someone tell me that?" Madeline said and then chimed in *I tried to hold you back but you were stronger, and now it seems my only chance is giving up the fight...* and shook her butt through the tight fabric of her dress. "God, I'd give anything to be twenty-one again!"

She laughed wickedly and innocently, both at once, and this made Nat laugh, too.

Nat liked Madeline. Though she was a striking woman, Nat didn't feel at all unFresh in her presence; on the contrary, she felt pretty and feminine, even in her jeans and with her hair uncombed. The way Madeline looked at her—looked at anyone—was extraordinary. Not really maternal, but with a gaze that seemed as if it could see only the lovely one had to offer and none of the flaws, the ugliness, that usually showed when one was in the presence of other females. Madeline wasn't conscious of her beauty in the way so many other woman appeared to be. Maybe because of that, she seemed unconscious of others' lack of it; and for this, Nat fell immediately in love with Madeline in the way she supposed girls loved one another.

"I don't know," Madeline sighed, eyeing herself in the full-length mirror. "I guess we all gotta go sometime."

The second floor apartment occupied the same square footage as the dingy bar below, but its open floor plan and sparse furnishings made it seem almost palatial in comparison. It was long and narrow and mostly dark, except for a few colorful lanterns strung across the ceiling and some white Christmas lights that framed two large picture windows through which one could see the brilliant, blinking horizon of the strip.

Although there were only a few pieces of real furniture, there were mounds of pillows and throws scattered about the hardwood floor, from beneath which came the bass of the girl band and, during breaks, the jukebox downstairs. Near the record player was a white wicker loveseat with splintered, wobbly legs. The colored cotton cushions on it were faded but still garish; they sagged in the center where people were most likely to take a seat when invited to.

Beside the loveseat was a small ornate table with fake gilding that was cracked and had peeled away in some parts, exposing the pale blond wood underneath. On top of this was a desk lamp with a tattered shade that was partially hidden underneath a gold silk scarf. It was little feminine touches like these—paper lanterns, silk scarves, the smell of perfume—that gave the room its warm, golden hue. That made it feel like home.

At the far end of the room was a small, bare kitchenette populated only by an empty, unplugged fridge and a 50s-style dinette with black-and-gold-speckled vinyl seats. Against the long wall with no windows was a bamboo room divider, over which were strung piles of brightly colored clothes, an old-fashioned steamer trunk, and two garment racks, upon which were hung dozens of elaborate, showy costumes made mostly of fringe, lots of sequins, and feathers and velvet. All were dresses, except for one silver pantsuit made of stretch polyester that reminded Nat of the twirling Styrofoam galaxies downstairs.

Beside the garment racks were two hat stands, both overflowing, and beside those, an Art Deco vanity table with an enormous circular mirror. Photos—some in frames, some lying about like tossed-away slips of paper upon which were written the phone numbers of strangers Madeline said you might like to fuck but never call—buried the surface of the vanity like a January snowdrift. Dozens of others were taped crookedly to the mirror, to the walls—to any available surface—and cluttered Nat's view of her reflection. At the other end of the room sat a double bed with a dull brass frame.

Nat walked tentatively around the room, experiencing Madeline's persona not through questions or conversation but through the sensory revelations the woman had created in the little room upstairs. Rubbing her palm over a textured bedspread, letting her splayed fingers dangle in the burgundy tassels that hung from an antique lampshade in the corner, touching the fabrics and photos and even the woodwork, Nat made a sweep of the apartment and took in the lingering scent of some tropical flower that might have lived there in a vase, or in a perfume bottle, now long gone. Like a blind woman would acquaint herself with what at first is dark, unknowable, and terrifying, she maneuvered the corners of the room and, in the process, began to feel a sense of comfort and belonging.

Trina sprinted across the floor and dove onto the bed, squealing and giggling like an eight-year-old whose parents had just that moment pulled out of the driveway.

"I love this bed!" she yelled as she buried her face in the big fluffy pillows and rolled from side to side. "Can I sleep here?"

"Mi casa es tu casa, cherie," Madeline said. "Of course, you can—you can both have the bed. I'm going to spend the night at Bob's."

"Oh, but...I'm not..." Nat started to protest, believing still somewhere in the back of her mind that she might make it out of there before sunup and get to Utah.

"Best seat in the house," Madeline said, winking.

"Yeah, but..." Nat started again and realized she had once more been put in the unenviable position of breaking up the party. It wasn't anything like love, she thought, that kept her in Vegas "just a few more minutes." Rather, there came to her a sense that, for the first time in ages, she was making a connection, she was making friends of women and it wasn't false or forced or uncomfortable. She just smiled and looked forward to the drinks the dreamy bartender would soon be bringing, and resolved to slip out after she'd rested a while and had a chance to say goodbye to Trina privately. She took a seat on the floor, leaning against the bed where Trina was splayed out.

"Oh, God!" Trina suddenly exclaimed, flinging herself over onto her back and staring at the ceiling. "I'm tired like a thousand days!" She sat up and stared at them. "Really," she said. "I don't think I've slept in months."

Madeline gracefully walked the room in her bare feet, stretching her neck and her arms and even her toes when she walked. She took a seat on the small vanity stool and started to remove her jewelry.

"How's Oz?" she asked Trina.

"Good," Trina said. "He's good."

It was the second time the subject of Arizona had come up since they'd arrived, but Trina hadn't yet said anything about the wedding. It wasn't like an elopement, a lovely secret that must be kept from parents and others. Getting married in prison was about as sanctioned as a wedding could get, so Nat wondered why she wasn't spreading the good news.

"Ugh!" Madeline said, "I wish there was something I could do for that sweet boy." She opened the lower right drawer and removed a small silver box, into which she placed her rings.

"Bake him some cookies," Trina said, winking at Nat. "Deep down, aren't you really a homemaker at heart?"

Madeline snorted. "Home*wrecker* you mean."

Nat suddenly caught Madeline's eye in the mirror. At first, she stirred a little uncomfortably, like she'd been caught peeping in someone's window. But for that briefest of moments, she felt an immediate connection with the woman staring back at her. The whole thing took less than two seconds at most, but left in Nat a warmth that came from bonding with someone without saying, or doing, a thing.

"Are you okay?" Madeline asked her. "You look a little ill."

"I'm good—drinking too much, I think," Nat said, and felt Trina's hand tap her lightly on the head.

"She *is* good," Trina said, praising her like she would the dog.

The dreamy bartender, who was introduced as Griff,

arrived with two pitchers, one containing Kamikazes and the other plain tomato juice.

"You're not drinking?" Madeline asked Trina with shock. "What is it, planets out of alignment or something?"

"Trying to cut down, is all," Trina replied, shrugging it off. "You know what happens when you drink too much."

"Actually," Madeline said, "if you've drunk too much, you have no idea what happened."

"True." Trina winked and poured Nat a drink. "Maybe that's what you need, Natalie."

Nat stretched her legs and kicked off her new hiking boots. They'd been pinching her little toes for nearly four hundred miles, and she was glad to be rid of them. She wished she'd brought some flip-flops or tennis shoes, anything but the damned hiking boots, which might take her to the top of Mt. Kilimanjaro but couldn't be worn comfortably in the car.

"So, tell us about your fella," Madeline said coyly.

Nat went blank; it had been hours since she'd contemplated the lovely Guy and what wonderful possibility waited for her in the north. Still reeling from the realization that she'd left LA little more than twelve hours earlier, she seemed now to be deep within the rabbit hole, a place where nobody she knew was likely to find her and where the residents just assumed she, like them, was meant to be there. Upon remembering The Plan, she smiled broadly and blushed a little, trying to muster the strength to share her wonderful love story with another new female acquaintance.

"Oh, he's a great...man," she said, stumbling over that silly awkward way of describing him.

"No, no!" Trina scolded. "Not Guy! The other one!"

"Oh, there are two?" Madeline said with great interest. "You *are* full of secrets."

"The husband!" Trina replied with great emphasis. "Tell us about your husband!"

"Oh, my God, you mean that old bat was right?" Madeline laughed. "I'll be damned; she is worth sixty dollars."

"The Madame knew," Trina said, "but I didn't...and I'm hurt." She feigned a pout in Nat's direction. "Girlfriends share, Nat."

"If that were true," Madeline said, "I would be wearing that Mackie I had my eye on."

Did girlfriends share, Nat wondered. Was it really their business—everyone else's?

"Think of us as therapists," Madeline said, "and remember, it's not therapy until you cry."

Question answered; Natalie began at the end. Trying to encapsulate the whole affair into a few compact sentences, she tried, "It didn't work out" and "We were too young to know what we were doing," but the girlfriends would have none of it and demanded she start from the beginning: when they met, fell in love, why they married, how they blew it, and everything in between.

So, girls really were as difficult as she'd imagined, Nat thought as she forced herself to conjure up the unremarkable memory of how she and her ex-husband had met and married.

"I was waitressing. He was temping in the office across the street," she stated, trying her best to make the whole thing seem too trivial to even mention. "We went out a few times, and that's kind of it."

"Oh, come on," Madeline groaned. "What kind of tragic love story is that?"

It was an old tragic love story, Nat thought. It was a story that was over a long time ago, and it was hard to muster up much enthusiasm for sharing, with nearly complete strangers, one of the most hidden details of her past. Few of Nat's friends, even her closest ones, knew of her marriage and subsequent divorce. She'd so effectively put it behind her that when filling out insurance forms or loan applications or anything else that required some degree of personal history she automatically checked the "single" box instead of "divorced."

"He was an office worker-slash-musician-slash-writer," she said with a slight smile. "His name was Wesley, but he hated that. He liked to be called just Wes." She withdrew a cigarette from a fresh pack and lit it.

"Musicians are the worst," Trina said as she waved the smoke away from her face. "They never pay for anything."

They had dated for less than six weeks when struck with the notion to get married.

"It was so romantic, you know?" Nat remembered. "He wrote me this song, a song about me and being in love with me, and it was just so perfect. I thought, 'This is what people spend their whole lives looking for,' right? So I did it."

Unharmed, unprepared for the pain they could inflict upon one another, true virgins in nearly every sense of the word—and the world—the young couple drove up to Reno in the band's bus one weekend and were married in a small blue-and-white chapel off the lobby of a large casino. Not even old enough to gamble, they promptly returned to LA and moved into a tiny studio apartment in Echo Park, where the rent was cheap; and Nat was finally out of the Valley and her mother's home. She worked two jobs and went to school in between while Wes and his band struggled for local gigs that usually lasted a couple of days at most.

They started out poor and happy and, after eight months, could look forward to remaining just poor.

Theirs was a lifestyle others thought romantic and envied, but that Nat could never really get her hands around. She didn't like to party, and loathed people who spoke the word as if they were drunk even when they were not. "Hey, let's pa-tay!" they'd holler as they piled through her front door, and Nat would cringe.

She wanted to keep pets and other things that required routine, but she never knew exactly when her husband was likely to show up—or leave, for that matter. It pissed her off to wake to the six a.m. alarm and find people she didn't even know in her living room or bathroom, people who hadn't been to bed yet and showed no signs of leaving. She wasn't the kind of girl who could ever be described as "laid back," like Wes. She wanted order, purpose, and liked having short-term goals, like paying the bills or buying a new TV.

"Maybe that's what we loved about each other," Nat supposed out loud. "You know, that whole opposites attracting thing."

"'Opposites attract' is what people say when they really want to fall in love with someone they know they shouldn't," Trina said, and then added, "At least that's been my experience."

"Ditto," Madeline agreed. "Pure BS."

Wes was the complete opposite of Natalie. He wrote her poems and then put them to music and turned them into songs. He herded his pissed-off friends out of the house whenever Nat got her panties in a bunch. He tried to cook her dinner—when he was home and not too stoned to work the knobs of the gas stove. He picked flowers from the neighbors' yards and left them on the bed for her, but never remembered to shake the dirt off first. He seemed incapable of thinking any bad thoughts about his new young wife, no matter how hard she tried to make him.

He did all of the things Nat thought she wanted him to do, but as she had learned from her mother that long summer when she was still a child, it seemed there was always room for another request and could it really hurt to ask?

"I started not liking myself around him," Natalie remembered. "Do you know what it's like to be the uncool one? Well, that's what I was. I was definitely the uncool one. Everyone knew it."

"Like good cop, bad cop," Madeline observed.

"Exactly!" Natalie replied. "I was the bad cop. It was, like, my fucking job to be the bad cop." She was buzzed from the drinks and the cigarettes, neither of which she was used to consuming on such a regular basis. She kept saying "do you know?" even when not making a particular point, and constantly looked to the other girls for confirmation.

"I've always been the good cop," Trina said. "That's no walk in the park, either. I mean, people expect you to always be cool about everything, you know? And after awhile, you're not. You're not cool about anything because you're so fucking sick of being cool." She lit a cigarette. "I mean, really, when Oz went to prison there were these people who I thought were my friends—these fucking idiots!—would come up to me and say the stupidest things like 'Oh, Trina, it'll be okay, it's cool, at least nothing happened to you.'"

"They just meant because you two weren't—" Madeline offered.

"I know what they fucking meant," Trina snapped. "But it was totally not cool! I was not cool with it, with any of it! It just ruined our fucking lives, is all. Arrghh! I just wanted to explode, you know! I just wanted to tell them all to fuck off. See how cool you think I am then."

"Sometimes we all just wanna be the biggest asshole we can be," Nat said. "Just because we can!"

"Right!" Trina said, pointing her lit cigarette at Natalie and knocking a quarter-inch of ash onto the floor. "Sometimes, there's nothing wrong with being an asshole."

They all fell silent to consider this for a moment, and then Madeline said "Thank God!" and they laughed like drunk girls do, loud and boisterous and much more than the joke told would warrant.

Nat wished it were true, that there really was nothing wrong with being an asshole. But she'd been raised by one and knew better. It was a rare woman who did not, from early adolescence, nurture the terror of eventually becoming her own mother; and in this regard, Nat's fears were pure textbook. Psych 101.

"I swore I'd never be like her, never be her," Nat said, "but once I got out into the world...I don't know, it's like I just couldn't help myself! Suddenly, I was Barbara."

"Your mother," Madeline said matter-of-factly, and Trina gasped.

The girls were startled by a sudden knock at the door. It opened slowly, and fresh pitchers of Kamikazes and tomato juice magically appeared, followed by the dreamy 70s bartender, who set the drinks onto the floor in front of Nat.

"I thought you might be running low," he said with a wink to each of them in turn.

"I adore you," Madeline said, reaching out to touch him as he passed by, fluttering her fingertips over his leg like he was the Messiah.

"Don't burn the place down," was all he said as he disappeared into the dark hallway and shut the door behind him.

"Why can't I find a guy like that?" Nat said wistfully.

"If you have trouble finding guys to get you drunk, then I can safely say that you are looking in the wrong place," Madeline said.

"She likes his hair," Trina said to Madeline.

"I really loved Wes," Nat continued. "At least, I think I did. He was just so perfect, you know? And I was so...not. After awhile, it drove me crazy! His perfection glared against all the things that were wrong with me. I mean, nothing bothered him, and that made everything bother me!"

Wes was one of those guys who really could backpack through Europe on two dollars a day, she told them, sleeping in hostels and under trees and in the homes of people he'd just met at the train station. Unlike Nat, who couldn't imagine just picking up and doing anything without a plan. He could meet someone in line at the movies and before they'd reached the window would be inviting them home to party afterward.

The sweeter he got, the more Nat searched for the black that she knew was inside of him, looking for the button that, when pressed, would make him snap and stand up for himself and tell her to fuck off. She wanted him to say it. She got to the point where she needed to hear it. But he never would. He would only smile, kiss her neck, and say something like "Forget about it, baby. Let's make love," and Nat would be left to imagine a life where she would always be in control, she would be Barbara, and that frightened the shit out of her.

Natalie left home believing her mother to be the worst kind of female, the kind who would take her man's spirit from him. Only years later, while engrossed in the retelling of her and Wes did it occur to her that her mother may have had entirely other intentions.

"So, what happened?" Madeline asked. "Get to the good stuff."

"I cheated," Nat said. Just a few months into the marriage, she had entered into an affair with a co-worker, the manager at the café where she waitressed part time. He was grown up, older and more stable. He wore a shirt and tie to work every day. He owned a car that was still under the manufacturer's warranty, and he didn't live with roommates. She felt grown-up sneaking into his apartment in the middle of the day to make love, and for the longest time felt no guilt over leaving her boy-husband behind.

"Whatever happened to him?" Trina asked.

"I don't know," Nat replied truthfully, and added, "and I don't want to know." Secretly, she imagined that he married some nice girl and had six kids and took family vacations every year where nobody got depressed or divorced or committed suicide or did any of the other bad things Nat was sure she would have eventually visited upon her sweet husband.

"Oh...my...God. That is a sad story, Nat," Trina said. "You are breaking my heart."

She never thought about Wes, never talked about him, and this, she said to herself, was why. To consider him now would open the door to questions like "Did I do the right thing?" and "Was it my fault?" Remembering her marriage in all its gory detail was too painful, because any remembrance, even fleeting, would bring with it this sinking, dry-mouth dread. The kind that comes from realizing you've just driven your car off a bridge or performed some other reckless, stupid act from which you will never recover and which you will never live down.

In the end, Natalie explained away the complexities of her failed marriage simply, in that way many people explain away the first major catastrophe of their emotional lives—by blaming it on her age and inexperience.

"I mean," she said, "I was only eighteen, for Chrissakes."

Nat didn't know what time it was, but it felt like four in the morning. Being in that tiny upstairs apartment was like sensory deprivation—she had no sense of time or place other than her immediate surroundings. She was exhausted. Telling the story of Wes had sucked out the last bit of energy she'd been holding in reserve for the next leg of the trip, and all she could think of doing now was falling backward and passing out on the cushion of pillows that had been arranged on the floor. For the first time in a long time (ever?) Nat felt the sensation of just being. Not needing to be or do or think or say anything—just exist.

"Well," Madeline said, arching her back and stretching, "I give it a seven on a scale of ten."

"Eight," Trina offered with a warm, sad smile to Nat. "You know, since Madame Silvia was right about the marriage, maybe she's right about the other part, too—you know, about finding what you're looking for?"

"What's this about?" Madeline said, dramatically shuddering at the thought.

"She's going to get her soul mate," Trina explained.

"Is there a place," Madeline asked dryly, "where they are routinely kept? I'm just curious...for future reference."

Trina shrugged. "Nat's is in North Dakota."

On the heels of the story of the young, doomed marriage, the tale of Nat and Guy seemed, this night, sort of pathetic. Or, at least, made Nat feel pathetic.

"Who's this?" Madeline asked.

Trina told the story of Nat's first love, the premature separation, the meddling mothers and the hiking boots that reconnected them with the long tentacles of What Must Be. To Nat's relief and gratitude, she left out the part about the freak suicide attempt. Through it all, Madeline fixed her eyes on Nat and shook her head slowly, as if, indeed, regarding a pitiful sight.

"It is my experience," she said, "that people who feel

the sudden urge to find their 'first loves' have no idea what the fuck they are doing."

"Mad!" Trina shouted.

"So, what's the deal, Natalie? Why are you going? Really?" Madeline asked. She sat on the bed above Nat, who was still crouched on the floor, and patted her shoulder. "Had you talked to this man at all in the last fifteen years?"

"No," Nat replied.

"Had you written?"

"No."

"What do you think is going to happen when you get there?"

"I don't know..." Nat answered defensively. "Pick up where we left off?"

"Oh," Madeline said, "that would be walking one another to class and studying together? Or just give him a blowjob in the back of Daddy's car."

"Mad!" Trina shouted again.

"I take it back! I take it back!" Madeline said, raising her arms in surrender. "Ignore me, I'm talking out of my ass," she said. She smiled and bent over, pushing her high, rounded behind toward Nat. "Have you met my ass?" she teased. "It does most of the talking around here."

Trina slapped it playfully but hard and gave Madeline a stern but affectionate look. She patted the top of Nat's head and said, "Don't listen to her. What does she know about soul mates?"

"Nothing," Madeline said, as she lit a cigarette and inhaled deeply. "But I know a thing or two about love; and believe me, if you were in it you wouldn't be sitting here with us."

Further complications to the equation were the last thing Nat needed. She downed another drink and announced, "I'm leaving in a few minutes."

"You know you're too wrecked to drive tonight," Trina said sympathetically. "You'll wake early and go. It'll be okay."

Nat nodded. North Dakota might as well have been China that night, and she couldn't have felt further from Guy if she'd tried. But the psychic did say she'd find what she was looking for, and even though she didn't really believe in all that mystical shit the prediction was encouraging.

"What would Jesus do?" Nat drunkenly blurted out, and they all howled with laughter.

"He'd get over to his man's house before said man started calling all over town looking for him," Madeline said as she stood and slipped her large, narrow feet into her shoes. "You'll meet Bob in the morning. You're going to adore him, Trina."

Trina nodded. "I know I will. I can't wait to hear all about him."

"Well, then, you're in luck," Madeline replied. "Because if there's one thing Bob loves—other than me—it's talking about himself!"

Trina nodded. "Do I need to do anything here for you?"

There was nothing to do but enjoy the rest of the night, and try and keep Nat from getting sick. The girl band got off at midnight, at which time there was often an unofficial wet T-shirt contest that some of the regulars had concocted as a way of getting a free peek at some new girl's boobs.

Trina laughed and wanted to know if there was any prize money involved.

"Went up to fifty bucks last week," Madeline replied and then paused. "Am I running some kind of tittie Mustang Ranch that I don't even know about? Griff will lock up right after that. Feel free to join in," she winked at Trina. "Fifty bucks is fifty bucks."

"Oh, my God!" Nat suddenly groaned. "What time is it?"

"Eleven-thirty," Trina replied, and Nat groaned louder.

"Oh, my God, oh, my God, has time stopped completely or what?"

Madeline approached the spot where Nat lay writhing on the floor in anguish. She leaned over and tried to make eye contact, knowing that the best thing for a drunk girl was to get her to lock her gaze on something other than the spinning room; but Nat's eyes were wildly flailing about the walls and ceiling.

"Don't let her puke in my bed," Madeline warned.

"I won't," Trina promised.

"She doesn't get out much, does she?"

"Not much, I guess." Trina patted Nat's head and pushed her damp hair out from her face. "I'll take care of her."

Madeline turned for the door and stopped short. "Oh, I wonder if I should change..."

"I vote for comfy," Trina said, and Madeline nodded.

Nat struggled to place herself upright on the floor. Her bony elbows dug into the soft pillows, and she lifted her head, which by now felt like a thirty-pound water balloon, and watched Madeline. Whether it was the dreamlike surroundings of the apartment or just all that vodka she didn't know, but Madeline seemed to tower over her like a giant, iridescent goddess. Natalie watched in awe as Madeline touched her fingertips to her full, brunette head and, moving them in a lazy, circular motion, massaged her scalp. There came from deep within her chest soft groans of pleasure that were heard more like growls, and Nat was perfectly comfortable, in the midst of all that had gone wrong that day, to find herself sharing such a casual, but obviously intimate, girls-only moment.

Suddenly, Madeline grabbed a handful of her long, lustrous hair. Nat watched with rapt attention as her perfectly rounded fingernails, massaged her scalp, starting at her hairline and moving in gentle, widening circles over the crown of her head. Nat let her body sink further into the mattress of pillows on the floor. She tensed slightly, involuntarily, unable to imagine what special thing the three of them might share next.

It was a shock from which she would never really recover.

Madeline tugged at the jet-black cap that covered her head and slipped the flowing dark hair right off her head, exposing a completely bald scalp, and Nat was reminded of an old joke.

(That was no lady...)

Madeline scratched her—his?—head vigorously and then twirled the wig around on her long index finger, like an NBA pro spinning the game ball after a slam-dunk.

"Jesus, that feels good," she growled in a deep, masculine voice.

With sheer will, Nat fused herself to the floor. Her eyes drained of all expression. Her expression blank, her eyes fixed on nothing but air, in that way that amnesiacs suddenly remember their trauma in the most casual of places—on the bus, doing the dishes, sitting on the toilet.

Madeline wrapped a peach terrycloth turban around her head and tucked the ends in to keep it from falling off.

"Ugh! That's much better!" She gently draped the wig over a white, expressionless Styrofoam likeness of a woman's head and picked up a small valise that was placed next to the door. "Sleep tight, girlies!"

There was still time to clear Utah by dawn, Nat

thought, but only if she hadn't drunk so much. She could have been out of there and into the next county within the hour if she could only get her ass out of that bed and into the car.

Girl Business. Was there really such a thing, or was it just another ruse, a way that others had of tricking her into saying something she would later regret. Like those goddamned girls in the fifth grade who wandered the halls in packs, asking unsuspecting, uncool others, "Are you a Catholic or a Prostitute?"

There was nothing Nat had so far learned in Trina's or Madeline's business that would help her clarify, for herself, What Girls Do. How to know love. How to work it, how to solve it. There were no pieces discovered that could be applied to her and Guy. Like the missing components to an algebraic equation, the rational and irrational numbers, integers and all the other bits that add up to the mathematical certainty that X really does equal Y.

"How do girls do it?" she asked aloud, as Trina held a cool washcloth to her forehead and steadied her over the toilet bowl, where Nat threw up all she had taken in that day but could not keep down.

six

Like the countless pitiable migrants who come to Vegas as nobodies but leave as man and wife, Natalie awoke in the Capital of Love to the utter and divine completeness of finding herself in the aftermath of a wedding night. She lay supine, eyes closed and arms pressed lightly against her sides, enjoying the sensation of floating on the still, slate surface of a lake. The mattress gave beneath her body, creating gentle ripples in the sheets and tickling her flesh like tiny waves of warm, frothy breakwater. She looked not at the ceiling, not at her toes, able to focus coherently on neither objects nor thoughts; mildly anesthetized by the lingering affects of liquor and a sleepy denial of all that had assaulted her in the previous twelve hours, she simply lay on the waves. She felt herself just be.

She played with memories of a wedding night— memories or premonitions?—as if they were nothing more than leftovers of an erotic dream, delightful sensations of lust and longing that would with a simple

stroke of her fingers come literally to life beneath the
thin blanket that fell over her body like a gentle, swirling vapor rising from the surface of a warm pool. They
were wonderful, sinful remembrances made all the more
pleasurable by the sleepy contentment in knowing upon
waking they, like the involuntary twitch of a consciousness falling into a deep, dead sleep, would lessen in intensity until they were felt no more.

The buoyancy with which she began to awake called
to mind her eighth summer, the last she would spend
in the comforting bosom of a family still in love with
one another. It would be a year before her eldest sib-
ling, Anna, would lose her mind for no apparent reason, plunging herself and the others into years of mood
swings, violent tantrums, and, ultimately, suicide. Most
of that time Anna was sedated, left by the doctors to
aimlessly wander the rooms of the house when nobody
was about, ducking in avoidance into any open doorway, even the closet or the bathroom, when they were
about. Her only answer to any question put to her—why
she had cut off all her hair, why she had tried to cut off
Nat's—was to sigh wearily and, with her drooping gray
eyes, implore the asker to just leave her be.

"Just leave me be," she would say, moving like a
restless ghost through the house, levitating down the
hallway on her stocking feet past the fat yellow cat that
the year before she herself had named Punkin. Her condition was, to Nat, a constant puzzlement. She suffered
no physical ailment; she had not overdosed on drugs or
endured a violent blow to the head. Years after growing
up and gaining perspective, it occurred to Nat that even
cancer—something her own mother was terrified of—
would have been, at nine, a more finite comfort than
depression. "Depression" was a word Nat's mother and
father used often, first in whispers but later, as their
frustration grew, with sobs and shouts the whole neigh-

borhood would hear.

"Anna gave Punkin away," Nat remembered hearing one of her brothers wail one afternoon. Anna hit me; Anna threw my clothes out the window; why does Anna cry so much?—these were the mantras of '72 in Nat's home. "It's the depression," became the answer to all the mysteries of life; and in less than six months, her illness had become like an evil talisman strung around her neck, worn like a favorite pendant. The other children recognized it as clearly as if it were a topaz on a gold chain lying against her pasty white flesh, the stone shimmering in the light—when she would step into the light at all. They all hated it, for there was not one of them who did not wonder if it was a cursed birthright that each child, in due time, would inherit.

Anna never emerged from her depression, and as the strain became too great to bear, it looked as though Nat's mother might follow into the pit of that hopelessness as well; but as it turned out her demons were not sick at all, only angry and bitter at having been cheated out of something, the same thing that everyone in the family eventually came to feel cheated out of. Even at such a young age, Nat knew instinctively she would never again feel the euphoria of being eight years old and in love with her family.

Before the illness had taken everything—their energy, their money, their time, and, in the end, Anna's life—their last great holiday was at the lake. They rented a Winnebago big enough to sleep ten and packed enough supplies for a two-week journey to a wide lake somewhere in northern California. Nat's endless, sunny days were spent floating on an inner tube near the shore, treading water like an oil spill in a broad, indiscriminate path, but always under the watchful, protective eye of her father. They swam and fished and sunned themselves on the rocky shore, and lots of days

Nat didn't even wear a shirt. They ate fresh fish almost every night—sometimes Nat's mother made beans and franks—and at mealtime they would crowd around a wobbly table that doubled at night as Nat's bed.

There were other amenities: a gas stove with three burners, and a tiny sink that could hold three or four coffee cups at most. There was a toilet and a shower, but Nat's father bathed nude in the lake, like a pioneer. He would trudge barefoot to the shore every morning and, while the women were occupied doing dishes in the Winnebago, would lather up with a bar of soap and douse himself with the cold, clear water. He was a good father to the girls, and he let them indulge in the spoiled comfort of a hot shower; but he insisted his young sons wash in the lake "like men."

Nat's brothers, each having at one time felt the imminent threat some children feel when a baby is brought into the family, on those happy days coveted their baby sister with the enthusiasm they pretended not to have at home. They took turns teaching her how to swim, and throw, and bait a hook. And when the boys were off alone, Nat's mother would forget herself and simply enjoy her daughter's company, shampooing her hair in the lake, using a Dixie cup to rinse her hair until the water flooded her ears and dribbled into the corners of her upturned lips. It wasn't like the ocean—briny crud cold as ice and full of seaweed and other things that repulsed Nat. The lake was pure, undiluted; and although Nat, like any other eight-year-old tomboy, would rather have not washed her hair, it was something she was willing to tolerate to be with her mom.

Those happy years the family treated Nat like a precious gift, laughing at her silly jokes and listening to her nonsensical explanations of things like where the stars come from. At night they'd all meet back at the Winnebago, where underneath the retractable awning there had been neatly arranged a semicircle of lawn chairs.

Nat spent countless hours that summer sitting beside her father in the dimly lit cabin of that magnificent castle on wheels as they hopped from one campsite to another, savoring the best of what far from home could offer. While the others slept, she rode shotgun, fetching coffee for her old man, fishing his lighter out of the center console and trying to refold the road maps that had directed them into the further reaches of California. The hum of the highway underneath those huge tires sang like a lullaby; she would stay awake for as long as she could, which was never more than an hour, and eventually would fall asleep watching the broken white line disappear into the undercarriage of their vehicle. She let that summer happen in its own time; the experiences, both good and bad, were of their own design. It was a moment of life she would never be able to recreate.

On their fifth night out, after a long, satisfying day of fishing, Nat, in her underpants and nothing more, the gentle evening breeze caressing her slight, sunburned chest and shoulders, sat in one of the lawn chairs outside the Winnebago. She dangled her legs over the side of the chair, wriggling her toes in utter freedom, and watched with rapt attention as her father and brothers cleaned the fish they had caught that day. Before, on the dock, she had lain on her belly and watched the fish swim tentatively around the edge, their murky silhouettes visible six or seven inches below the water. They moved slowly in an unchoreographed pack, individually tethered by a nylon string that ran from the handle of her father's aluminum bucket to the tiny stainless steel hooks that skewered their fat lower lips. They looked almost magical, and Nat liked to think of them as tiny leprechauns of the deep that, once snared, would ensure for their captors endless years of good luck and fortune.

But lying in the bucket, their mouths agape and eyes as lifeless and black as the sky above the campsite, they looked only dead. Nat's brother Daniel, the second youngest, joined them and, with their father's pocket-knife, extracted a black eyeball from one of the fish and then flung it to the ground like snot from his nose. Nat looked on, horrified, as he bent over and inspected the tiny orb where it lay in the dirt and then, grasping it between his thumb and forefinger, dug it out of the sand, blew it off until it was shiny and black again, and, with a sadistic leer, pinched it hard until it popped. Nat had nightmares for three days and never ate a fish stick after that.

They were true Americans then, deliciously suburban in their pursuit of the California wilderness, to be found with complimentary maps provided by the triple-A. It was, as far as Nat could remember, the best time she had ever had.

The memories of that last summer came to her that morning in Vegas. They came on the first rays of sunshine and with the first warm breeze that tried to make itself known in the dank, cramped yellow room that had seemed such a comfort the night before. Remembering the sound of that poor fish's eyeball popping—the grayish liquid squirting out like overripe lemon juice and sending Nat screaming indoors for her mother—elicited in her a melancholy she felt like sharing.

She rolled over onto her right side to find Trina, snoring softly and oblivious to any fantasies—nostalgic or otherwise—Nat might be harboring. Nat wondered if Trina regretted getting married; if, given a choice, she'd have rather had it done by a look-alike Elvis in a chapel fashioned to look like Graceland. She wondered if this was all Trina would remember of her wedding day—the yellow room, the bad psychic, and Nat throwing up. Would she remember any of it in a year?

Suddenly, Nat realized her clothes were gone, and that she was dressed only in a pair of men's under-wear—not her own—and a short t-shirt that barely covered her belly.

She had no memory past the throwing up, and could barely recall that. She knew it must be daylight but had little point of reference.

The two picture windows framed in sparkling lights the night before were now hidden behind a thick shade that had been lowered sometime during the night, leaving the room shrouded in shadow when it should have been lit up in morning sun. Everything that had seemed golden, iridescent, the night before this morning was tinted brown, colored with tobacco vapors that hovered a foot above the floor and nested in the corners, like the evening fog coming into San Francisco Bay. It reminded Nat of flying low, just below the clouds.

She had no desire to move, not to get up, get dressed, or get on the road. Her joints had rusted over while she slept, and the slightest movement produced a pounding in her head; and so she just settled back into the crease her body had made in the sheets. She batted her eyes repeatedly until the ceiling came into focus, and she listened to P breathing deeply at the foot of the bed, sleeping in a pocket of covers between Trina's shins.

Nat peeked under the covers, holding her breath, not sure what she would find when she looked at Trina's sleeping body but excited and frightened both at the same time. Trina was sleeping on her stomach, with her head turned away. She, like Nat, had been relieved of her street clothes sometime during the night, and was wearing only a thin cotton nightie. It had worn spaghetti straps that hung off her shoulder, exposing another, smaller tattoo that had previously been hidden by her bra strap. The hem had hiked up around her hips, exposing her bare behind.

Nat dropped the sheet back over Trina's sleeping body and pressed into the mattress, trying to remember how she had come to lead herself so far astray.

She was already a full day behind schedule, and it was time that could never be made up, on so many levels. It was more than the weeks of preparation, more than the years of waiting for just the right Guy, just the right moment. There were hours that could never be accounted for, lapses in time that would forever be at the mercy of another's memory, leaving Nat vulnerable and out of control. She'd fucked up more than her ETA by stopping at the prison, by driving through Vegas. She could spend the rest of his life staring into Guy's green—blue?—eyes; but she'd never forget, or be able to tell, of the day she woke up in bed with another woman.

There were guys...and then there was Guy, the girls used to say in high school. Had she fucked things up her second first chance already?

Seconds passed like hours, and Nat could still not adjust her eyes in the smoky haze that settled like volcanic ash on the blankets. She wanted to go to the window, open it wide and breathe in some of that fresh desert air until her lungs would nearly explode with the promise of a new day. She wished she could look upon the Capital of Love through her rearview mirror and give a nod to all the others who'd done it last night, who'd gotten complimentary champagne and organ music and who this morning would wake up side by side, peering into one another's bloodshot eyes and calculating in their heads how far in the red they were.

She tallied the events of the trip so far but didn't know if she were dreaming it all, if it were nothing more than a bizarre blend of images seen on TV or extracted from ancient memories that had sometime in her sleep been strung together so as to form the illusion of actual occurrences.

The smell of Trina beside her, the floral in the air, and P's soft, rhythmic snoring told her it was most likely real.

She suddenly felt ashamed for what she might have done the night before, and she could not shake the feeling of impending doom that suddenly rushed in.

What bad thing had she done for love, and what part had Trina taken in her bad deed?

There was a reason Nat didn't drink, and it was sleeping beside her—an inability to hold her liquor, her tongue, her thoughts, and her actions while under the influence of anything more than one or two lite beers.

To lie still and contemplate the possibility of what she might have done the night before with another woman was almost unbearable. Even worse was the realization that no matter how many times she retraced her steps or tried to visualize the events as they might have happened, they were gone from her consciousness for good. There was no way to know

Did we make love?

without asking Trina, which Nat could not ever, under any circumstances, bring herself to do.

What if she answered yes, Nat thought, horrified. *What if she answered no?*

Nat grinned in the semi-dark. Since watching Trina undress in her car—no, that's not right, earlier than that—she had wondered what it might be like. Sometimes, when making love with Paul, or another, the sensations provided by a man could be given an extra push when imagined to be coming from a woman. She often wondered if she could have the nerve to go through with it, and had mostly decided no, probably not. It was exciting to plan, though. A breathless—but controlled—one-night stand with a woman she liked but would never see again. Just once, just to see what it would be like.

It was the after part that frightened her: the getting up, saying goodbye and leaving; driving home and hoping you didn't leave your address or phone number; praying you weren't followed. That seemed the truly hard part, the part that, for Nat, always kept those thoughts somewhere out there, like skydiving or visiting the Great Pyramids, something she could imagine would be fantastic to do but would never know for real.

But Trina wasn't anonymous; she knew more about Nat than just her first name. She might have memorized Nat's license plate, and after all, what was to stop her from showing up at her and Guy's front door in ten years and claiming Nat's love as something she had gotten to first?

Nat wished that Trina had woken up first, wondered what might be different if she had.

She braced herself for the waking then heaved her feet up and onto the floor. She locked her knees and stood up, trying to find her bearings in yet another impossible circumstance. The air was no fresher above than below. She dropped the covers over the foot of the bed, not even trying to cover up Trina's nakedness, thinking it would wake her. Thinking it would set things—the day, their lives—in motion.

Nat's side of the bed sagged with the impression of her body, like a chalk outline drawn at the scene of a most heinous crime. The air was filled with the stale smell of dried liquor and sweat and something else, something that made her queasy. The stink permeated the bedclothes; it clung to the furniture like the rank odor of something eaten three days ago, the leftovers now piled high under a swarming, crusted cover of bugs in the sink.

A smell like that turned a fantasy of one tender kiss into making love into getting it on and then into just a fuck. Nat had never tasted such a lurid thrill as a married partner, much less a married woman; and now, as she teetered on the brink of marriage herself, their deed from the night before seemed doubly offensive. Nat acknowledged with an acquiescent horror that the smell was coming from her—her hair and her clothes. Everything smelled bad this morning, and she wanted a shower more than anything.

In the fantasy she had originally taken great pains to construct —idle thoughts of North Dakota and what would come afterward—she would run to Guy over fields of wildflowers, places where the wind's caress was like a lover's and where nothing bad could ever come. She loved him still, after all these years, wanted him even more; yet even before she had rinsed the smell of another girl from her body, she could not help but find some small measure of pride in the bad thing she might have done for love. The corners of her mouth turned up slightly into a quiet, secret grin, and Nat bit her lip.

Trina lay motionless, maybe dead. The smooth limbs that might have wrapped themselves so skillfully about Nat the night before now were tangled and twisted like she'd just thrown herself off the roof of her apartment building.

With Nat, thoughts of love usually lingered like a lovely perfume in an empty bedroom. All she'd wanted was the smell of balm, an afternoon nap on chenille where drawn shades diffused the light. But since embarking on this journey, the straight and narrow wasn't so anymore. It was hard to know which gave her more pleasure—longing or guilt, ecstasy or devastation. It was hard to know which was which and to know how she would ever be able to tell the difference anymore. Trina snored lightly, and Nat would have given anything for some music, anything, to drown out the one intimacy that wouldn't leave.

She labored in spontaneity. Closer to Trina, near the

foot of the bed, she stood and waited, as if her mere presence were weight enough that it would press upon Trina's soft flesh and rouse her from even the deepest sleep. She waited with anxious dread for Trina to wake, knowing that the simple, involuntary movement of her eyelids rising would, like a checkered flag, signal the night's end.

Nat stubbed her toe on the bed and, cursing the dark, moved away from Trina and next to the vanity where Madeline kept her makeup, perfume bottles, and other girl things.

The vanity was small, and looked smaller still bordered by photographs and letters that had been taped there over nearly every bare spot on the edges of the mirror and frame. She read a few—"We miss you, love you too" was written over the back of one of the cards that was postmarked Orlando, Florida.

"Come soon, xxoo"

And then, a second time:

"We miss you bad."

Nat peeled the postcard off the face of the mirror, taking care not to tear the yellowed, hardened tape that would need to be replaced. The blue ink was smudged but the picture on the front was of a sunset beach scene. Nat wondered if that's where Madeline was from and if it was did they know he liked to be called Madeline?

Trina rustled on top of the sheets and rolled onto her side. Natalie held her breath and wondered if she would finally wake, but she just exhaled loudly and turned over again.

There were more cards from Florida—letters, too— all strung over the top of the mirror like Christmas bulbs dead in the spring.

"Missed you this summer, it's been hot...please come for Christmas."

Nat gently pulled some of the cards down one at a

time and laid them in her open palm. Some were blank on the front, some showed photos, mostly of beach scenes. Most were signed "Love, Mom," but some were not signed at all. Nat thought about the postcards she could send home from Vegas. Thirty-foot neon high heels and lap dancers with their nipples air-brushed out. It was just as well. Best that nobody knew she was even there.

Today is the day, Nat thought, *to set things right.*

She pulled an orange-and-black kimono from the rack where the sequined costumes were hung. The silky material chilled her flesh as she slipped both arms into the sleeves and let the billowing trail of material fall over her bare legs. Even tied shut in the front, it offered little warmth. Her own clothes smelled like mutt and other, worse things; and she needed at that moment to get a clean change of clothes and a shower.

With a quick glance back toward Trina, Nat slipped out the door and headed downstairs, grabbing a short stack of postcards and letters on the way.

It was cool downstairs in the club, but already the desert sun had started to rise, climbing the outside stucco of The Star Struck Room, searching for a way to get inside. There was only a shade more light downstairs than up, but that suited Nat fine in her condition. She walked through the main room like some kind of geisha ghost, the tails of Madeline's kimono dragging in sludge across the floor and the front flaps gaping symmetrically down the front of her half-naked body. She picked her way carefully across the unswept floor, peppered like a minefield with cold cigarette butts and bottle caps; and her toes curled at the touch of anything foreign.

It was quiet this morning. She maneuvered a wide turn to the right to avoid a strip of toilet paper that had been trailed out of the ladies' room on the heel of someone's shoe. The black lights were colorless and cold, and the solar system showed its nicks and cuts and places where the paint didn't cover the white underneath. Some red planet smacked her like it had the night before, and without turning around she reached back and yanked it off the string from which it was hung.

The jukebox was silent, but the flimsy plywood door did little to mute the sounds of traffic coming from the boulevard outside. Key customers, Nat thought wryly to herself. Vegas was loud. It was always in a hurry.

An empty phone booth in the corner this morning beckoned her, mocked her as she stood in the center of the Day-glo universe, nearly naked underneath the silky robe, holding no change and having no idea of what to say to him now. She took a seat at the wide bamboo bar, adjusting the robe to shield her bare thighs from the cold, sticky vinyl stool. She picked up a letter addressed to a PO box in Vegas that began "Dear Richard."

Nat set the others aside.

"Did you receive my last letter? It was sent about two months ago and I wonder if you ever got it. Because we haven't heard back from you, I am just going to assume that you didn't..." Overhead, the air conditioner kicked on, sending the planets into a violent maelstrom.

"Everyone misses you. They ask all the time about your work and if you've ever seen Liberace's house. I once saw Lucille Ball's."

There was more, mention of a kitten stillborn and somebody's daughter's grammar school graduation. Stuff that happens only at home, always when you're away. Nat felt the pangs of domesticity like a dog bite in the belly. How she had taken the road to Vegas. How her sweet adolescent memories had been seduced by the wife of a felon. How she dawdled while the minutes ticked away and time all but stood still. These were the mysteries of life that morning.

Nat set the card down and made her way behind the bar to where the liquor was kept in neat rows on glass shelves. She went looking for orange juice and instead picked out a bottle of flavored Stoli and a clean rocks glass from a rack under the sink. Nat could count on one hand the times she'd gotten sick from drinking, and was no expert on the science of recovery from hangovers. But more than once she'd been given the sage advice to fight fire with fire. Meaning to make herself a good-morning Kamikaze, she discovered there were no limes and she couldn't find the triple sec, so instead she made a strong screwdriver and returned to her seat. Mixing the drink with her forefinger, she caught sight of her reflection in the massive smoky mirror that hung behind the bar.

Her hair was too short, she decided, and vowed that from that moment on it would not be cut again for at least a year. She'd not spotted any gray hairs yet, and was thankful for that.

She looked thin—gaunt, even—in the low light and without the sun on her face. She looked like she'd come from a cold place, and those who didn't know her would probably not guess she'd come from Southern California. It was the liquor, she told herself. It was sleeping in a strange bed. It was the stress of the trip and wondering what the hell was going to happen when she finally came to his door. Driving there, getting there, was supposed to be more than half the fun—it was supposed to be bliss. So much time and freedom to contemplate the possibilities. The journey was so forgiving; the destination, she feared, might not be.

Her wide, round eyes gave her a youthful, naïve appearance. Even dressed in someone else's clothes, sitting at the bar before breakfast after a night of throwing up and confessing divorce, the lack of lines in her face and the brightness in her eyes presented a wonderful dichotomy to those who took the time to get close. At least, to try. She remembered one boyfriend describing her, at twenty-eight, as "well-preserved." Not the same as "fresh," but implying that a certain quality of freshness did once exist.

Poor dead kitten.

It was nearly eight, but darkness was not giving up to the sunlight just yet. The walls, the ceiling, the jukebox were shrouded in shadow, the only illumination at all being some red neon lettering that spelled out "Bud Light" above the mirror. The light was anemic, like in deep space, but in the mirror it warmed Nat's reflection like a Venusian sun.

There were more cards, mostly plain declarations of love and promises to remember the next birthday as well. There were no goodbye letters, though, no angry diatribes and no threats of expulsion from the family, or the will. The most recent letter from home was dated eight months earlier.

"Don't worry about your dad and me. Everything is fine here. It sounds like things are going well for you, you're probably a big shot by now. How is the desert? Hot, I'll bet. I don't mind the heat..."

It's the humidity, Nat snorted with cynicism.

"...can you get tickets to Tony Bennett?"

And that was it. The letter ended abruptly, and Nat felt gypped. Then, on the back, written hastily before the envelope was stuffed and sealed

"Love, M"

Nat was suddenly ashamed for taking the letters, humbled at having peeped in someone's window, too eager to see their cancer and then gasping at the sight of it.

"You shouldn't be reading those," Trina said sleepily from the bottom of the stairs.

Nat turned to face her; she, too, was dressed in

someone else's clothes. She wore a thin lavender chenille
robe that barely covered her knees and was missing the
tie. The opaque fabric of the cotton nightie underneath
held her tightly in some places and fell loosely in others,
keeping what Nat already knew to be the texture and
shape of Trina's body hidden. Her glasses were perched
on the top of her head, and her hair stuck out in all directions, as if attracted outward by some wild magnetic
field that emanated from all corners of the room.

Barefoot, Trina made her way through the maze of
tables and chairs and approached the bar, moving in a
way that reflected total ease with her surroundings, her
situation, herself.

"I know," Nat replied. "I couldn't help it."

Trina came to stand close to her; and for a moment,
Nat panicked, thinking she was going to try and kiss
her, but she did not. Nor did she say anything about
how it felt to wake up married. Trina ran the palm of
her hand over the short platinum stubble on the side of
her head.

"Wow," she said. "Some night, huh?"

"Yeah," Nat replied vaguely.

"Pretty wild," she smirked; Nat just grinned. "You
don't remember a thing...do you?" Trina grinned then,
and Nat's smile turned sheepish. "I'd be surprised if you
did."

"Lotta liquor, huh?" Nat asked.

"A lot?" She tapped the pack of cigarettes on the bar.
"That's putting it mildly."

Nat fingered the letters on the bar in front of her,
thinking that she must get them back upstairs before
Madeline returned.

"You didn't know...did you?" Trina asked.

"About Madeline? No, I didn't."

"I guess I shoulda told you."

"No big deal," Nat said, half truthfully, half not. A

mind fuck was still a fuck, she thought cynically, and the unveiling of Madeline should not have come as a surprise at all, although it did.

The murky bar was still except for the muffled sounds of life coming from under the door and through the cracks in the windows.

"You gonna be leaving soon?" Trina asked.

"Yeah," Nat replied, not with excitement or anxiousness but in a matter-of-fact tone, as if simply acknowledging another impending everyday task like doing the laundry or taking out the trash.

"You don't have to," Trina said. "You could...you know, hang for awhile."

"I have to go, Trina," Nat said. "I have to." Trina just nodded.

They made small talk that centered, at times, around Nat's trip—what sort of weather she could expect and how long did she think she had left to go—and at other times wandered into subjects completely unrelated: finding shoes that fit and how to teach a dog to stay. Nat could sense life, on the other side of the thin walls, going on without her. In LA or in North Dakota, there were people—people she knew!—getting on with their day, their lives, not affected at all by how much Nat had drunk the night before, or with whom she had spent the night.

She should have been halfway up the stairs and already making plans about how many miles to conquer before lunch. But even with the tenacious reminder, in the back of her mind, of what she was supposed to be doing out there in the first place, she could not make herself rise from the stool and leave.

"Hey!" Trina said suddenly. "You won the contest!"

"Contest?"

As Trina reached for the front of Nat's robe, Nat

instinctively flinched. Spreading the folds apart, Trina pointed to the baby tee that had mysteriously appeared on Nat's person sometime while she slept. Nat pinched the hem of the shirt and pulled it away from her body so she could read the pink letters on the front: "Wet 'n' Wild. No 1." She stared at Trina blankly.

"You won the wet T-shirt contest, Nat!"

It was difficult enough to imagine even entering such a contest. Taking into account Nat's unfortunate and sometimes unnerving resemblance to a pre-pubescent boy, it was inconceivable that she would win.

"Well, the judges were obviously drunker than I was," she said.

"You could say it was more a style thing than substance."

"What do you mean?" Nat said, self-consciously checking out the flat front of her top.

"You took your shirt off and flashed the crowd."

"And I still won?"

"Well, you beat one other person."

"I thought you said I won."

"You did," Trina replied. "There were only two of you."

It wasn't like she expected that she'd beaten out a dozen or so female mud wrestlers anyway. She shrugged, "Well, what did I win?"

"Forty-five bucks," Trina said. "But you blew it all on a round for the house, so..."

"It's all gone." Nat nodded her head, as if to say *Of course, it is.*

"It's all gone." Trina took a sip of Nat's drink and winced. "You also made a new friend last night...if you know what I mean."

"Yeah," she said, like a question but not.

"*Do* you know what I mean?"

Nat hesitated, afraid to say yes and then be challenged to recount some intimate detail of Trina's body, like a mole that was shaped like Italy, or a particularly sensitive tickle spot. Afraid to say no and risk hurting Trina's feelings for not remembering a single thing except the throwing up.

"You don't," Trina said.

"I don't," Nat replied.

"Hmm," Trina said thoughtfully and paused for several minutes. She cocked her head and pursed her lips like she was weighing in her head the pros and cons of revealing some stupid thing Nat might have done the night before. To tell your friend that in her drunken state she'd peed in the kitchen sink—that was something that would need to be told. To tell her that she'd slept with another woman's husband or something unsavory like that—that was something that wanted to be revealed with carefully chosen words, and at just the right moment.

"He's not going to like that," she finally said and spun around on her stool, turning to face away from Nat.

Nat cocked her head like P. *He?*

"Griffin!"

Nat only stared back blankly. "Me and Griff?"

"I wouldn't consider it cheating or anything like that," Trina said, presumably referring to the Guy situation. "Consider it a bachelorette party sort of thing. You know, one last fling."

It wasn't what Nat had expected to hear.

"Dancing?" Trina asked her, trying to jog Nat's drunken memory. "Kamikazes? Doing shots off his chest? Strip poker? Do you remember any of this?"

It was no use; Nat remembered none of the fantastic drunken deeds Trina rattled off. In a way, it was a blessing in disguise. Sure, it would have been great to remember a drunken night of unapologetic, unashamed and completely wild sex with a total stranger, but it kind of made for a better story that she didn't. It certainly made for a better excuse.

"I came up to bed about three, but you guys were still going at it." She looked around the obviously empty bar to indicate his absence and shrugged. "I guess he had someplace else to be this morning."

Griffin. Griff, for short. *Of course his name is Griff,* Nat thought. *What else would he be called?* Griff was such a fake, cheesy name. So porno. It suited him perfectly.

"I guess," Nat replied, surprised to be more than a little disappointed that the one wild time she couldn't remember was not with Trina but with just another guy who couldn't be bothered to stick around till she woke the fuck up. The drunken orgy Trina revealed would have been perfect for her first girl-on-girl experience. There was liquor involved—lots of it—which by the rules of straight girls would have automatically absolved Nat from any responsibility for her actions. It wasn't that she'd ever really planned on making it with another woman, not that she'd ever really sat in her house and considered how to do it, go about it. But in the missing hours from the night before lay one of those golden opportunities she knew didn't come along very often. To have wasted one free turn on just another guy disappointed her more than she'd have thought it would.

"Is that all...I mean, did anything else happen?" Nat asked, trying to sound as if she had only the most fleeting of interest in what twisted, depraved acts her body might have committed.

"What do you mean?"

Nat knew Trina knew exactly what she meant. She also knew Trina wanted her to ask it outright. Say it plain. *Did we do it?*

"Nothing, just wondered..."

"As far as I know," Trina said as she circled the bar and headed for the fridge, "that's all that happened."

Touché, Nat thought. It was as if Trina could read her mind, as if she were now playing the same Get Out of Jail Free card Nat had hoped to use that morning. The girls eyed one another with suspicious affection. They grinned like each held a fantastic secret about the other.

Trina pulled a plastic bottle of orange juice out of the small cooler under the bar and filled Nat's glass to the top. "That's better," she said, and poured one for herself with no vodka in it.

"To last night," she said, as she raised her glass to Nat.

"To last night," Nat agreed. They clinked glasses and gulped their drinks.

"We'll never tell," Trina added with a wink.

"Hey," Nat said as she picked up one of the personal postcards that she'd stacked on the bar. "Do you think they know his name is Madeline?"

"Don't know," Trina said with uncertainty. "Even if they did, I doubt if they would call him that," she added.

She told Nat that when she was younger she wanted to be named Marguerite, after her best friend in the second grade, and nothing—not crying, pouting, starvation, even self-mutilation by felt tip marker—could get her parents to call her anything but Trina.

"Once, my dad accidentally called me 'Lucy'" Trina said. "It was kind of exciting for that minute to be someone else. Even if it was only an accident."

The temptation to be someone else had come to Nat several times in the past twenty-four hours, and she was surprised to realize it was a fantasy she'd never consciously harbored before. Being where she was that morning—not just the physical space she occupied but including the places her imagination had taken her—felt as near to being someone else as she could possibly get. *My name is Natalie,* she said firmly inside of herself. *I am going to be with Guy. He loves me. Nothing will change that.*

She stated these thoughts as facts, despite what Madeline had warned her of. She spoke this not as a wish or possibility, or even an eventuality. There were hundreds of miles left to contemplate the night before and what had occurred between her and Griff, a thousand ways in which to re-route this new information so as not to upset the linear thinking she had always come to depend upon in times of upset or stress. A shower, a meal, a clean change of clothes, and a full tank of gas would do more to make amends than a thousand what-ifs.

Trina crossed her arms over the front of her body and walked toward the center of the dark, stuffy room. She raised her nose into the air, the way a dog does when smelling drive-through burgers and other delicious things that blow in the breeze along the highway.

She closed her eyes, sighed heavily and wondered aloud, "What now?"

seven

With each moment spent in the company of Trina, Nat's grand love gesture began to diminish, first in urgency and next, subtly, in importance. The morning her plan would have her leaving Utah and breaking into the second leg of her journey, dreamily passing white mile markers and signaling with clenched fist for truckers to sound their horns, was instead spent lounging on the roof of The Star Struck Room, exposing her bare legs to the tepid springtime sun and basking in the gentle radiance of her second screwdriver. Adding to the numbing effects of her early buzz was half of a dusty white pill Madeline had found at the bottom of her bag. Dramamine, she said, a "natural" remedy for the hangover that was preventing Nat from fully appreciating the bad things she was alleged to have done for love the night before.

It was Madeline's suggestion to take the party onto the roof. It was still hours before the club had to be opened, and there was time enough for Nat to pack and leave. The liquor consumed, the reminiscing shared, and the confession revealed the night before needed time to be fully absorbed before anyone, including Nat, could gather the energy to get back to real life—whatever, for each of them, that may have meant.

In any other city, populated with people who went to bed at a decent hour and usually with someone of their own sober choosing, it would have been disgraceful to see a pair such as Nat, in the silk kimono, and Trina, in a babydoll nightie and threadbare robe, stumble barefoot out of a dark bar at nearly ten o'clock in the morning, clutching their heads with one hand and their drinks with the other. But in Vegas, a city where not re-membering where or with whom you slept the previous night was not only acceptable but was the city's biggest draw, they fit right in.

Nat shielded her eyes from the light as she tentative-ly maneuvered across the carpet of cold, sparkly white gravel that crunched beneath Madeline's mules. Tour-ists on their way to the casinos on the strip streaked past on the busy boulevard; some honked at the sight of what they mistook for a couple of working girls trawl-ing for dates.

The unwanted attention mortified Nat—she grasped the folds of her open robe and held them tight around her bare midriff. Trina took the opportunity to flash a passing telephone repair van whose occupants howled and screamed their approval.

"Hey," she shrugged in response to Nat's mock shock, "I've got a need for acceptance, what can I say?"

The accused gigolo Griff was discovered in the parking lot, washing Nat's car. Nat at first imagined this some sweet morning-after gesture, like making scrambled eggs while she slept in his shirt. She regret-ted thinking him a screw-'em-and-leave-'em kind of guy. She considered, for the briefest of moments, the Possibility of Griff.

But then it was revealed that the chore was part of "the deal" (revealed by Trina, between fits of giggles, to be "loser washes winner's car"), and that winner and loser had been determined by the competition Nat had swept the night before. She was horrified to realize that the only way she could win a wet T-shirt contest was to beat a boy.

She wondered what the feminists would make of such a paradox, and if she should just accept the victory anyway. After all, a girl learns early on, you just don't beat a boy every day.

Griff smiled and waved, asked how their heads were feeling, and Nat searched his voice and face for clues they had been lovers. There were no furtive glances; no winks or blushes that would indicate an intimate familiarity with the way Nat's body felt under the covers. She posed leading questions—How was your night? How did you sleep?—but his casual, vague responses gave up nothing. He could have fucked her. He could have not. Either way, she was convinced, he had probably taken her wallet while she slept. It was immediately, and bitterly, confirmed in Nat's mind that he probably was a gigolo.

The rooftop patio, an eight-by-twelve-foot area cordoned off with bamboo and overgrown, undomesticated houseplants, was reached by a narrow, haphazardly built staircase that clung precariously to the rear wall of the bar. Not for regular customers, enjoyed by invitation only, it was an oasis of greenery in a sea of neon. The view was three hundred-sixty degrees: you could look for Hoover Dam or toward Red Rock Canyon; you could see the big circular drive at Caesar's but not too far beyond because at its peak the deck was, at best, twenty-five feet above ground. Mexican Bob had built it for Madeline the year before, before the Wanna-Lei-

A-Girl Bar went under and The Star Struck Room took its place.

Aside from meager cosmetic touches here and there—tiki torches that leaned off-center in sand-filled coffee cans and a couple of Tropicana beach towels slung over high-backed beach chairs—they had made few improvements since covering the tarpaper roofing and, like Columbus, declaring a brave new world.

Madeline had brought in some sand from the desert, buckets and buckets of coarse, putty-colored dust she'd sifted into containers from where the wind formed miniature dunes alongside the roads that led out of town. She had tried to make the rooftop more like the beach, but, of course, all the sand blew away on the first good wind. It fell like confetti onto the parked cars below, and after taking a garden hose to the job there was little evidence of that one good idea. Cacti and ice plants anchored in heavy clay pots now bordered the sitting area on top of The Star Struck Room, and that, Madeline said, would have to do as far as ambience.

Nat liked it. It had been, she guessed, a natural extension of Wanna-Lei-A's tropical motif, and she was glad it had been spared the barren, lunar transformation the club had undergone when it became The Star Struck Room. After all, she wondered, how much fun could it be to sit on the moon?

Surrounded by tiki paraphernalia and wicker, listening to Jimmy Buffett on the Walkman provided by Griff, and feeling the slight spin of alcohol furthered by the Dramamine in her system, it was hard to imagine being anywhere else at all. It was impossible in this sated funk to imagine even having to descend those stairs to go take a pee. Nat lay with her eyes half closed, listening to Griff's favorite songs and then rewinding the tape to hear them again, and enjoyed the affects of the pill and the liquor. It was the Dramamine, Madeline told her. It had the same affect on her, accomplishing the exact opposite of what the label said it was supposed to do.

Nat waited patiently for whatever would come along next—a change of mind, an epiphany, Mexican Bob. She resolved to comply with whichever arrived first and took a giddy, drunken pleasure in imagining all manner of possibility that might present itself before the end of the day.

Madeline and Trina talked about the last year, what they had been doing, and with whom; and for the fourth time in a row, Trina passed up the opportunity to segue into her marriage to Arizona at the prison. Nat was beginning to wonder what she had to hide, and why it had not been hidden from her.

She was growing more curious about Mexican Bob—why he was named so, and why the anticipation of his arrival was like a wonderful contagion, even among those whom he'd never met. Asking where Bob was—regardless if you even knew who Bob was—brought the asker into immediate accord with everyone else, like uttering "Swordfish" through the priest hole.

"He'll be along soon," someone would say, and that cryptic explanation was all that was usually offered—like spies utter "The blue swallows have perched in the church tower."

She and Mexican Bob were partners in every sense of the word, Madeline said with a wink. He was her guardian angel, and had come to her as the answer to so many prayers. While Madeline was a great hostess, she was a lousy businesswoman, and just the year before was in the process of driving the Wanna Lei-A-Girl Bar into bankruptcy and herself into some dramatic, made-for-TV suicide. Then, one Thursday, she said, Bob walked in. He was clutching a blue-beaded clutch he'd found in the parking lot as he exited the key shop next door, and he had come to return it.

It was love at first sight, Madeline remembered with a sigh. He was handsome and polite and uncomplicated. Within weeks, he had purchased a half-interest in the club and had taken over its finances, to keep her from going under. She had moved from the second-floor apartment above the club into his modern split-level home on the outskirts of town, where they settled into a wonderful state of domesticity. They spent their days like retirees—shopping, lunching, walking Bob's three dogs (round-faced bichon frises named Marilyn, Barbra, and Bette)—and spent their evenings apart, she at the club and he at the dance studio where he gave lessons to elderly women and singles who were trying to meet that someone special.

They'd been together only eight months; but Madeline confessed it felt like they'd been married forever, and she liked it. She liked finding new recipes to cook together; she liked making friends with the neighbors—and she especially liked that none of them knew her "little secret." Growing up, she said, she knew that she'd always wanted to be a woman but never dreamed she'd like being a wife.

They had remade the club and were almost out of the red. Madeline had been clean for eight months, and Bob had given up red meat entirely.

On the brink of losing it all, Madeline said, is where you have to be when the real thing comes along. Otherwise, you just don't see it, and could end up passing it by entirely.

Nat picked up an old newspaper from underneath the lounge chair and made a cursory pass of the front page, but it was eventually tossed—unread, folded over—onto the floor where she found it. There was little need to keep up on current events, weather reports would be useless, and politics meant even less here than they did when she was home. Instead, she watched the sky, ingesting the graduating intensity of blue as her eyes moved from the horizon upward. In a very unNat-like state, she began to enjoy the blissful ignorance of time and reality that comes from either total madness or the utter abandon of wandering aimlessly into other people's time zones. There was only a mild acknowledgement that Los Angeles lay somewhere to the south and that life there did, indeed, go on without her; but these facts in themselves meant shit and she was only twenty-four hours into the trip.

"Bob's danced on Broadway," Madeline stated suddenly, as if reminding herself of some trivial fact, like Today is Friday.

Nat nodded with mild interest, but Trina squealed with excitement, as if it had just been revealed that his true identity was Santa Claus. "Really?"

Nat shut her eyes and listened to them having girl times over there on the other side of the patio, without her. Going through photos Madeline had stashed in her pocketbook, sharing memories of things that had happened to them separately.

"Do you dance?" Trina turned and asked Nat, who just shook her head and hoped she would not have to illustrate just how much she did not dance.

Bob had always wanted to dance professionally, Madeline told them, to choreograph movie stars and musicals, but somehow just ended up in Vegas. He gave dance lessons three nights a week at a franchise school just off the strip. This was only remotely in the field of dance—everyone knew that—and it wasn't long before Bob discovered that teaching grown men to wriggle their butts like Diana Ross was, like so many tasks that had once lived as dreams, a somewhat bitter pill to swallow. Though these things he did dutifully, it was competition ballroom Bob loved.

Nat loved music more than almost anything, but she

lacked any internal rhythm, and she eventually grew to hate dancing as a man with allergies would grow to hate the progression of winter to spring. She had made hardly any attempts except when, fortified by great amounts of liquor, she would succumb to her own woefully inept rhythms and would flail about the dance floor with some poor guy until he either managed to escape into the crowd or, if he were especially polite, would feign a leg cramp and instead offer another round at the bar. These times more often that not left Nat driving home alone at two a.m., repentant with embarrassment and consumed with the desire to cut off both left feet and bury them in the dirt.

Madeline had tried it a few times but said she preferred "waltzing horizontally," and this made Trina giggle and Nat blush.

Nat wished she could dance like Bob. Wished she could be swept up in a man's arms, her bosom pressed against his and her lips whispering breathless obscenities only he could hear. She wished she could hear Sinatra in her head, and she wished the Dramamine hadn't laid her out so effectively or she would have tried it with Griff. She once overheard her brother say that a woman who can't dance can't fuck, and she hated to think it might be true. She wished, briefly, that North Dakota were farther than three days' travel, that it was yesterday all over again and there were options she might not have yet considered.

But these wishes were like any other—wanting to be a ballerina or a blonde or learn to play the drums. Wishes never lasted; their effect was felt only briefly, and then they, too, became another nostalgic remembrance that began, usually, "When I was a child..."

Bob's favorite times, Madeline said, were the ones at the auditorium on the south side of town. Most days they played heavy rock or sometimes a square dance, but on the first and third Tuesdays of every month there was ballroom dancing. He told of nights when the cavernous room would fill with lovely music and every couple, sometimes as many as a hundred and fifty, would suddenly fall into the same swirling cadence, clutching one another tightly and spiriting into the night in romantic bliss the likes of which Nat, since the year her grandparents died, could barely imagine. Walking into the ballroom on those nights, Madeline said wistfully, was like opening a giant, satin-lined jewelry box.

"So, what's your story, Griff?" Trina asked, and Nat pretended not to hear.

"Oh, Griff is very mysterious," Madeline said. "He's like some lost little puppy we found along the side of the road and decided to keep." She smiled broadly at Griff, who grinned with embarrassment.

"That's about the sum of it," he said.

"Oh, no," Trina insisted. "There must be more to you than that. What do you think, Nat? Do you think there's more to Griff than that?"

Nat scowled and wished she could remember exactly what there was to Griff. It was probably awesome, she thought. Probably the best sex she'd ever had, probably went on for hours, and she had probably climaxed three times just from screwing. And now she couldn't remember a moment of it.

Although Griff's penchant for sudden appearances with no explanation might give him an air of mystery—unknown and fresh in the way that you thought of strangers whose last name you did not know but under whose body you had spent the previous night—he revealed his past to anyone who cared to know.

He had no family that he called as such anymore; he was a drifter, a transient in the purest sense of the word, having never found his roots in any of the towns or people he had known along his way. He had been on his own since he was fourteen, leaving behind an era that could not accurately be described as "childhood" one day when he mounted his father's 1960 Duo Glide and simply drove away for good.

Griff had no money in the bank, had never finished high school, didn't know the names of any of his long-lost relatives, and this, it was speculated by Madeline and the regulars who had come to know him, disturbed him less than everything else put together. He had been known to answer to "mister" and "sweetie," but was not above coming to "Hey, shithead!" when the circumstances warranted; and to this Madeline would personally testify.

Griff was rumored around the club to be somewhat of a ladies' man, although this was something to which none of the patrons of The Star Struck Room could personally attest. What was known was that the women he dated were always divorced—or widowed—and that fact alone revealed more than Nat cared to know. Trina was delighted to have found someone so disreputable among them and begged for more. Did they buy him expensive gifts? she wanted to know. Did they take him on cruises and use him to make their married friends jealous? Did they leave money in his pants pocket while he showered, and had he ever been bought off by a jealous but impotent husband?

Juicy gossip for a weekday morning. It should have eased Nat's angst over why he had not given her a second glance all morning, but instead, this new knowledge just instilled in her the fear he might have called her "ma'am" in their moment of passion.

Griff looked much younger in the daylight, and sober—he might have been as much as ten years younger than Nat, maybe even more. She had always dated older men; she would never have considered anyone her own age, much less someone younger. Guy was the exception, not the rule—just another breakthrough moment in her plot to Alter Life's Plan.

She watched him from the lounge chair where she splayed under the warming sun. It had been thrilling, at first, to learn secondhand of their exploits. And then she had to learn that he favored older women. How much worse, she thought, can this get?

Nat suddenly felt old. It wasn't the aging face that bothered her, or the ass that seemed to drop inches while she slept. Unlike the other tanned, implanted denizens of West Los Angeles, she didn't cling to her youth with a tight grip that sported a fake French manicure. Getting old, in itself, was nothing to fear. It was all that went with the process that frightened her. She feared not what might happen, but what might not happen, or worse, what she would not let happen.

It was during these moods Nat would remember most vividly what it felt like to be young. She had always said she would never, not for a million dollars, be eighteen again. What she missed about eighteen was not the smooth skin or bright eyes or freedom or lack of responsibility. It was the fearlessness. Life on your plate and the glorious courage that comes from knowing you have absolutely nothing to lose.

Let others succeed, she would think. *Let them find the best husbands, succeed in the best careers, birth the most beautiful children. As long as I am eighteen, nineteen, or even twenty-five, there is time. Time really is on my side.*

Nat watched, in her early thirties, others little more than half her age rewarded with the things she had wished for herself, and it became harder to keep the faith and not wonder what had gone wrong.

As her birthdays racked up, she began to realize that time was not on her side, nor were any of the other clichés she could think of true: there was nothing to get while the getting was good, and when the going gets tough, the tough sometimes fold completely.

Now, on the roof, she started to feel old in Griff's eyes. Old and ashamed for the things Trina said she'd done the night before; and she feared that, once out of Vegas, she would remember that night with embarrassment and regret, like some self-pitying beast lying helpless in its own mire while family members and strangers shook their heads and wrung their hands. She longed for the normalcy of Guy's voice and his touch—could she even remember what that felt like?—but sensed even then that such longings, in light of her bad deeds, were nothing more than platitudes of the worst kind.

"Honey, you know I how much love you, but sometimes, these things just happen..."

Screwing Griff was no big deal. In fact, all that morning she had ducked in and out of thoughts of making love to Griff and wondering how fantastic she might have been under such drunken circumstances. But as her mood darkened, she became to dread that she had fucked not only Griff but herself as well. And knowing that screwing oneself was always performed with more mastery than one would ever squander on a mere other, from fantasies of the night before Nat would soon lose all pleasure.

It had been her conviction that anticipation would carry her through California, would bloom over the first thousand or so miles; and that, like rolling thunder in a wet, black sky, her passion would be set loose upon both her and Guy once she had actually found him. Such was Nat's understanding of the world, of love; it was, at the very least, her understanding of how this trip would turn out, and so it was for this reason she began to now worry about the color of his eyes and how his hair lay about his face and if she actually remembered any of these things at all.

All she had hoped for the night before was a clean bed in a quiet room. That morning, she would have traded everything to be rid of the sour stomach and grinding headache; and sitting upright behind the wheel of the a car, at that moment, seemed as likely as sprouting wings and flying the rest of the way. That shifting priority, Nat knew, was a tacit betrayal of The Dream.

"Would you ladies like to see my bike?" Griff said, startling her.

"I would," she said before Trina could reply.

"C'mon," he said, heaving out of the chair and extending his hand to help Nat out of hers.

As she stood, she swayed backward, and Griff grabbed her elbow. They started toward the unstable staircase, and she clung to him tighter.

"I'm afraid of heights," she admitted as she looked down at the gravel pit below, which she was sure to stumble into.

"I'm afraid of bees," Griff replied.

"Heights, bees...how pedestrian," Madeline said. "Everyone's afraid of bees and heights."

"I'm not," Trina said. "I'm afraid of a meteor crashing to earth and ending all life as we know it."

Nat grinned at Trina's comment and followed Griff down the steps. At the bottom of the stairs, they turned right and headed for a small nook between the key shop and the bar. Nat winced at the sharp pebbles that wedged between her toes and pressed into the tender white skin on the arch of her foot. She gripped Griff's forearm, and he flexed his muscle under her touch—probably didn't even realize it, she thought cynically. How typical. How male, she mused, as she recalled the boys whose bodies puffed up like a blowfish at the slightest touch of a female body part.

"Here she is," Griff said proudly, pointing at a misshapen heap of something that lay against the side wall of The Star Struck Room. "I got on that bike one day," he said, "and I just kept going."

At first unimpressed, Nat's second thought was that it was old and crusty and for that reason alone, Trina would like it. Like the silhouette of a huge crustacean, it lay low to the ground; the seat was short and looked like it might fit two girls easy but only Griff alone. It was black in most parts, a faded, bleached turquoise in others; and throughout it ran a maze of dulled chrome. In some spots the metal had turned a burnt orange. It didn't look like it could run at all, much less out of town.

"Oh, it runs," Griff said, reading Nat's doubtful expression, and with that he walked over, lifted it from a nest of flattened-out cardboard boxes, and with one hard kick brought it to life. It sputtered and gasped for only a minute and then hummed low and evenly. Not like those fiberglass insects that screeched down Santa Monica Boulevard at two a.m., waking everyone in a five-mile radius. Like the whisper of a confidante, it spoke softly and to one person at a time.

To one side, partially hidden behind a dented gray dumpster, was stashed a cruddy platform trailer with one low tire and rusted hinges and upon which Griff's last "ladyfriend" (emphasis his), Marie, had asked that the motorcycle be towed behind her Cadillac. Griff had traded some good weed to a man in Michigan for the trailer. It was cumbersome and heavy and held together with patches of nails and short boards and even rope in some places. There were times, Griff said, when it was useful; and so, rather than dump it along the highway, he had jury-rigged the motorcycle to tow it and used the trailer to haul whatever, if anything, he was leaving town with.

The bike was Griff's father's, but that was incidental to its appeal. Griff never got to ride on the back when he was little, didn't have any memories of flying recklessly through the streets holding his old man's jacket till the fabric shredded under his bitten-off fingernails. Didn't even get to see him disappear into the horizon, his hair blown back, his jacket flapping behind in utter abandon. No, that would have been too good of an ending.

Instead, Griff came home from the fifth grade one day to find his father being escorted out of the house and marched diagonally across the front lawn by two policemen. Not much of a sight to carry around and tell your friends about.

Griff's uncle came to stay in the house next. He spent evenings at the dinner table, getting drunk and talking about how Griff's dad was framed for that crime and that the lying bastards would pay for their misdeed. They never did, and eventually Griff's uncle moved to Florida; and next into the house came a distant relative by marriage.

The Harley stayed where it had been parked that afternoon, leaning up against the outside of the garage. It remained there for two years, huddled against the wall like a wounded beast, resting its bones and waiting for the strength to rise up and face its only natural enemy once again. You could see it through the kitchen window. You could watch it from behind—like it was crouched over, sleeping standing up. Griff watched it while he did dishes and yard chores. Nobody else did, though. Nobody touched it after that day Griff's dad left—not his uncle, not his distant relatives, not the women who cared for him nor their boyfriends who occasionally beat on his ass for no good reason at all.

It got rained on and snowed on, it got peed on by the dogs who lived in the neighborhood, birds shit all over it, and spiders trapped flies in the sticky threads they'd woven between the spokes. But no person touched it until Griff's fourteenth birthday. That day he went outside and, with his fingernails, dug the leaves out of the tailpipe. He pulled twigs from the carburetor and replaced the front tire, and he cleaned as much sap off the chrome as he could. He siphoned gas from the mower and filled the tank and planned on taking it once around the block, but the wind in his ears drowned out all else up to that point and once he turned the corner he kept on going. There were times over the years when he thought about going back there, but by then he didn't even remember where back there was. Missouri, maybe Mississippi. Something with esses.

That was fifteen years ago, and still he wondered if anybody was mad that he'd taken it without asking.

"I've ridden this girl over a hundred thousand miles, I'll bet."

"Don't you ever wonder if you're almost there?" Nat said, half-teasing, and winked at Griff, who nodded thoughtfully.

"You know what, Nat?" he said with a wide grin. "I sometimes do." He shut off the bike and laid it down gently, patting its gas tank affectionately.

They climbed the stairs back to the patio and found Bob, who had arrived just moments before, enchanting both Trina and Madeline. Despite Madeline's effusive praise, Nat found herself somewhat disappointed at the reality of Bob—or, at least, disappointed that she had imagined him so inaccurately. She had expected Mexican Bob to be at least forty, maybe nearing fifty. She fully imagined him to be stout, to have at his disposal a virtual library of dirty jokes and, to accompany these, a forced, contagious laugh. He would possess a lecherous, maybe toothless grin and a well-weathered face; and he might even make a pass at Trina when Madeline was not looking but Nat was. She prided herself on this insight, but she was shocked to finally see such a person as Mexican Bob when she stepped onto the top stair of the rooftop patio.

He was beautiful in the way that makes others want to immediately leave the room.

Bob was a natural blond, Nat guessed. This was evidenced not by his hair color (which was dyed to jet black) but from the paleness of his eyes and his fair complexion. Bob had been born Terry, she would learn, and used to be a surfer, having been raised on the beaches of Orange County by his third-generation Republican parents, only to leave home one day, dye his hair, and take up ballroom dancing. And men.

Nat tried to fathom under what wild circumstance he could call himself Mexican and what possible reasons he would have for changing his name to Bob.

Bob was very tall—effortlessly reaching over six feet—a physical trait that was made even more obvious by the way he rhythmically bent both knees just slightly and then straightened up again, as if he were bobbing to some strange, distant mariachi beat that only he could hear. Even with his purposely narrowed eyes and black hair—cut and combed precisely, parted on the left and kept in place by streaks of dried, transparent goo—even with his thorough desert tan, he was obviously not Mexican; he was German or Swedish or of some other Nordic descent.

When he spoke, it was with a chipped Latin accent, an affectation that suited him; and this fascinated Nat, who wondered almost aloud what could drive a person to such depths of fantasy.

Bob was dressed smartly in a pair of dark blue jeans, a perfectly pressed white dress shirt, a silver-and-turquoise bolo tie, and a pair of too-shiny red cowboy boots. He wore the costume convincingly, like the abuelos who gathered with their extended families in park on Sunday after church.

Bob stepped away from the edge of the rooftop and

began to weave his way through the handmade jungle, working the small but adoring crowd of four like an incumbent senator, but with sincerity. He hugged Trina—Nat heard him say he'd heard so much about her. He touched Madeline every time he passed within arm's length of her, and this made Nat even more jealous.

Griff and Bob shook hands, and then the tall ersatz-Mexican hugged the dreamy bartender, as if to acknowledge that it had been a long, long time, although they had probably seen one another just the day before. Griff and Bob bent their heads in collusion, and this was noticed only by Nat. Suddenly, Bob laughed uproariously and slapped Griff's back and, spinning gracefully on one stiff toe of his boot, turned to face Nat, who looked away just as quickly, as if she had never even noticed him standing there.

"Isn't he gorgeous?" Madeline squealed to Trina. "Didn't I tell you so? Didn't I?"

Bob waved her compliment off with humility and sought out Nat, who was studying like make-work the growth of ice plant along the lattice on the southern border. When they shook hands, she tried with her touch to read the man like the lady psychics did on Venice Beach, but there was little she could learn before Bob released his grip. His eyes bored into hers, as if reading the thoughts she could not admit even to herself. She looked away first, and dropped back into her lounge chair.

"Natalie," Bob said sincerely "it is my pleasure to welcome you. I hope that all your needs have been met."

Trina snorted and said to herself, but loudly enough for everyone to hear, "That's an understatement."

They were a quixotic pair —an ex-surfer turned ballroom dancer and his drag queen lover. Nat could only shake her head in amazement and wonder who back at work was plotting an escape to dance or sing or to seek out some other seemingly unattainable dream. She wondered who would be next to dye their hair and change their name.

Madeline leaned casually against Bob, leaving a trail of warm, dry kisses on his smooth, pale cheek, providing for Nat a take on love that she had rarely seen. She watched with an almost pubescent voyuerism—innocent and lewd both at once, curious, unashamed but a little self-conscious. Soon the sight of Madeline and Bob elicited in her a renewed lust for some of that stuff that had set her out on the highway.

The clouds came quickly, with little warning, and seemed to color the entire sky at once.

"We were just revealing our deepest fears," Madeline told Bob, "if you can believe that."

"Nothing like a little light conversation," Bob said, and winked at Nat. "Tell me before I begin," he asked Madeline, "is there a right or a wrong answer?"

"Well, Nat's afraid of heights and Griff is afraid of bees," Madeline recounted. "I know, I know, not very deep and, yes, a little dull, but pour a few more drinks into that girl and I'm sure it'll get a lot more interesting."

"I am afraid of spiders," Bob said, and Madeline shushed him. He laughed and slung his arm around her and kissed her bare shoulder. What about you, *mija*?" he asked her. "What are you afraid of?"

"I'm afraid capri pants will never go out of style," she deadpanned and lit a cigarette.

For the next twenty minutes everyone recounted the most acceptable fear they could cop to: spiders, sharks, tornadoes, maniacs with butcher knives hiding in the closet when one is alone at night.

"I'm afraid I'll lose my girlish looks before my time and you'll be seduced by one of those big-breasted students of yours down at the studio," Madeline confessed. She took a deep drag and blew the smoke directly into Bob's smiling face.

"Impossible, mija," he said, shrugging her off.

"What—that I'll lose my looks or that you'll be seduced?"

"Both."

"I will one day, you know," she said. "One day I'll grow old and wrinkly and maybe you won't love me anymore."

"I will love you forever, *mija*," he said. "Even when you are old and wrinkled. Especially when you are old and wrinkled."

Nat caught Trina's eye; and they smiled at one another, thinking the same thought, missing the thing in their own lives that Bob and Madeline had found.

"Oh, really?" Madeline asked Bob. "What if I become sick, will you take care of me and still love me?"

"Forever," Bob said, squeezing her hand.

"And what if I am in a terrible automobile accident and I'm disfigured. Will you still love me then?"

"How terrible?"

"Oh!" Madeline yelled and playfully slapped his thigh.

"I mean," Bob said, "are we talking wheelchairs or prosthetics?"

"Does it matter?" she asked, incredulous, but Bob only laughed with delight at the ease with which he could tease her.

"The worst!" she said. "Think of the worst that could happen to me. And then tell me you would still love me!"

"Let me think..." he said.

"Would you still love me if I had no arms?"

The question took everyone on the patio by surprise. It occurred to Nat that this was not some off-the-cuff statement, not something that had just popped into Madeline's head. Her true fear was present, and it was revealed to be the worst fear of everyone on the rooftop that day.

"Would you still love me if I had no arms?" she repeated.

"The more to love your legs, and your toes," he said and kissed her sweetly, tenderly, on the lips.

It wasn't the loss of limb that Madeline feared, although Nat had to admit it was a pretty bleak possibility to contemplate. Not going through life and never finding your soul mate, but to have found him, or her, just to lose them again was an unimaginable hell that made Nat shudder to think of.

"Nat's afraid of North Dakota," Trina said, laughing.

"I can see it," Madeline said thoughtfully. "Personally, I'd be more afraid of Iowa, but North Dakota makes sense in that weird, square-state sort of way."

Nat tensed at Trina's comment. It had been hours since she'd been required to do anything more than to simply exist. The reminder of North Dakota brought thoughts that felt like bad memories, even though she had never been there before and was still days away.

"I'm afraid of Florida," Griff chimed in, "but that's more a law-enforcement thing than anything about that state in particular."

Nat *was* afraid of North Dakota. North Dakota scared the shit out of her, more than twenty crazed maniacs in the closet with butcher knives. She was afraid to go; she was afraid to stay. If the Dramamine and the vodka hadn't laid her out so effectively, she'd be afraid she would be swept away on a strong desert breeze, fluttering over the sand and rocks like a dream or a thought that never really existed in the first place. There was nobody waiting for her in the north; nobody even knew she was coming. There was nobody waiting impatiently for her in LA, checking their answering machine and wondering to themselves how much longer she'd be.

It had never occurred to Nat, up until then, that her Plan would be anything but fully realized. She wondered if that was how Arizona felt in the moments before he walked into the Quickie-Shop with an unloaded gun. She was suddenly furious for allowing herself to wake up to the awareness that anything and everything could go horribly wrong at any moment, and could, for all she knew, stay that way for the rest of time.

Better to fear bees, she thought.

Nat wriggled her toes in the small, sporadic drops of rain that had begun to fall from the darkening sky. She was already committed to driving through the night, hopefully all the way through to Wyoming or even as far as South Dakota, but she knew the rain might slow her down. Trina wrapped a King of Spades beach towel around her slight, drooping shoulders and shivered at the slight chill that had crept up the stairs and onto the patio, but Nat made no effort to cover her thin, dampening body from the quickening wind.

She tightened her muscles and locked her joints, feeling a sudden, swelling panic course through her body like a flash flood, looking for an outlet, searching for a weak spot, a way to escape her private consciousness and make itself known to everyone within earshot. With all her effort she lay motionless and didn't speak a word, knowing that if she allowed herself to even part her lips there would come a torrent of fear and dread that was likely to never go back inside.

"Well, now, how did we all get so morose?" Madeline said. "How about some music to liven this party up?" The drizzle had slowed; and the clouds had started to part, revealing a blue Nat did not often get to see in Los Angeles, where the horizon usually faded to white.

Madeline opened a large straw bag that had been stowed by her feet and pulled out a small radio. "We have a few hours before we have to open up," she said, checking her watch. "Let's see if we can liven things up a little before we send this thing on her way."

"Tell us about dancing," Trina said to Bob as Madeline fiddled with the radio buttons and found some soft jazz on the FM dial.

Nat listened with interest to Bob's stories about dancing the night away; but with all secrets revealed came melancholy, and soon her mind wandered randomly like the clouds. She let it go west, to the prison, and then north to the snowcapped mountains and road that would be sheathed in ice. It was cold everywhere in between, but still Nat lay there, exposed to the chill, either because she simply did not know enough to get in out of the rain or because just once she finally said, *Fuck it, let's get wet.*

While the soft music played and Madeline painted her toenails, Mexican Bob rose from his chair, bowed before Trina, and delicately extended his hand.

"May I?" he asked, and Trina giggled.

He took her hand and pulled her close and there on the roof, in the rain, led her in a graceful sweep of the rooftop, his fantastically eloquent feet lifting them both above the surface and through the gentle shower that dusted their shoulders. Nat applauded heartily but her smile grew wooden and envy soon turned to jealousy.

They twirled like the tiny painted figurines in a music box, clutching one another and spinning round the rooftop. Nat watched with envy their every breathless step toward the edge and then back again to the safety of the center. Trina laughed like a little girl; wildly she clung to Bob as they swirled round and kicked up the fine sand that had been blown in from the east.

After just a few pirouettes, Trina pulled back from

Bob and threw up over the side rail of the patio.

"Are you alright, sweetie?" Madeline asked.

Trina waved her off and threw her head over the side of the rail again. "All the excitement, I guess. Maybe something I ate."

This was a place, Nat knew, she would miss.

Madeline declined Griff's invitation to dance, but Natalie was just tight enough to accept when he approached and bowed before her, his fingers extended eagerly. She awkwardly moved her hands up his biceps and shoulders, trying to find the fit she couldn't imagine would have come so easily the night before.

"Just relax," he whispered to her, and she did.

Her hands found their way to his shoulders and her head dropped back slightly. The grand, empty sky above them had taken on a turquoise hue, and instead of concentrating on her feet and where they were supposed to be placed, this was the view she chose to enjoy.

They started out slowly, like amateurs, struggling to find a shared rhythm in which to move their hips and feet. Griff led; Nat followed by instinct alone; the strain of his muscles beneath her fingertips told her in which direction to move, when to slow and when to quicken her pace. Trina and Bob literally danced circles around the pair in the center of the rooftop patio, but even with the occasional stepping on of toes, they eventually found the tempo that would take them through the remainder of one song and the entirety of two more.

For the first two days of her trip she could think of nothing but what would come; but once having lived in Vegas—and that is how Nat thought of her twenty-four hours there, as having lived there—once having met Madeline, Griff, and the wondrous, enigmatic Mexican Bob, her thoughts were reluctant to move beyond what already was.

It's the liquor, she told herself, downing a beer and

expertly tossing the empty over the edge and into the cavernous trash bin in the alleyway next to where the Harley was laid out in the gravel. The bottle shattered in the bottom of the empty bin, signaling to Nat and to the others that their time together would soon be over.

By four o'clock it was obvious to everyone that each of them had at least one damn good reason for not wanting to leave the tiny tiki patio and have to face whatever was waiting for them at the bottom of the stairs. For Trina, the prospect of returning to Barstow was a bleak chore. Griff could have stayed or not; it honestly wouldn't have mattered. And so when Nat passed out completely after having swallowed a second half of the Dramamine, which Madeline soon discovered was actually a Quaalude that she swore was "BB" (before Bob), Trina stepped up to the job.

"She is going to be p-i-s-s *pissed* when she wakes up and finds herself still here," she said as they surrounded Nat, who lay splayed out in the lounge chair, oblivious to the wind pushing open the folds of the silk kimono robe she never did change out of. All nodded in agreement.

"If she's so afraid of North Dakota," Madeline asked, "why the hell is she going? I mean, does she really think that she's just going to pick up where they left off?"

"Dunno," Trina replied. "Guess it's a girl thing."

"Poor thing, I'd hate to be there when she got to him," Madeline said and, checking her watch, said to Bob, "It's almost time to open up, sweetie."

"I'm going to drive her," Trina announced. "At least through Utah. It's the least I can do."

Griff was recruited to come along so he could bring Trina back.

"It's a plan," Trina said decisively; and she, Griff and Bob each grabbed a piece of Nat and lifted her out of the lounge chair, shuffling in baby steps as they struggled to get her down the narrow, rickety staircase without dropping her over the edge.

The next hour was spent quietly gathering Nat and Trina's things and looking for her keys. Nat had been tucked into the backseat along with P, who curled up against her belly and rested his nose on her thigh. Griff loaded the bike onto the trailer and hooked it up to the rear of Nat's car. With a small hand pump he filled the one flat tire, and then the four hugged and said see you later.

Nat didn't get to say goodbye, didn't get to take a last, long look around the place that had likely changed more than her perspective. She lay passed out, drooling and snoring comfortably, as the three of them and the dog unceremoniously drove away from the place she had never visited before, things she had never seen or done, and probably never would again.

eight

Trina made herself comfortable behind the wheel and settled in to make good on her vow to get Nat through Utah by the time the drugs wore off. The Nevada/Utah border was a little over an hour away, but it was agreed before they left that anything less than five hundred miles might appear as a half-assed gesture and would probably not make up for the time Nat had lost.

Griff rode shotgun, passing time with small talk—guessing how long it might be before Nat would again regain consciousness—and going through her things. Under the passenger side seat, he found a small folder containing her carefully laid out itinerary, along with highway maps, driving directions, motel recommendations, and other points of interest that she had downloaded and printed out from a website that catered to vacationers traveling by car.

She had outlined four legs of the journey from LA to her final destination—Los Angeles to Vegas, Vegas to Salt Lake City, Salt Lake to Laramie, Wyoming, and

Wyoming to North Dakota—and each leg was painstakingly outlined in its own succinct, one-page report that featured a detailed map with interstate highways, major cities along the route, and a thick yellow trail to indicate the most expedient path. Along with each of these was provided detailed driving directions ("Take the I-55 S/US-95-S/US-93S exit, exit number 75B, toward Cashman Field...") that were so precise as to be confusing. Mileage charts and estimated driving times were highlighted at the bottom of each sheet.

"Holy shit!" Griff exclaimed as he read the top page of the stack, a neatly typed summary of the major departure points: Las Vegas, Salt lake City, Laramie, and, finally, Bismarck, which according to Nat's notes was only fifteen minutes from Ruune, North Dakota, her final destination. "Going by to this, she should be in Wyoming by now."

"Well, how far is that?"

"Where she's going?" he asked, riffling through the stack of maps and doing the math in his head. "Jesus, it's gotta be a thousand miles, at least! She's still got a long way to go."

"Don't look at me," Trina replied. "I have nothing to do with this."

"I thought you were traveling together."

"Well, no...well, yeah, sorta. We were. I mean, she was just giving me a lift to Indian Springs, is all..."

"The prison?"

"Yeah, you know it?"

"I know *of* it," he stressed and grinned and shook his head.

Griff read Nat's itinerary aloud like chapters of a suspenseful novel, telling each leg of her trip with a growing, dramatic anticipation, as if somewhere along the way the journey had grown from a simple matter of point A to point B into an insurmountable trek of almost biblical dimensions. "Do you know it's almost two thousand miles total?" Griff said with disbelief. "And she's got it laid out here in less than three days."

"Is that not a lot?"

He shook his head. "Not if you're one of America's Most Wanted. Must be in one hell of a hurry."

Trina shook her head in Nat's defense. "She just wants to get there, is all. She's got a plan."

In the back of the folder was another, larger map of the entire United States, upon which Nat had traced in yellow highlighter the path she would take northeast from sunny, suburban Los Angeles to Ruune. The last destination marked with an X was Vegas, and scribbled next to it was written "dinner—2 hrs."

"Oh, I am *so* responsible for this," Trina said and gasped.

They passed through the rest of Nevada contemplating details about the life they imagined Nat had left behind in Los Angeles.

"Maybe she's left her husband," Griff said, but Trina said no, definitely not.

"Maybe she's faked her own death!" she said excitedly, even though she knew that to not be true.

After some fantastic speculation that included everything from a secret government mission to bodies that had not yet been discovered, Griff observed, "Maybe she just had to get out of town for awhile."

Trina nodded, as if yes, that was probably it.

They passed the Utah state line with little notice, and Griff talked about the places he had been. Having never been further south than Los Angeles nor east than Las Vegas, Trina was impressed he had lived at one time in every state in the continental United States except for Alaska, and he would have liked to see Hawaii if he could have found a way to get there on his bike. He'd landed in Vegas seven months earlier, having been asked to vacate his last girlfriend's home in Reno on very short notice and having no desire to see the Bay Area. How he'd hooked up with Madeline and Mexican Bob made for a pretty funny story, he said, except for the part where they mistook him for a male prostitute.

"Next week would have been seven months in one place," he said, as if even he were unable to imagine such amazing longevity. "That's the longest so far. I'm thinking about heading out again, you know, after I drop you back."

Sometime between Saint George and Cedar City, Nat began to stir in the backseat. She did not awake completely, not enough to know if she were alive or dead but only enough to know that, whether in heaven or hell, there were others there, too, and that was some at least some comfort. She hoped they weren't just girls.

"Are all your exes really old ladies?" Trina asked with a leering grin in the front seat.

"Disappointed?" Griff said.

"Just curious," she replied with a shrug.

"What's the matter?" Griff smirked and poked his index finger into her ribs, tickling her. She giggled and pulled away. "Don't ya like boys?"

"Asking me if I like boys is like asking me if I like potatoes," she said. "Maybe I like them fried and mashed, but not baked. But I can't say that I like them all."

Griff stared at her blankly. "Are you saying you like fried boys?"

"I'm saying," she said with emphasis, "'boys' is too generic for me to say if I like them or not. You have to be specific, you know? Maybe I like some, maybe I don't like others."

"Oh, I get it," Griff said and leaned back against the door. "You like girls...I mean..." He cupped his hands and held them over his pecs for emphasis. "...you like melons better than potatoes."

"Shit, that is so tacky!" she laughed out loud. "But yeah, I guess so...honeydew, cantaloupe, casaba...the juicier the better."

"Ahh," Griff said with a shrug, "you're too young for me anyway. What about Natalie?" He nodded toward the backseat. "What's her story?"

In the back seat, Nat began the arduous chore of trying to open her eyes fully. First one eyelid batted, then the other. She tried to concentrate on opening both at once but drifted helplessly on to the next thought.

(I cannot feel my tongue)

"Oh, she's a potato kind of girl, straight up!" Trina said and nodded firmly.

"Fried, baked, mashed..." Griff said.

"...even raw," Trina replied, and all Nat could wonder was *What restaurant is this and why am I ordering potatoes?*

It was hard to tell how long she had been dreaming. To outer space, to the wildflowers that grew alongside the highway, maybe just to the rainstorm just outside of Barstow. There was that car, the red import that nearly drove her off the side of the road. Those memories triggered another, and another—Guy and North Dakota and wanting it all so much—but she did not trust these initial conscious thoughts. In this place, which could have been the trunk of the car, for all she knew, it was still hard to know what was real and what was not.

Nat wiped her eyes with one finger and waited for the pounding in her temples to subside. She tried to stretch her neck but the muscles had stiffened during her sleep. She tried to remember how she had come to land in a heap beside the stinky brown dog that lay nestled against her chest. Trina was right. His feet did smell like popcorn.

She had been unconscious only once before, when she was seven, by the errant swing of her own aluminum bat that, instead of delivering one final fantastic pop fly far beyond the back fence, clipped her own ear and sent her spiraling backwards into the Little League dugout. The abject humiliation of being driven from the field that day, her ear canal plugged with bloodied, ragged tissues pulled from team mothers' sleeves and handbags, listening to the cheers of her little teammates as they rallied toward victory, in spite of, or because of, her absence, was a memory that refused to die. Like so many other childhood traumas, it was resurrected every time anyone in the family suffered even the slightest injury—a stubbed toe, a bloody nose; all of these and more would precipitate Nat's agonizing recollections of defeat when her mother would say, almost wistfully, "Remember when Natty knocked herself unconscious?"

Nat quit baseball and took up the clarinet. At this moment, lying fetal beside the stinky dog in the backseat of her car as it rumbled to some unknown destination, she longed for such a simple choice.

"I wouldn't exactly call them girlfriends," Griff confessed after a few moments of considering Trina's question. "More like lady friends."

"Ooh, I hate that term—lady friend," Trina replied. "Once I went out with this guy who introduced me as his lady, and that was it. So, it's true. You do date old ladies?"

"Only the rich ones."

"Is that a money thing, or is that a weird sex thing?"

"Oh, it's definitely a weird sex thing," he said, and then added with a laugh, "occasionally involving large amounts of money."

They laughed in the front seat, her front seat, and Nat began to awaken. She slid the dog off her belly but stayed where she was, listening to the two of them make small talk that occasionally landed on the subject of how Trina had come to find herself in Nat's path. Nothing terribly interesting, no breathless confessions of love from either of them.

(Of course.)

"Do you tell them you love them?" Trina asked Griff.

After considering this for a few moments, he replied, "Only if I do."

Nat tried peering out the side window, tried to deduce in which direction they were driving—north, east, maybe southwest back to Barstow? She could only imagine what fantastic criminal plot she'd become party to while under the influence of the pill-popping, cross-dressing Madeline and her band of misfits.

Trina messed with the preset buttons on the stereo but because of the vastness of the land all she could get was country and gospel. Either was more than sufficient to remind anyone of the miserable path upon which they tread. But the rhythmic rumbling of the road beneath the trailer was mistaken for the hum of the Winnebago; and Nat, in her stupor, imagined herself ten years old all over again and was reminded of her father. It was with thoughts of her grandparents she usually consoled herself—other than sporadic memories that came unsolicited and usually in dreams like the lovely memories of the lake and grappling in the garden shed—and she was not wont to reminisce about her dad.

It was hot in the backseat. Trina had the heat blasting up front, but all the air pushed toward the back and that, combined with the body heat emanating from P, was drenching Nat in sweat.

She hated the heat. She was reminded, any time the thermometer passed eighty-five, of bad memories of her dad. For some, balmy temperatures elicited fantasies of surf and sand and family barbeques in late July, but for Nat the heat brought only uncomfortable memories of long, sun-scorched Sundays spent in her father's breeze-less, stale apartment somewhere in what they euphemistically called the "Inland Empire." Summer break, when other girls her age were at the mall or at the pool, trolling for boys, Nat could be found sitting on the edge of her father's sofa wearing shorts and an undershirt, fanning herself with a TV Guide and pressing an iced tea to her forehead while she waited for one of her brothers to come and pick her up.

She wondered if her father had ever bought that window air conditioner he talked about getting. Eighty-five hundred BTUs, he told Nat. "Not even your mother can put out that kind of chill."

There were days when her brothers were too busy with their girlfriends or too lazy to come that far to fetch her, days when Nat's mother was sick of her lot in life or just too tired to make the drive herself; and those days Nat remembered as the worst. Because her father had lost his car in the divorce and had never regained the desire to buy another, Nat was, on these days, a big girl, and this meant only that she could ride the bus alone. She would be sent off by her father, who packed her bag with emergency phone numbers and the exact change she would need for the trip from Rancho Cucamonga to Reseda. A dollar-eighty-five in dimes, nickels, and quarters jingled in her pocket like Christmas bells, a constant reminder that should she lose even one coin she was fucked.

It was an awful ride—hours spent in a wheezing bus that labored through neighborhoods Nat did not know, crammed shoulder to shoulder with people who sweat profusely and seemed not to give a damn that their damp clothes were touching hers. Through some neighborhoods more than others, she was nearly paralyzed with the fear of losing even a nickel under the seat where it could not be reached. Only five cents made the difference between a safe ride home and a hellish phone call home to say she'd screwed up. Again.

She would try and pass the time by watching the blur of Mexican markets and electronics stores that crowded the landscape for miles in every direction. Sometimes she wished she could ride the bus to the end of the line, to see what really lay on the valley's faded horizon. Maybe it would take her all the way to Mexico, she used to think, maybe she would be sold into servitude by some banditos who would take her dollar-eighty-five and rename her Maria or Consuela, turning her into a girl that not even her own mother would recognize.

"They'll be sorry," she would say sullenly, alone on the bus, her face pressed closely to the glass but her breath dry like the desert wind.

It would be years before Nat would learn there was no such thing as the end of the line and the busses didn't go as far as Mexico—maybe Tarzana, maybe Calabasas or Simi Valley, but no farther. And even then, all they ever did was turn around and come back again the same way. The busses never took you anyplace at all.

Later, her dad moved to New Mexico and all she could do then was write letters and hope for a postcard or a phone call; she stopped riding the bus altogether.

Those trips depressed Nat. It was not just the heat; it was the weekly reminder that her father was living someplace else, living in a crummy apartment off some wide, desolate boulevard littered up both sides with sagging, parched palm trees. The man was a pioneer. He bathed nude in the lake, for Chrissakes. He kept a shotgun in the closet behind the suits that hung sheathed in plastic wrap. Maybe he had even killed a man.

Nat was never aware of what her father did for a living, never conscious of anything her father did outside of the house other than the faint knowledge that he, like other fathers, was "in business." This knowledge was disproven one afternoon when, crouched in her parent's bedroom closet, playing kissing games with a boy from three blocks over, she saw a shotgun tucked behind a row of perfectly pressed blue suits.

Although she had never seen her father leave the house in one of those suits, she knew instinctively, as any daughter would, there must be very important occasions, indeed, on which they were worn. Maybe he was the president of some big company, maybe he worked for the government. Maybe that's why the gun and the suits were hidden there in the closet together. Maybe he was a double agent and could not be trusted with even the most trivial of information.

It didn't seem fair that a man who could catch, clean, and cook his own dinner should live like he did; it seemed impossible that a man who kept a hidden gun was anything less than magnificent and dangerous, and so it was just another cruel surprise one day when Nat was driven by her mother to the small dry cleaning store in El Monte where her father managed a few part-time hourly employees. Barbara was delighted to show her young daughter that her father pressed trousers for a living and spent his long, dull days accompanied by the drone of a black-and-white TV that sat below the counter, playing Spanish soap operas and matinee movies about the war. It was as if she couldn't wait to show Nat what sort of man she could come to expect for herself.

When, one day in the summer, glory finally came to Nat's father, when her dad's greatest achievement finally came—and even then only accidentally—Nat didn't care that in the brilliant glare of working for NASA and sailing around the tip of Africa, things she was sure other girls' fathers had done, her own father's fame was painfully undeserved.

Nat's father provided information that had led to the arrest of a man who was said to be responsible for seven armed robberies and one murder, committed in the course of a liquor store hold-up in the west Valley. The suspect's likeness was put on all the news channels and in the local papers; and a few days later, Nat's father recognized him as a recent customer who had brought in eight blue shirts and requested "no starch." Later, as TV cameras captured the police ambushing the dumb ass as he entered his apartment, he came to be identified by Nat's father as Jack Hanson of Monrovia. He was behind bars within a matter of hours; and only a day after that, Nat's father collected a fifteen-thousand-dollar reward the city council put up as part of their Take a Bite Out of Crime campaign.

Nat's father was hailed by the press and local businesses as a hero. He had, they had said, acted selflessly and with no concern for his own safety. It was during those days of TV interviews and photo opportunities that Nat often saw him on local TV, standing proudly in one of his finely pressed blue suits, and she could not have been happier if he had just landed on the moon.

Nat saved every newspaper clipping—which after just a few days became too worn and threadbare to read to her astonished and envious classmates anymore—in her shirt pocket until they all but disintegrated; and when there came no more feats of heroism, Nat put these away in a book somewhere for safekeeping, a place over the years she was to forget entirely.

Only a month later, Nat's father withdrew his reward money from the bank, quit his job, and moved to New Mexico—she had never known it was her father's dream to live in the severe Southwest—taking none of the furnished accoutrements from the dive she had used to visit, taking only a suitcase full of rayon clothes and his girlfriend, Chrissie, a health nut who tended bar near the Ontario airport and in the evening made Caesar salads and mango milkshakes.

Chrissie saw Nat as the little sister she never had, and seemed genuinely pleased when she came to stay at the apartment, although there were times Nat might have preferred she were cruel to her or lazy or fat. None of Nat's brothers would come to see their father once Chrissie moved in, and that seemed to suit everybody just fine. Chrissie was forever grateful for Nat's meager friendship; later, Nat learned she had lost her own three children in a house fire. According to Nat's father, their tiny Jesus nightlight burned too hot one evening, igniting His plastic shell and sparking a fire that in less than twenty minutes burned the whole place to the ground. She sought solace with the Church, and this disgusted Nat's father, who saw that whole religion business as nothing more than ass-kissing of the worst kind.

When they moved to New Mexico—a place hotter than the valley would ever be, heat she knew her father would be all but unable to endure—Nat came to know a true fact of love.

What you do not for love, you do for lack of.

Nat wished Trina would crack a window and let some cool air into the backseat to dry the perspiration on her forehead and cheeks and dissipate the stifled, unhappy memories of the heat. She wished she had a cool drink.

Griff reached underneath the passenger side seat.

"Anything else under there?" Trina asked.

At first, it was thrilling listening to them, even though most of their talk was small, about things such as the weather and the landscape. It was like being invisible, like crouching under the dinner table as a child, wishing to hear surprise birthday plans and Christmas lists but hearing only petty talk about which neighbor said what about some other neighbor. Eventually growing bored, Nat would climb off the floor and take her seat among her family, and one of her brothers would remark, "Oh, there's Nat!" as if they had not known her whereabouts all along.

"I'm looking," Griff said, and pulled out a brown envelope with a rubber band around it.

"This is seriously snooping, you know," Trina warned. "I'm supposed to be her friend."

"Then you should want to learn more about her, right? You know, to help her."

Griff peered over the backseat, and Nat quickly shut her eyes. She tried to breathe steadily, as if she were still sleeping, and lie still while P alternately licked his feet and then her face. She barely stirred as his fat pink tongue dragged across her cheek.

"Do you think she's dead, or what?" Griff laughed, sliding the rubber band off the envelope and opening the flap to inspect the contents. Inside were her passport, its blank pages a testament to places Nat had never been, her birth certificate, and an employee ID badge bearing an uncomplimentary likeness of her.

"What's that?" Trina asked.

"It's an employee ID," he replied and held it up. "She's a teacher!" he said with surprise. "She's a fucking grade school teacher!" Griff flipped through the rest of her documents, some of which were legal and all of which were highly personal. A Social Security card, a list of bank accounts, and more. "You know what it looks like?" he said.

"What?"

"It looks like she's pulling a Bob."

"What do you mean?"

"Well, all her stuff is here, you know, all her documents and things. Things you'd need if you were disappearing."

"She's not going back at all?" Trina said.

"Maybe not," he considered.

Pulling a Bob, Nat thought disgustedly. Leaving

home as one person and returning as another? Or not even returning at all—just going off to become someone else entirely? Impossible.

"I wonder what else she's got around here?" Griff said as he lowered the passenger side visor and rooted through the vinyl pockets on the door, looking for more incriminating evidence of Nat's surreptitious plans.

"Maybe you'd like to roll me over and strip-search me," Nat suddenly snapped from the backseat, rising to face the spies who were busily deconstructing her life.

"Feeling better, Nat?" Trina asked in her sweetest voice, and Griff stowed the things he had been snooping through back under the passenger seat.

"Where are we?" Nat asked groggily.

"Somewhere in Utah," Griff said.

"What time is it?"

"It's nine o'clock," Trina said. "Hungry? We can stop."

Nat's apparently sudden departure from Vegas and appearance in the middle of Utah in the middle of night would have had much more impact had the affects of the Quaalude completely worn off. Trina's presence was less of a concern than Griff's—they were girlfriends, after all. They'd shared things: jokes, confessions, clothes, a bed.

But Griff slept with old ladies in exchange for gifts of cash and casualness. He surely didn't sense in Nat any promise of large sums of money or an aversion to commitment. What the fuck, she wondered, for a brief moment, was he doing here?

Then the Quaalude's fog quickly took over, and so the why's and how's of such events were at that moment significantly less important than just getting a cool drink and a breath of fresh air.

"We're taking you to Salt Lake City!" Trina told her excitedly, as if revealing some fantastic gift for which she had yearned.

"What happened to me?" Nat said, rubbing her temples.

"You got slipped a Mickey, sweetie," Trina said.

"You cannot hold your drugs, woman," Griff added with a smirk.

"And you were going on about being so far behind schedule and all," Trina continued, "...and you were in no condition to drive..."

"None," Griff concurred.

"And so I just felt, well, I owed you, you know? I wanted to help you out, help you get to North Dakota."

"We're going to take you as far as Salt Lake City," Griff said, "and then you're on your own."

"What...what about you guys?" Nat asked, feeling again that same weird, unnamed disappointment she'd felt the morning she woke up in bed with Trina and discovered she'd been with Griff.

"Taking her back," Griff said simply as he nodded toward Trina. "Then who knows what."

Nat and Trina locked eyes in the rearview mirror. They smiled at one another, and for the first time in the past few days, Nat began to wonder if she were the stupidest girl alive. In this funk, with this shit in her system, on this road at this time, she could barely remember the plan, let alone its purpose. Sometime during the past forty-eight hours, what had started out as a magnificent gesture of love and devotion had turned into one of those silly, trite placards that you see at the Hallmark Store and Giftshop: Life is a journey, not a destination.

God, she thought, *how maudlin.* Her life had become one of those little inspirational sayings that are supposed to get you through life-altering events like cancer, as well as the little shit like forgetting to mail the electric bill.

Well, which is it? she wondered. Was it the journey, or the destination that was keeping her going? She hadn't spoken with Guy once from the road. She'd planned to talk with him at least a couple of times, just to say hi, hello, how are you doing? Plant little hints of the fantastic surprise he didn't even know was coming. But every time she picked up the phone to call—in the prison, the club, while everyone danced on the rooftop—there always seemed to be a better reason not to.

With no more personal affects to rifle through, Griff busied himself with Nat's CD collection, picking out the ones he wanted to hear and filing away the ones he said weren't worth it.

"Jazz is good," he said, nodding his approval at some John Coltrane and Stan Getz. "Retro is very bad," he added, holding up *Rock Ballads of the 80s*.

Trina filled the long gaps between highway rest stops with little-known facts on everything from the life cycles of desert plants to the lavender Bo-Kay air freshener she'd bought before leaving Vegas, which everyone referred to now only as "back there."

"So, Nat," Griff said, throwing his left elbow over the back of the seat and turning to face her. "What's this about hooking up with this guy?"

"Not 'this guy,'" Trina corrected him. "Guy. His name is Guy."

"We used to date," Nat said defensively.

"Where you serious?" he asked. "I mean, I only ask 'cause if some chick that I dated two decades ago suddenly showed up on my doorstep I'd be thinking one of two things."

"Such as?" Nat asked.

"Either her life is fucked up, or she needs money."

"I don't need money," Nat snapped.

"And she's not fucked up," Trina added.

"Guys don't understand," Nat said. "It's a love thing."

"Well..." Griff pondered. "If guys don't understand, what makes you think this guy, Guy, will?"

The car was only six hundred miles from LA; and not only Nat, but others, complete strangers with whom she just happened to be sharing a ride, had begun to question the wisdom and motivation of such an undertaking. Was it Guy, was it love—or was it the wish for those things that kept her going. Were they really soulmates, or was this just a pathetic life version of last call? The older she got, the more fondly he was remembered. *Jesus*, she thought, *when I'm forty will I be picking them out of my grammar school class pictures?*

Ever the square peg in the round hole, Nat was worn from the slamming she took whenever she tried too hard to make things fit. There was something to be said for effort, she thought. There was always that, the knowledge that she had at least tried. But along with it came the risk of failure, and such an outcome could be even more devastating than never having lifted a finger in the first place.

Guy. No therapists need tell him he was in love, no one-night stands or those horrifying stories of others being left at the altar. No regrets and no looking back. The plan was the most important thing; Nat knew this to be true. Work your plan, or your plan will work you. Besides, she thought, how much harm could be visited by another thousand or so miles?

Sitting in the backseat, smelling of dog, her head pounding and her tongue coated with green fuzz, Nat set about the business of getting her shit together. She began, in her mind and heart, toeing the boundaries of North Dakota, miles ahead of the car and a lifetime ahead of Trina and Griff. She would get there sometime that evening, when—with a little luck and a lot of concentration—her mindset would be securely in place and her fantasy would, with the strength of a steel wrecking ball, once again find its core. Daydreaming, anticipating, by Provo she would be at it again. It was of little importance that the car would not physically arrive for at least two more days.

"I have to eat," Trina said, sometime around ten o'clock. "If we're going to drive straight through I need to get something in my system." Nat would have been fine with not even peeing till they reached Wyoming. Not just to make up for lost time, but because of the sight she knew the three of them must be, driving through God's Green Earth. A man who'd wooed rich elderly women, one bisexual adulteress, and one general heathen—not to mention a dog named P, of all things—and in a land of blond heads and equally whitened souls, these three sinners would be instantly pegged as imposters. She was glad they were driving at night, when the blackness of their souls was not so obvious.

They passed a UPS truck with a bumper sticker that read See You in Heaven, and she thought how much she was starting to hate irony.

"Do you know any jokes, Griff?" Trina said, but before he could answer said, "That's okay, I know one." She cleared her throat. "Whaddya call a guy with no arms and no legs and he's laying in a ditch?"

Nat grinned. She knew this one.

"Phil!" Trina squealed, as if that were the funniest goddamn joke she'd ever heard.

"Oh, that is so old," Nat groaned.

"I got another!" she gasped. "Whaddya call a guy with no arms and no legs and who's water-skiing?"

Nat rolled her eyes. "Are these the only kind of jokes you know?"

"Skip!" she laughed, waving Nat silent with her

hand so as not to make her lose her thought.

Griff told one about the Pope; and while they were all gasping for breath, Nat reached over the seat for the can of Pepsi nestled between Trina's thighs. Trina squirmed in her seat and parted her legs slightly, so as to allow Nat to take it. In the process, Nat's fingers brushed softly against Trina's legs.

"It's so fucking hot in this car," she sighed, her face red. "Jesus, the temperature never even reaches seventy—how come it's so fucking hot?"

They were silent. The radio signal was lost, only static came from the speakers; and neither Trina nor Griff made a move to turn the dial and find another. There was a long silence, and they listened to the soothing soundtrack of the radio's white noise and the hum of the tires over the highway, thumping like a quickening heartbeat in places where the big rigs had split the concrete into checkerboard.

"Trina," Nat began innocently enough, as she sat back in the seat and downed the last of the Pepsi. "Why don't you ever tell anyone about the wedding?"

"No reason," she said glibly, shifting her left hand underneath her thigh and gripping the steering wheel with her right.

"What wedding?" Griff asked as he began to flip through Nat's CD collection, not having any idea what he would start with that simple question.

Nat's face froze in a silly, stupid grin, and she asked, "What do you mean 'it's nothing'? A wedding's not nothing."

"What wedding?" Griff asked again.

"It's nothing," Trina said to Griff, and then reiterated to Nat, "It's nothing!"

"What wedding?"

"Her wedding," Nat replied, and immediately wished she could take it back. It was a secret, she knew that, one that Trina entrusted to her, one like girlfriends share. But Nat was a lousy girlfriend; she wasn't good with girls, and that was no secret.

"Whoa!" Griff shouted. "What this? Wedding? As in, 'I do'? As in, 'till death do us part?'? So it's true...you do have a taste for potatoes after all!"

"Shut up," Trina said and slapped his leg. She shot Nat a look via the rearview mirror that said to her, without words, thanks a lot...friend. "It's nothing," she said to Griff. "I was married...that's all."

"The plot thickens," he joked, but nobody laughed. "When?"

"It's nothing...forget it," Trina replied, but Nat could not.

"Yesterday," she said.

"Yesterday!" Griff shouted. "What the fuck is it with you chicks?" He laughed to himself and shook his head. "I thought y'all were gay."

"What?" Nat shouted. "You thought I was gay?"

Trina laughed out loud.

"How could you say that?" Nat asked, "after, after...you know..."

"After what?" Griff replied.

If Nat had been watching closely, she would have seen the blue veins in Trina's neck start to protrude. She would have seen her entire body begin to vibrate with energy and emotion.

"I know I saw you exchange rings," Nat said, carefully entering a conversation she knew to be loaded with booby traps.

"Yeah?" Trina replied. "And?"

"So, what'd you even get married for?" Nat asked. A question she had been dying to ask since the first time Trina announced it in the car. *What possible reason could a lesbian have for marrying a man serving felony time,* is how she wanted to put it, but didn't. Not even giving Trina time to answer, she added, a thought accidentally spoken, "That's fucked up."

Even Nat was surprised to hear it out loud, but there was no time to make it right because the look on Trina's face said it had in a fraction of a second fully sunk in. Nat knew it wasn't any of her business, and if she could just tell her never mind, they might stop at a Denny's and have a nice dinner and forget the whole thing. It wasn't too late to salvage the rest of the trip—only another two days to Guy—and really, in her heart, she did not want to know any more of what she had just asked Trina to reveal. Not so soon after the tenuous realignment of her increasingly impossible fantasy life.

"Fucked up?" Trina asked incredulously. "I'm fucked up? Excuse me, Miss 'I'm on my way to rekindle a love that never existed.' Talk about fucked up!"

They fell silent; not even Griff could think of anything to head off the girl fight that was brewing before him.

"Miss 'I wouldn't know love if it stopped the car, laid me out on the highway and bit me in the ass!'" Trina continued.

It was true after all. Nat was not good with girls. What she had started as a sort of social experiment was destined from the start to go horribly wrong, and that was something, she thought grimly, she should have recognized back in Barstow.

"Oh, oh, really?" Nat replied. "Look who's talking, Miss 'I'm so fucked up I like girls but I married a man. No, a felon!'" Even she was shocked by the sting in her statement.

Griff looked out the window and whistled a tune, feigning great interest in a completely darkened landscape that had not changed in over two hundred miles.

Trina's eyes grew wide like saucers. She gasped loudly, like a dog does when spying a cat in the distance, and drew in a long breath.

"Well, look at the fucking pot calling the kettle black!" she yelled, and lit into Nat. "Miss 'I'm so fucked up I don't know *what* I like!'"

"Trina," Nat said softly, in vain trying to retract what had already been spoken. "C'mon, let's stop all this..."

"Miss 'I'm so afraid of girls but I'll do the first guy that comes along,'" She gasped, her right arm flailing at Griff, indicating that he was, at least on that trip, the first guy that came along.

"What the hell?" Griff said from the passenger seat. "What did I do?"

"Oh, yeah, not like you," Nat spewed at Trina. "Oh, so sorry I'm not gay, I mean, I'm so uncool, aren't I? Not like you. It must be so cool to be gay..."

"Maybe where you're from," Trina spat.

"Jesus," Nat said, and kicked the seatback behind Trina. "Excuse me for trying to improve my life."

"You call this..." She waved her arm through the interior of the car, indicating not the occupants but the circumstances. "...an improvement? Getting drunk, throwing up, screwing strangers?"

"Well, I was sure it was an improvement for at least one of us," Nat replied cattily and looked away. "Maybe it wasn't me after all."

"Nat," Trina said, her tone softened, "you are so fucked up you cannot even see how fucked up you are."

"Really."

"Really. You are basically betting your entire future on your high school boyfriend," she said. "A guy you dated for two weeks, over twenty years ago. You go on and on about being soulmates with this Guy—oh, excuse me, with this man—but then you practically wet your panties when you think you've made it with Griff!

Even though you can't remember a fucking thing! How pathetic is that?" Trina pulled out a cigarette and lit it. "Jesus, I could have told you you'd done the dog last night, and you wouldn't know any different. Except maybe you'd value the experience."

"Ssssh, everyone!" Nat yelled. "The lesbian who married a felon in a secret wedding is about to impart some wisdom on the rest of us. Everyone hush!"

Nat had nearly snapped. Trina, as well. Griff and the dog merely pretended to be interested in other things.

"Furthermore..." Trina continued, ignoring Nat. "Furthermore, you have no friends 'cause you say you don't understand girls. You're not 'good with girls,' right? Isn't that how you put it? Well, I got news for you, Nat, and you'd better get a grip 'cause this is gonna blow your fucking mind..."

"I don't want to hear it," Nat said.

"She doesn't want to hear it," Griff said.

"You weren't with Griff last night, Nat. Griff never touched you, he wasn't even there."

"Don't say it, Trina," Nat warned.

"You were with me!" Trina yelled at her through the rearview mirror. "Me! A girl! And you don't even remember! How fucked up is that? Not good with girls. Ha! That's a laugh." After a short, punctuated silence, she added, "Oh, wait, I take that back. You really *aren't* good with girls."

Nat's jaw dropped, and she slumped in her seat as she felt the wind knocked out of her. This was the shoe that never should have dropped, the one she had suspected, in the back of her mind, eventually would. Despite all indications otherwise, in the dwindling distance between her and Guy she had begun to harbor a hope that everything—everything—that had happened in Vegas was just a freak chain of events. Like Arizona and the cooler and the clerk who electrocuted himself.

A unique set of circumstances that were mathematically precluded from ever occurring again. Her growing fondness for Trina was a girlfriend thing, she had told herself. It was normal, she had said. It had no effect on her life in any way other than the fact that she could expect to send Trina the occasional birthday or Christmas card, that she would remember their getting drunk as some girlfriend rite of passage, like some crazy bachelorette party.

But if what Trina had confessed was true, it was a whole new pile of emotional shit she was going to have to sift through before giving herself completely to Guy. She was already dangerously behind schedule, and this revelation was promising to fuck things up but good.

"I would have told you sooner," Trina said with a bite. "I would have told you right away, but I knew how...*disappointed* you would be." Her eyes narrowed, and she focused on the white line in the center of the highway.

"We didn't do it?" Nat asked Griff.

He just shook his head and shrugged. "News to me if we did."

"Nat," Trina said cautiously, as if talking a jumper off a very high bridge. "Nat, listen to me..."

"Oh, my fucking God," Nat said, traumatized into a string of expletives directed at everyone in the car. "Who the fuck *am* I? Who the fuck are *you?* This is your idea of doing me a favor?"

Trina opened her mouth to speak, but before she could say anything, the car was struck from the side by unseen force. She clutched the steering wheel and struggled to guide the car back from the far left lane, from where the impact had pushed them. Nat yelped and so did the dog. Griff, who of the three of them had probably seen more shit than anyone, muttered, "Jesus H. Christ, what the hell was that?"

"That," Nat said, "was my world."

"Pull over," Griff told Trina. "Something's hit the car."

Hyperventilating, Trina rolled her window down and pulled over to the side of the road. The interior was filled with the pungent aroma of fear and sweat and excitement, and none of it was coming from the dog.

It was obvious, once the initial shock of the collision wore off, that what actually happened could be described as a bird that had lost its way. It had splattered the back window with blood and feathers and tiny bird bones that stuck to the car like Elmer's Glue; and Nat winced, thinking of the sludge that was going to be pasted all down the side of her car.

Trina took this as a terrible omen.

"Oh, shit, not a bird," she whispered with horror. Her hands clenched in tight fists, and these she shoved up against her gaping mouth, as if she were trying to stifle the terrible acknowledgement of what had just happened. "Did you see that?" her voice cracked. "It killed itself on your car!"

Nat would buy none of this; she knew it to be just bad luck on the bird's part, having probably been sucked up in the back draft of that eighteen-wheeler that was going at least ninety when it passed the wagon.

Griff got out; and Nat pushed her door open, struggling to escape the confines of the backseat. Once on the shoulder of the road, she thrashed about in fury and confusion as she pounded her thighs and screamed at the sky.

What the fuck? What the fuck?

In the middle of the night, in the middle of Utah, in the company of persons whose last names she did not even know, Nat felt slip between her fingers the one loose thread of self-control that had been unraveling—for hours, days, years?—while she wasn't looking. It was like a giant ball of yarn on which events were pulling and pulling while the ball got smaller and smaller and smaller until it simply existed no more, finding nothing inside—just the other end of the string. Loose. Connected to nothing.

Nat's breakdown was about more than what Trina had said, about more than the fight or feeling tricked or even embarrassed at how she must have looked now, especially now, in Griff's eyes. It was that disconnect, like the piece of string you find attached to nothing at all. It was experiencing a disconnect from herself in the largest sense possible.

I am Bob, she admitted with defeat. *I have left my home as myself and have somewhere along the way become someone else entirely.*

"Birds don't commit suicide, Trina," Griff said. "They just don't."

"Don't you know what that means?" Trina demanded of the two of them. "Do you *know?*"

They didn't. Nat continued her fitful dance along the side of the road, stomping brush, pebbles, empty soda cans and chips bags with her nearly new hiking boots and kicking up a cloud of dust and sand in a ten-foot perimeter.

"It's bad when birds die," Trina said simply. "It means death. It means someone is going to die."

Nat sank to the ground and sat cross-legged in the cold dirt. Her feet were cold; she was tired and feeling sick. There were people—all these people—with her in her car, but she felt like the stranger, the one who did not belong.

It was only eleven o'clock, and they were still hours away from Salt Lake City. They were in the middle of nowhere, in the middle of nothing, and everything, it seemed, was falling apart. A big rig flew by, throwing into their bodies a gust of pebbles from the road and big chunks of grease and dirt that, in the wind, had wrested free of the undercarriage of the truck.

"When a bird gets killed," Trina yelled over the truck's roaring aftermath, "it means someone's gonna die."

"That's not how it goes," Nat said angrily. "It's when they fly into your house!" She'd never believed in superstitions until her aunt Judy died two weeks after a sparrow flew down the chimney.

Nat popped the trunk and retrieved a rag and some windshield cleaner. Not like bird shit, this was great red gobs of bird guts and feathers plastered to the glass. It would be a bitch to clean up.

"I can't stand to see things die," Griff said.

They stood in silence, save for the roar of the occasional produce truck peeling past in a rumble of rock and loose weed. Nat removed as much as she could, then flung the bloodied rag into the brush alongside the road. She dropped the Windex into the trunk and slammed it shut, then pushed Trina over to the passenger side and took the driver's seat. Griff and the dog crouched in the backseat.

They all knew the next thing said would be either incredibly insightful or insanely cruel, and none of them felt up to the responsibility.

"Who am I?" Nat finally said in a tiny, wretched voice.

Trina sighed heavily and forced a slight grin. "'Miss I got drunk and had a good time and shouldn't make too much of it cause it was a one-time thing and doesn't have to mean shit'. That's you, Nat. That's who you are. Nothing's changed."

Natalie started the engine. Slowly pulling off shoulder, she headed into the black horizon, where, somewhere, Guy was asleep in his bed and maybe dreaming of a nice, normal life with a nice, normal girl.

She's the Girl

Perhaps Sinatra said it best, Nat thought as she pulled a CD from the case and popped it into the stereo.
(Love is the tender trap)
or was it Ted Bundy
(I want what I cannot have.)

nine

Had love's truth come to Nat just once in the days preceding Ruune—had it not uttered the spiteful lies of obligation or dependency but instead told the simple truth of eternal devotion—the rest of the trip would have been like coasting downhill. But by the time she had conquered nearly a thousand miles and still did not see the truth for the trees, love had become just another fuck, this time cleverly disguised as a sixty-eight-year-old virgin and a marriage that would be consummated in heaven.

Miles past the bird incident, and Nat's sudden and uncharacteristic breakdown, nothing else had yet died. The caveat of death foretold by the bird's demise on the back window was, so far, unfulfilled, and for that good fortune all were relieved. But the chaos of those concurrent events, one seemingly random, the other an eventuality like a slow-moving freight train in the distance that only the most ignorant would not have seen coming, threw the three companions into an awkward, contemplative silence spent pondering life, death, love, breakfast, tornadoes, and whatever else might have been foremost in their minds.

Trina kept a watchful eye on Nat and Griff. Unable to shake her simple faith in superstition, she stood sentinel for a hint of impending trauma or early signs of disease—melanoma on the tip of a nose, perhaps, or a slowly clogging artery that would with only seconds' notice seize up and bring to its victim a painful, swift death. She rubbed her belly and ran her stubby fingers down her cheek and neck, as if needing that constant reassurance of her own existence. She watched P, too, because she knew it was usually fate's way to take somebody's dog for no reason.

Griff thought of the women he had loved and those who had loved him back. With less than fifty dollars in his wallet, he knew he'd soon be wondering where his next meal would come from, and he speculated how he would ever meet a woman of substance while in the company of two crazy girls, one bisexual who passed for gay and one just nuts.

Nat, for nearly fifty miles, showed no appreciable signs of life except for the slight, almost imperceptible movements of her fingers and toes that kept the car moving forward. Her mind, filled now to capacity with the expectations and imaginings she'd brought with her along with the insistent ironies that dogged her every thought, was simply unable to react. She simply shut down. By dawn, just before the eastern sky began to warm with the light of what she was sure would be another doomed day, they had driven over four hundred miles. They could have stopped, slept in a motel, turned around and gone back to Vegas, eaten breakfast, done nearly anything but keep driving. But at that time of day, one exit led easily to another, and before long they had passed through Salt Lake without incident and were on the way out of the state entirely.

The determination to simply keep the car pointed north had, when Nat wasn't looking, morphed from the most profound and intense human yearning for a like personal connection to a seemingly meaningless task performed simply by rote. Life, in that car and at that moment, wasn't the journey; it *was* the destination. It was the conquering of all that fucking asphalt that became the thing.

People often say of challenges and tragedies that just showing up is half the battle, but Nat knew that to be just more motivational bullshit. Getting there was the battle, and it was one she was determined to win, no matter what the cost.

Breaking the silence, Trina spoke up to announce that several small meals were better for her body than one or two large ones, and that she would like to stop for pancakes.

In misery, the kind that unfaithful lovers and loneliness in other forms brings, time passes always so slowly. With an apathetic disregard for schedules, appointments, or commitments of any kind, minutes pass like hours; and even the most mindless tasks, such as brushing one's teeth or buttoning a shirt, are slowed to an excruciating crawl. A punishment of love, Nat was sure, to imbue the sufferer's experience of loss with that extra dollop of despair, the one that tastes of metal in one's mouth and makes life seem as if it were being lived underwater.

True anguish, though, the kind that cannot be assuaged by the phone call from another to say "I'm sorry" or cannot be eased by the taking back of hurtful words, is a wretchedness that comes from a permanent loss—the death of a child, the death of one's dreams, or of one's self. That sort of misery swallows time whole. Entire days, weeks—sometimes years—are simply removed from the sufferer's life and absorbed into others', those who walk or drive past closed curtains, oblivious to what, inside, cannot even muster the strength to peek outside. They go about their daily business, free of the burden that cripples those forlorn souls who wake from their daze like those waking from a coma not knowing who is President or what fantastic technology is now being taken for granted. Their lucid moments come few and far between.

Nat, for as long as she could remember, had been stuck in stage one. The sense of yearning, disappointment, and, ultimately, misery she carried with her from early childhood had not matured. When her body began to change, when she began to witness the progression from girl to woman, it was, for her, a purely physical fact and had no impact at all on her expectations of adulthood—both her own and that of others.

True wretchedness could be hiding somewhere down the highway, could be coming nearer still with every confession or revelation in the car, in her mind. Like an unpredictable, deadly tornado, it could be out there as they spoke, swirling in the darkness, gaining momentum and waiting for her to turn her head just enough so it might approach swiftly, severely, in her one blind spot.

They found an IHOP and ate blueberry pancakes and sausage. Conversation was light and consisted mostly of the décor, the food, and the waitress, who moved with such a happy obedience she could as well have been one of those automatons on loan from Disneyland.

When they were done, Griff went outside to tend to other things, and Nat and Trina faced off over a table-top of greasy leftovers and cold coffee.

"Jesus fucking Christ, I don't know what's happening anymore," Nat said as she lit a cigarette and blew the smoke over the top of Trina's head. She tucked it into the corner of her mouth and cradled her head in her hands, digging her short fingernails into her scalp and twirling wide swaths of greasy hair around her fingers. Her clothes were wrinkled and damp with perspiration; the insides of her shoes felt muggy and wet. She was, at that moment, the least Fresh she had ever been in her entire life.

She pinched the neckline of her T-shirt between her thumb and forefinger and sniffed it, wrinkling her nose at the putrid tang. "God, did I puke on myself or something?"

Trina laughed. "Nah, I think you drooled a little, but that's about it."

"I'm sorry," Nat said to her.

"Sorry about what? Forget it."

"This is all my fault."

"What's your fault? What are you talking about?"

"That everything is so fucked up! I mean, look at this, it's so...fucked up!"

"You think this is fucked up? This is nothing. It'll be fine."

"I don't know what the hell I'm doing anymore."

"Hey, who does?" Trina said. "Hang in there. You've got a plan, remember?"

Nat huffed. "Yeah." Writing it all down in her planner, researching the details and determining the most expedient path meant shit that morning. All of her planning, second-guessing, and musing were about as concrete as wishing on a penny and then tossing it into a fountain.

"I'm sorry about the things I said," she told Trina.

Trina waved it off like a bug that had just flown into her line of sight. "Ppfff," she said. "Things. What things?"

"God, I'm tired," Nat sighed.

"Like a thousand days," Trina agreed.

"Am I making a mistake?" she asked.

"I don't believe in mistakes," Trina replied.

"How do you mean?"

"Well, okay, I mean there are some things you do that are a mistake. Like jumping off the roof into the kiddie pool. That's a mistake. Pouring gasoline down the carburetor when your car won't start and then sticking your nose under the hood while your girlfriend turns the key—that's a mistake."

Nat grinned.

"But I don't think that things you do from here, in your heart," Trina said as she touched a fingertip to her chest, "I don't believe anything you do from your heart should be called a mistake."

"Even if it turns out badly?"

"Just because it doesn't work out the way you thought they would doesn't mean it wasn't the right decision."

"Are you telling me to keep going?"

Trina cocked her head and tapped her plate with her fingertip while she contemplated Nat's question. "Are you saying you need be told that?"

"Arrrghh!" Nat cried out in exasperation. "Two days ago everything was so clear. Now it's like a puzzle that I just can't do. Everything's all mixed up and doesn't read right, and it's like I think I see the words, you know, I think I see what I'm supposed to do, but between my eyes and my brain I lose the connection."

"You're just tired," Trina said sympathetically. "You need a bath. You'll feel better."

Trina left the tip; and she and Nat joined Griff, who was in the parking lot checking the trailer hookup and trying to determine the extent of damage the bird had wrought on Nat's car. Only a marble-sized dent and a hairline crack in the back window. There were some wet red feathers stuck to the glass with some deeply colored viscous fluid, some smears Nat had missed in the darkness.

Trina and Nat fed P bits of sausage and syrupy pieces of blue pancake. Nat held a small cup with water, which the dog lapped and spilled all over her hiking boots. Griff got some water from the men's room and, one cup at a time, washed all the bird goo off the paint before it had the chance to completely harden and ruin the finish.

The sun rose brightly in Utah, as anyone would expect it to in such an open, American kind of place. Nat wondered aloud if this was where the buffalo roamed, and Trina observed that the skies were not cloudy all day. They grinned at one another, and Trina socked Nat playfully in the arm.

Trina cleared the trash off the dashboard and the floor—empty chips bags, soda cans, bottles of flat, warm soda nobody would miss. Nat stood in the parking lot and faced the road, watching the normalcy of the new day like it was the most amazing thing she had ever seen. Commuters in station wagons, compacts, and carpools buzzed past in both directions. People dressed in shirts and ties, skirts and stockings, with their coffee in the cup holder, listening to morning radio shows, barely gave them a pass on the way to work. Nat's normal life, the one she had left back in LA, the one where she woke up at seven a.m. like everyone else and showered and ate and drank her coffee and was at her desk by eight-thirty, seemed like another person's life entirely.

Watching one young woman in a clean mid-sized sedan primping at the red light in front of the pancake house, her significant other (Husband? Boyfriend? Roommate?) beside her with his paper and extra-large coffee, Nat wondered, *Is that me?*

It was like one of those out-of-body experiences she had read about, the ones where while just sitting and watching TV or napping on the sofa, one's self, one's essence, just rises into the air, floating free of gravity and other earthbound forces, watching the scenes below from another angle entirely and thinking, Is that what I really look like?

Maybe I am not here at all, Nat thought, standing like an unperceived spirit on the side of the road. She studied the woman at the red light and thought, *I am at the scene of some horrible crash and I am watching paramedics slam my chest and wrest the jagged metal from my flesh while my vitals slow and my body simply gives in. And now I am free to walk away.*

Trina blended well into Vegas—hell, Trina was made for Vegas—but here in Utah she looked like she might be picked up by the police at any moment and taken in for questioning. She'd borrowed a pair of Griff's jeans and one of Nat's pastel-colored tees, but with her shaved head and tiger tattoo, she was the ultimate party crasher at the Normal People's Ball.

That morning, owning the experiences of the last few days spent with Trina and in the places they'd been, standing in the parking lot and watching the normal ones—those she used to think herself one of—was like standing on the moon and watching the brightly lit Earth below.

With no place else to go, with nobody really watching the clock for their arrival, Griff and Trina decided to accompany Nat a while longer. The weather was nice, the drive had been interesting (to say the least, according to Griff), and it didn't seem right to end it all in a place like Utah.

Griff took the wheel; some time later, Trina pointed out the huge highway sign depicting the outline of a cowboy on a bucking bronc, and they entered Wyoming.

Nat wondered if it was just by some cosmic coincidence that the farther north she drove the less inhabited the world seemed. Not many tourists traveling in the spring, she observed, and their only company for miles at a time was either truckers on their way to another state or locals en route to those mysterious, hidden communities that could not be seen from the highway.

She watched out the passenger side window for signs of life but even in her own opaque reflection saw none. The uppermost slopes of the mountain ranges were still sheathed in white, and as the wagon climbed in elevation it grew colder in the car, even with the heat turned up all the way and even when the sun was high in the sky. There was not much to look at through Wyoming; Trina read facts from an almanac Nat had forgotten she'd packed, and from the infrequent billboards and highway signs that peppered the road they learned things not found in the usual guidebooks. A giant likeness of Abe Lincoln's head, one billboard teased, could be viewed in Laramie—which was still hours away, Trina was disappointed to realize. Griff, who had had a torrid romance with a widow in Douglas, Wyoming, several years earlier delighted them with the legend of the jackalope, a mythical creature along the lines of Bigfoot and the Loch Ness Monster.

"I want to see that! I want to see that!" Trina exclaimed.

"For real?" Nat said.

"We don't have anything like that in Barstow," Trina pouted. "There's the world's biggest thermometer down in Baker," she recalled, "but it's not like...alive or anything."

Nat sighed. Los Angeles held none of the fantastic oddities of nature road trips to other states happily provided. Beguiling, sometimes frightening creatures that could be found only in roadside stands that sold sodas, cigarettes, snacks, and, for an additional fee, a peek at something those back home would never believe. They were usually fake, she knew. The man who was billed as half snake wasn't, the dog who could speak wouldn't—at least, in front of strangers—and even Griff admitted that the jackalope was really the result of a creative taxidermist looking to make a few extra bucks by sewing some antlers onto the head of a stuffed rabbit, despite the legend of periodic and fearsome attacks on small children and pets.

Little, they agreed, could be counted upon to be as authentic as it first appeared to be.

As they neared Laramie, Nat gave in and agreed that a visit to the giant Abe Lincoln head might be just what she needed to break out of the funk in which she'd spent the last twelve hours. They exited the main highway and took a narrow two-lane road that paralleled I-80 for a few miles then curved slightly to the north, entering, the signs indicated, Baldwin, Wyoming, population 3,732.

Ivy, and all that only she could represent, came upon Nat abruptly and accidentally; and this was the only way in which she could have come upon her, for even in her wildest imaginings Nat could not have pictured such a temptation to fall back into fantasy as Ivy. After finding her, learning how she had come to be who she was, Nat could think only of the hours preceding her and shrug her shoulders and say to herself, *Yeah, but what's the catch?*

It was while arguing over the giant head—would it be as fantastic as could be seen on Mount Rushmore? Was it some stupid sculpture made of twine? Was this really a good idea after all—that they did not see one of the town's three stoplights turn red and entered the intersection just as Ivy stepped off the curb.

Nat, who was driving, saw her first. Only the top of her head was visible over the long hood of the wagon; and at the moment of her sighting, it was surreal, like seeing an angel or other apparition that really isn't there at all.

"Holy shit!" she yelled, and the others caught sight of her next, but only in time to see her head disappear behind the front of the car, as if she had been swallowed whole by the pavement.

"Holy fuck!" Trina screamed as Nat slammed the brakes, and they all three threw open their doors and ran to the front of the car.

"The bird! The bird!" Trina kept saying. "I told you—it was that damned bird!"

"Did I hit her?" Nat started to cry as pedestrians and others began to take notice of what had happened. "Is she dead?"

Like a fallen baby bird, Ivy, with her eyes closed, lay delicately on the asphalt just inches in front of the bumper. Not crumpled in pain, as Nat had dreaded finding her. Not covered in blood or disheveled, she lay peacefully, as if someone had gingerly picked her up and put her in that exact position, taking care to cross her ankles and making sure her skirt was not hiked too high up her legs.

"Oh God oh God oh God," was all Nat could say.

Griff touched his hand to Ivy's throat and lowered his ear to her mouth. "She's not dead, Nat."

Ivy's eyes fluttered, and a voice from the crowd said, "Jesus, Mary and Joseph, they've run over Ivy."

"I didn't run over her!" Nat shouted to the crowd. "I didn't even touch her, really!"

Griff spoke to Ivy softly, as to a child. "Hello, there. Are you all right? Do you feel any pain?"

Ivy's eyes opened wide and skimmed over the worried, frantic faces huddled over her in the middle of the street.

"Hello, Lucy," she said to one, and to another, "Hello, Frank, how is Mary?"

"Hello, Ivy," they responded in kind, one at a time.

"I'm well, how are you?"

As Ivy's gaze landed on Griff, Trina, and then Nat, faces she did not recognize, she smiled sweetly and cooed, "Hello. I don't think I've had the pleasure."

Griff slid behind Ivy and lifted her gently by the back and shoulders, nestling her tiny body against his chest.

"Somebody better call Mother, or Gary," a voice from the crowd said.

"Somebody call the doctor," another chimed in.

"No, no," Ivy insisted, wiping her bangs from her face as she straightened up. "I'm fine, honestly. I just got a scare, that's all."

"Did I hit you?" Nat asked tearfully.

Ivy took her hand and stroked it softly. "No, sweetheart, you just gave me a start, is all." Then, to Griff, she said in a knowing way, "I'm hypoglycemic."

Trina stood and faced the crowd. "You guys can all, like, you know, move on. Everything's okay. We'll take her to the doctor."

"Oh, no," Ivy protested. "Just take me home—I tell you I'm fine." And to illustrate this point, she held on to Griff's forearm and lifted herself onto her feet, standing exactly on the spot where Nat had feared she had mowed her down. "See? No harm, I'm fine."

"I think we should call an ambulance," Trina said, and Nat agreed. "We don't know if she's got internal injuries, or what."

"I just slipped on the pavement," Ivy protested. "I was startled. My blood sugar is low. I'll be fine once I get home and have a bite to eat."

"I'll take you home," Griff said, smiling sweetly and in his most charming way. "Don't you worry about a thing."

Despite Nat's protests, Griff placed the old woman gingerly in the backseat of the car, nestled between himself on the left and P on the right.

"We can't do this," Nat whispered to Trina angrily. "We've got to go!"

"How long can this take?" Trina reassured her. "Really, we'll be in and out before you know it. You'll see."

"We'd better get going before someone calls Mother," Ivy warned from the backseat. "She won't like this. She won't like this at all."

Ivy was petite, as it seemed all women eventually grew to be. She was plain, like the landscape. It could not be said that she was once very beautiful, not in a feminine way; but she was good-looking, with defined, symmetrical features. She wore little makeup, just a light wash on her lips that was the color of an LA sunset shrouded in smog. Her long gray hair was swept off her neck and piled casually on top of her head. Loose strands dangled over the tops of her ears and the nape of her neck; but in the front, her bangs, clipped with a silver barrette to keep them from falling in her eyes, might have fallen only to chin level.

Ivy brought her hand up to touch her lips, and Nat was surprised at how delicate and graceful her fingers were. The skin was clear and smooth, the palms pink and probably warm and moist when cupped to the cheek of her grandchildren. Nat imagined she must have at least ten of them, not having any knowledge yet that this was a simple medical impossibility. Nat daydreamed of her sitting on the lawn surrounded by little ones who ranged in age from two to ten, their shoes kicked aside and iced tea waiting on the porch while they painted lemon-yellow suns and stick people in gabled houses.

Ivy's hands seemed to have aged more slowly than any other part of her body; and although she said she was sixty-eight years old, there was none of her, of what Nat could see, that seemed barren or dry. Not like Wyoming and what surrounded them in all directions.

Upon closer inspection, Nat noticed that Ivy's eyes were two different colors, and that a splattering of very light, girlish freckles dotted her face. A small red blemish, about the size of a pen point, scarred the right side of her nose where, Nat would later learn, she had been bitten by a puppy when she was only eight.

Suddenly, Ivy announced, like telling I'm an Aquarius or a Lutheran, "I'm a virgin." At first Nat had thought she just hadn't heard the woman correctly, that the wind rushing by or a big rock bouncing against the undercarriage of the Volvo had distorted her words, making Nat think she had spoken something she truly had not. But then Ivy said it again.

"That's right," she sighed and looked out the window at nothing in particular. "It's true that I am intact."

Griff sidled up closer and patted her head. "It's nice to meet a traditional woman," he said, and Ivy blushed.

Ivy's family had always lived in Wyoming. Her father died when she was young; and so it was another, more distant relative who marched her down the aisle and gave her up to Buzz, her beloved dead husband and the man she barely got to kiss before he was called away to defend his country in the last world war. Her older sister, a woman everyone called Mother, was "in charge," Ivy said. Mother had been married as well, and, like Ivy, her husband had died prematurely. Although, Ivy added with a whisper, Mother was not a virgin. Her boy Gary was thirty-eight the previous December. He was a Christmas baby, Ivy said. She said he was a gift from God, just like the baby Jesus. Gary had been married for almost five years to a girl named Susanna. She had no middle name, and Ivy thought that exotic.

At first, the thought of running down an elderly virgin in the middle of the road was like some macabre comedy of errors, Nat thought. It was too perfect an ending for a trip that was already fraught with the bizarre and unbelievable. But if it were true that this old woman had been carrying a torch between her legs for all these decades, just for the memory and reverence of her one true love, it would make the trip and all that had happened thus far worthwhile. It would lead the way to Ruune more clearly than the green-and-white highway signs or those faded red dots that read, always with a sneer, YOU ARE HERE.

A desire that had blossomed over the years into practically its own religion. Nat wanted to believe it was so—hoped it was—and found a reluctant but nonetheless wonderful anticipation in thinking that this woman had been sleeping all those years with only the memory of her love. Here, now, tentatively taking the turns to Ivy's house, she found her anticipation growing and her excitement flourishing as she played a twisted game of Beat the Clock. With Ivy on her mind—she and her Buzz—maybe Nat could get to Ivy's Love Place before it really was too late, before reason got there first and wrecked this new good thing she'd found.

Possibility. Hopelessness. How—or when—either might come to her was impossible to guess at this point. She wearily resigned to placing herself somewhere in the middle and let it ride.

She eyed Ivy in the rearview mirror, longing clouding suspicion, doubt diluting desire. She watched as more and more of this fresh territory disappeared over her shoulder, seeing all that land swallowed up by moments just past. They passed a historical marker on the right, something about a Flaming Gorge, but before Trina could look it up in the AAA guidebook it was just another piece of history gone by.

At Ivy's direction, Nat took a narrow unnamed street off the main drag. The tires hit dirt, and she slowed as the landscape before them revealed a subdivision of rundown duplexes and ratty single-family homes that seemed eerily desolate and barren.

Most of the houses they passed on the way up the block lay in decay—weeds sprouting out of the asphalt and the sidewalks, trees bare near the top and front windows mended with cardboard and duct tape. On the right they passed what was once a yellow house that had faded in the arid days to a sun-bleached shack; through an opaque rectangular window on the side Nat could see the outline of shampoo bottles. There was a Camaro on bricks in one yard; beneath a tree in the next an engine hung from thick rope.

Ivy's house lay at the end of the wide street and, maybe as recently as only twenty years ago, might have stood in solitude on acreage that had been passed down through generations of her family. At one time they probably buried their dead in the backyard; and maybe a hundred years ago they had even hanged a man from one of the old, stooped-over trees on the south side of the house. They were probably mayors and judges and sheriffs. But it would have taken only one greedy brother-in-law to screw the legacy and parcel up the land like it was day-old birthday cake, selling for a profit to real estate speculators who would happily seed the land with cheap housing that, from the moment of its christening, was nothing more than a ghetto.

Ivy leaned forward from the backseat, tapped Nat's shoulder with a sharp finger, and declared, "Get ready now, almost there..."

It was an ominous statement, and Nat wondered if policemen would be waiting, or just angry relatives who wanted to beat the shit out of her.

Nat could see a sensation of coming home all over Ivy's face. Even if returning from just a ten-minute walk to the market, she knew Ivy would always ascend the porch steps with a spontaneous joy she herself had longed for since those first afternoons spent curbside at her grandparents' home. After the divorce, coming home was a thrill that was lost forever.

P whimpered from the backseat. He nervously licked his chops, and Ivy said he could roam the woods behind the house.

Ivy's house stood alone. A neat white picket fence bordered the property on the front and sides. Guarding the walk that led up to the front door was a low wooden archway entangled with leafy green vines and small, pea-like buds that hinted at the beauty that, in a few short weeks, would emerge from within. Just beyond the backyard, which could be seen from where they parked, was wild brush and brambles that led into nothing. That, Ivy said, was where the dogs went for fun. The lawn was a shade of green that, in April, could have been described as lush; and it was impeccably manicured, the stiff blades of grass cut precisely along the edges of the sidewalk and drive, rising at an exact ninety-degree angle from the earth.

Had she seen it somewhere before? On television? In her dreams? Nat wasn't sure she was seeing it at all, feared that it was more like a mirage on the highway, nothing but vapors rising from spilled oil. Her mind immediately set at ease, the highway the last thing on her agenda at the moment, she took in the sight of the grand old home and felt a rush of something—belonging, safety—something she couldn't put her finger on.

The exterior of the house was painted pale blue bordered in white, with pastel yellow shutters. Three stories up was a turret with open archways from which you could probably see the whole county—the whole north side of the town, at the very least.

Trees sprang up behind the house, cradling it in a cool, springtime shade you could probably feel in the hallways, in the front room, where the polished wood floors would smell of lemon oil and where your stocking feet would glide over the surface like skating on an iced pond. Behind every window was hung a delicate sheathing of white eyelet lace, an opaque shield against prying, envious eyes.

Home. There came from within structures such as these a seduction that not everyone could know, only those like Nat—searching, wandering, orphaned by their own transient longings, seeking solace in a simple home of four walls and a floor and maybe some flowers on the sill. To Natalie, it was simple: if you weren't going home, you were going nowhere. There was in Ivy's house that wonderful invitation to come in, kick your shoes off, and settle into a comfy chair. To wander aimlessly over the lush green lawn, to drink homemade sun tea and then, at dusk, call the children home from stickball and hear your voice carry over the rooftops of your neighbors' homes and down the side streets you couldn't see from the porch. She wanted to capture that experience, that moment, before going into the house. She wanted to indulge before this dream, too, was shattered on the shrill words of another or was lost in the careless, unthinking deed of someone who had not the slightest idea how lucky they were to call this house a home.

On the front porch, a slatted swing hung from thick chains. In the breezeless afternoon it rocked eerily back and forth in a gentle, buoyant movement, propelled by some unseen force as it shifted its center of gravity back and forth as if someone had just risen from that spot and disappeared into the house.

Nat sighed and shut off the car, listening to the soft pings and clicks of the engine's spent energy. It was a moment full of anticipation, and any errant movement could ruin that moment. But possibility was rife, and she didn't want to miss the next ecstatic discovery that was sure to be found behind the heavy front door.

She got out and reached for Ivy. The old woman held her first two fingers tightly, but it felt like a baby's lazy grasp; and Nat used her other hand to cup her elbow and hoist her tiny frame from the backseat. Ivy said thank you then wiped her gray bangs off her face and, leaning into Griff, who appeared suddenly on her right, made her way toward the house, her brittle bones rocking from left to right like that dead porch swing, buoyed by the weight of a sack containing some books and magazines.

Nat and Trina followed. Once free of the backseat, P lifted his nose into the air and broke into a sudden gallop for the backyard. Nat watched from the curb as the swing spent the last of its own energy, and then she slid her keys into her pocket, loving the sound they made jingling against one another and against the loose change in there.

Home.

Next, she knew—she hoped—would come the sound of the screen door creaking open and then slamming shut on its loose hinges—the sound of coming home, having company. Images like these were what Nat did best, even after having been out of practice for a few days. But then this dream, too, was killed—popped like a rising balloon against a lit cigarette.

"Well, who the hell are you?" someone—something—shrieked; and into Nat's consciousness, like a heavy rock tossed into a still, smooth lake, came the image of her own mother. She could see her with her eyes shut; she could imagine her dancing up there on the roof, pointing her slender finger at her only daughter and singing, like an evil owl, *Who? Who? Who the hell are you?*

Nat recoiled defensively as a woman who could only have been described as "in charge" came bounding down the porch steps with the furious energy of one who'd just been stung on the ass by a wasp. She was tall and handsome, exactly as Ivy had described her. She wore men's trousers in a soft gray fabric; the baggy material billowed down her legs and around her ankles as she fiercely strode nearer the pack of unwelcome visitors. The heels, and then the toes, of her stiff shoes tapped precisely on the pavement

(tap-TAP tap-TAP)

and Nat felt that punishment was imminent. Mother's prim, angular face wore an expression that said "Don't touch my family," and Nat was thankful to see her long fingers clutching a cordless phone and not a gun.

Concentrating only on the dwindling distance between herself and the suspicious visitors, Mother made her way down the front walk and intercepted them halfway between the curb and the arch, before Natalie could step under, before she had even gotten within sniffing distance of the peach pie she just knew would be cooling on the kitchen sill. From the clip in the woman's step and the determined look on her face, Nat expected she would slap her, maybe spit in her face; and she recoiled defensively.

Obviously, someone *had* called Mother.

The woman stopped abruptly less than three feet in front of Nat and furiously punched in a number on the portable phone.

"Never mind, she's here," Mother barked into the mouthpiece. Making a cursory inspection of Ivy and her belongings, Mother added reluctantly, "...seems to be all right..." and then glowered at Nat, whose hand dangled limply in mid-air before it dropped self-consciously to her thigh.

"Do you know what we do with reckless drivers around here?" Mother demanded; but before Nat could answer she turned to face Ivy and, bending slightly at the waist so as to look eye-level into her sister's face, lightly grasped Ivy's hand in hers and in some familial code conveyed her desperate, consuming worry. From behind them, Nat watched with a growing fear the purple veins in the woman's neck. Her mousy-brown hair was sheared close to her head but left long enough, in certain sections, to tuck behind her ears, which, Nat noticed, were not pierced.

Ivy dismissed Mother's doting with a gentle wave of her tiny arthritic hands; and then she smiled upon Nat, whom Mother slowly turned to face full on.

"We hang 'em," Mother said, answering her own question to Nat. "From that tree," she added, pointing somewhere behind her head.

"Oh, now, Mother," Ivy said, "I don't know what you've been told, but I am fine."

With her suspicious, probing eyes, Mother made a quick, clean sweep of Nat from head to toe, regarding with much disdain the intrusion she and her companions provided.

"Natalie Dresden," Nat said—her right hand again extended in hope—resisting the urge to add "sir" at the end. She imagined that next Mother would want to smell her breath; but she made no move. She only stared at Nat's cupped palm as if she knew exactly what she'd been doing with it, and as if such knowledge thoroughly disgusted her.

"And what, Natalie Dresden, do you think that name means to me?"

Well, Nat thought, *this week it means shit to you and me both*; but she was silent, knowing that when the words would finally come out they would come more like an apology.

Ivy introduced all three of them by name; but instead of soothing Mother's rage, Ivy's explanations of how they had come to meet only served to irritate the woman

that much more. It was useless to present the virgin Ivy
as unmarked, unbruised, for the horrors of which Nat
and the others were now suspect were doubtless the result not of a chrome bumper or a tire but of wicked intent; and that, Nat feared, Mother would see written all
over their faces.

Mother placed herself to Ivy's right and regarded the
tattooed, bleached, and pierced Trina with great suspicion and then rolled her eyes dramatically. She appeared
to sniff in Griff's direction and then, with an unwaver-
ing stare, turned her attention back to Nat, who tried to
quell her discomfort by ignoring the old woman, by no-
ticing with a sudden, feigned interest all things within
her line of vision—the basement windows that peeked
over the top of the lawn like another pair of curious,
suspicious eyes; the dirt flower bed, its barren surface
raked neatly in rows and roped off with wire fencing
coated in yellow plastic, the puddle of dog pee that had
lessened to just a damp spot in the dirt; an open book
and tea cup that sat on the porch just below the heavy
swing. But it was always the lure of the house—loom-
ing large just behind Mother's left shoulder—that drew
Nat's attention back from wherever it had strayed.

Using her thin but rigid body to block the path to the
house, Mother drew herself in for hard, probing questions and then back again to the perimeter of some invisible boundary, like a demented game of Hokey Pokey.

(put your left foot in and you shake it all about)

"Do you have any identification?" she asked casually,
as if she had said Do you have a tissue? Just as Nat was
about to reach into her purse for her wallet and driver's
license, she enjoyed a sudden reprieve by the abrupt appearance of a postal truck screeching to a halt in front
of the house, missing the rear of Griff's trailer by only
inches. Out stepped Ivy's nephew Gary—the dimwitted
boy Ivy had referred to—who, Trina would conclude

later, would likely be the next postal worker to snap.

When she was young, Natalie had often pondered, along with the mysteries of pubic hair and all-day jawbreakers, where it is that postmen come from. Enigmatic creatures—like white tigers and schoolteachers—they are never spotted in their natural habitat, never imagined to enjoy the mundane pleasures of a normal life

was it even possible to imagine the postman sitting on the toilet?

but instead were seen only walking their routes, and other places—places which they never arrived at or left, places in which they simply were. On those rare occasions when a mailman or some other such creature ventured out of bounds—spotted picnicking, at the movies or market or, worst of all, at the beach—they seemed strangely discrepant, upsetting some natural, unspoken order. It was a fact that to find oneself, at twelve, behind the object of your unrequited affection

Jesus H. Christ, and with his wife!

in the checkout line at the market was one of the most traumatic episodes to befall a pre-adolescent girl. Some twenty years later, Nat felt that same dreadful disorder at realizing that the red-blue-and-white postal truck now parked nose to tail with the trailer must be delivering not catalogs and bills, but Gary.

Those first moments of terrible realization recalled for her awkward moments at the taqueria down on Sherman Way, staring at the back of her pharmacist's balding head and praying the man would not turn around and recognize her.

"Well, hello there, Natalie Dresden!" her loathsome fear went. "How'd that vaginal cream work out for ya? Infection gone?" Nat knew that without the unspoken hierarchy enjoyed by those who do not wear a uniform to work she and her druggist should have been just people buying cabeza tacos. Small talk about green salsa vs.

red—seeing him actually eat, or smoke a cigarette—was the closest thing to intimacy anyone could share with their pharmacist, their postman or hairdresser; and Nat found it terrifying and awkward, even as an adult.

Gary, officially dressed in crisp blue woolen shorts and dark knee socks, leapt from the truck and ran, huffing, to Ivy. "Oh, Jesus, Auntie Ivy, I just heard you were run over by a truck!"

"Oh, Gary," Mother said. "For Chrissakes! Does she honestly look like she's been run over by a truck?"

"I'm perfectly fine," Ivy protested yet again. "I wasn't hit by a truck, I wasn't hit by anything. I was just startled and...fell down."

Gary removed a candy bar from his pocket, unwrapped it and tore off a piece for Ivy. "Low blood sugar?" he asked.

She nodded.

"Well, what do we have here? Visitors?" With his tired eyes, his tepid smile, he had addressed the group collectively.

"Perpetrators," Mother snarled.

"I don't know you," Gary said to Nat, with none of the suspicion that was Mother's. He cleared his throat as he approached, flinching almost imperceptibly as he passed Mother.

His ballooned fingers found first Nat—his right hand was blackened with ink and marred with dozens of miniscule paper cuts that would never heal—and shook her hand with a firm, friendly grasp.

"I'm Gary Goode," he said with a wink and a trace of playfulness, "and I want to thank you for bringing my aunt home safely."

Gary was Ivy's favorite—and only—nephew. He was a man who, even at thirty-eight, could have been described as large for his age. It was only after he was born that everyone started calling Leona "Mother." Up until then, she was just plain Leona, but with the birth of her son, she became "Mother"—in name only—to everyone in town.

Gary said hello to Trina next; he winked at her and shook her hand and, with a slight gesture of his forefinger to his head and a smile, indicated approval of her tattoo. He and Griff nodded in one another's direction but did not speak.

"Safely!" Mother choked on the word. "Gary, you idiot, these are the people that nearly killed your aunt!"

"Oh, Mother!" Ivy protested, waving the notion away with her tiny hand. "They saved my life!"

"Lord, how do you figure that?" Mother asked.

"By not running me over like some lump in the road," Ivy said and turned toward the house, still holding on to Griff's arm.

Nat was surprised at how different Gary was from Mother. She imagined that Gary might really be Ivy's baby, that she had birthed him out of wedlock when she was only thirteen and that, in order to save the family's name, Mother had raised him as her own. It sounded like something that would happen in a square state.

"Gary," Ivy said, pushing her tiny, rocking body between Mother and her favorite, and only, nephew. "Where do you think my new friends are going?" she asked anxiously.

"Where?" he asked.

"North Dakota!" she exclaimed with disbelief, like it might as well have been Jupiter.

"North Dakota!" he said. "Well, what do you think of that, Auntie?" he asked, punctuating his question with an affectionate squeeze of her shoulders.

"I think that's wonderful!"

"Well, I do, too."

Mother sighed dramatically in the background, and Ivy invited them all inside; Mother made a noise that sounded like choking on a chicken bone.

"We're going inside," she announced, and with that she took Ivy's left arm and gently wrested her from Griff's light but firm grasp. As she led her younger sister up the wide path that let to the house, she said, without turning around, "Do what you please."

Nat and the others followed and pressed into the foyer, enduring those first awkward moments of acquaintance when all one could hope for was to try not to breathe through one's nose or let any strange noise emit from one's body. Any such sound would have echoed through the front living rooms as if they were standing at the bottom of the Grand Canyon, for the stillness in the Goode home was like being in a vacuum; it engulfed the slightest tremor of sound in a millisecond and left in its wake the deafening absence of life.

The atmosphere indoors, despite Mother's constant edginess, seemed the antithesis of the suspicion and doubt that had hung over them on the front lawn. It elicited in Nat memories of home—a real home, not the one she chased like a wish through the northern skies. It was like standing in the Craftsman, giddy from the smell of balm. Such quiet was comforting after a thousand miles of wind in her ear. Other than the shuffling of their shoes on hard wood the only sound heard was the soft, rhythmic beat of a wall clock on the far side of the room. Like a countdown, ten...nine...eight...a gentle reminder of time slipping past.

Like the Craftsman, the rooms in the house were cavernous, even though filled with furniture and memorabilia. They were linked by wide, open doorways through which three adults walking abreast could easily pass. Nat noticed that when Gary stood in one of the doorways he was dwarfed by its enormity and made insignificant by the grandeur of his surroundings. The ceilings reached higher than any Christmas tree she

had ever seen—if she had stood on a chair in the center
of the room and extended her arms upward she would
still not be able to touch the ceiling. She had tried doing just that in the Craftsman when she was a girl—almost every weekend she tried, when the others were in
the kitchen, bitching about something—and had never
even come close to touching the top. Now, in the Goode
home, she had the sudden, nostalgic urge to try it again,
but she needn't stand on a chair to know that she would
still not reach it. She was glad it was not one of those
details children remember so poorly, embellishing the
facts as they get older until everything about their youth
is remembered as the biggest, the grandest, the deepest.

Through each of the many windows came a warm,
woody glow that lit up the room and warmed their faces, even Mother's, which in the harsh sun outside had
been colored a funny, metallic yellow.

From the far wall, papered with framed photographs
from floor to ceiling, peered generations of family and
friends at weddings, Christmases and other still, quiet
times. Denizens of their own protected enclave, they
smiled generously in black-and-white and color, waving
hello and giving rabbit ears to one another in the silly
way that families act when the camera is pointed their
way. Nat's family was not so generous in that way; they
huddled secretly in old albums kept in the credenza in
the dining room. They might smile at you if you went
looking for them, if you made the first move and didn't
mind riffling through all that other shit. Here, wearing a big welcome—bigger even than the one they had
passed coming into Utah—these faces smiled to Nat and
her friends, and for the first time in so long it truly was
like coming home.

She couldn't wait to sit in the dining room. She could
be convinced to spend with them a week or more, had
she been asked.

Unlikely, because in Mother's occasional sighs Nat detected a wish that they would just all get up and go. She tried to ignore Mother, concentrating only on her need to visit the rest of the house, the need to see Buzz and sit on the cool mound of his grave.

"Gary," a distorted voice moaned from above, shattering the perfect pitch of silence. "Gary, what's happened?"

At the top of the stairs stood a slight, blond-haired woman. She gripped the railing with one hand; the other was planted firmly on her hip. Her head was cocked; and she was looking directly into Gary's eyes, ignoring the small group of strangers gathered at the foot of the stairs.

She tapped her heel on the wood floor, in an effort, Nat guessed, to hold Gary's attention. She frowned and spoke again. "What's going on?"

Nat, mouth gaping, stared at the woman she guessed must be Gary's wife, Susanna. More than her sudden presence, it was her voice that had startled. It wasn't sharp or angry like Mother's, but out of place in that moment and totally unexpected. It was a frightening sound and took Nat completely off-guard.

"She's deaf," Trina whispered to her, tugging at her elbow. "Haven't you ever heard a hearing impaired person speak before?"

"I know what you're thinking," Gary suddenly said to Nat, who bristled with embarrassment at having been discovered staring. He grinned at Natalie in a weird, knowing way; and after all that had happened, she would not have been surprised in the least if he, in fact, did know what she was thinking.

"How does a guy like me end up with a woman like that?" he said.

"Um..." Nat could only say, not sure if that's what she was thinking or not.

"Gary!" Susanna cried out from the top of the stairs. "Will you tell me what the fuck is going on?"

Gary laughed and signed to her as he spoke aloud, "I'm sorry, Ivy had an accident." He opened his arms and welcomed her as she descended the stairs, but she passed him and went straight to Ivy.

"Are you all right?" she said, cupping Ivy's tiny face in her small hands. Ivy nodded with affection, and Susanna turned back toward Gary and grasped his hands. "Thank God! What the hell happened?"

Susanna had not yet acknowledged that there were others in the house. She and Gary appeared, to Nat, to be in deep discussion, probably telling of the near-accident and the commotion it had caused throughout the town.

Gary was right; he did know what Nat was thinking. She was wondering how he had ended up with someone like Susanna—or someone like Mother, for that matter—and she wondered how long it usually takes for one of a couple to start thinking in terms of balls and chains. She had heard her father say that same thing a thousand times—How in the world did I end up with that woman?—and she vowed on the spot to never let a circumstance arise where Guy might be tempted to pose that question, to himself or to perfect strangers.

"Must she use language like that?" Mother said of Susanna as she led the others into the front room and herded Ivy onto a soft-cushioned sofa. "Jesus H. Christ, doesn't she know how goddamned offensive that sounds?"

"Unlikely," Nat muttered under her breath as she edged into the front room slowly, taking a seat near the doorway that led to the bottom of the stairs, where Gary and Susanna were engaged in conversation using only their hands. Everyone else had completely forgotten about them, and Ivy had already pressed Trina and

Griff into more interesting topics of conversation—do tattoos hurt, and how does it feel to ride a motorcycle? Nat ignored them and continued to spy on Gary and Susanna, who hung back as if trying to blend into their grand surroundings.

Mother rose and started to slowly pace the room. She folded her thick arms over her chest and strode in front of Nat, seeming to deliberately block Nat's lovely view of two people in love.

"Where did you say your party was headed?" she asked Nat with much interest, as if trying to catch her in a lie.

"North Dakota."

"North Dakota," she repeated. "You've still got a long way to go." Meaning, Nat supposed, *so you'd better get your fat asses off my couch and back out onto the highway.*

"Oh, you can't go yet!" Ivy protested to the three of them, but while looking into Griff's eyes. "I have to thank you properly."

"Thank them for what?" Mother asked through bared teeth.

"I told you, for saving my life!" Ivy replied and then announced, "You must stay for dinner. Please say you'll be my guests."

"Do what you please," Mother muttered.

"I'm on it," Gary suddenly said from where he stood with Susanna. "I'll cook up something special for you and your new friends, Auntie. How does that sound?"

"Wonderful!" she exclaimed.

Nat shot Trina a glare demanding refusal, but Trina only shrugged, tapped her watch and mouthed, silently "one hour." Nat just shrugged.

Gary kissed Susanna on the cheek and, like a fighter pilot embarking on some deadly mission from which he foolishly expected to return, flashed thumbs-up then disappeared behind a huge door that swung as quietly as the draft that blew through the rooms. He left without anyone having said goodbye to him, without anyone having even acknowledged he had been talking; and suddenly Nat was overcome with the urge to leap from her seat and follow him to wherever he was going.

Susanna stood like an awkwardly painted stick girl in the absence left by her husband. Her arms and legs protruded uncomfortably from inside her dress, and she looked as if she would remain exactly where she stood until someone came along and picked her up then set her down again in another part of the house.

"A smart girl," Mother said of Susanna in a sharp tone, like reluctant praise, "but deaf as a stone."

It was an odd remark, as if implying Susanna was in some way at fault for her handicap. As if she, at one time, were mere moments from discovering the cure for cancer but instead had let herself be tempted into a world of silence and signing. *Hanging with the wrong crowd,* Nat imagined Mother cursing. *Those damned deaf ruffians.*

"Bitch," Nat mouthed silently of Mother when she was sure she would not be seen. Looking up, she made eye contact with Susanna, and the two smiled at one another. Susanna raised her eyebrows and nodded softly then took off up the stairs.

Nat settled back into the red velvet sofa while the ladies' conversation wafted through the still rooms like a quiet breeze. Listening to Ivy recount the days of Buzz was like watching a favorite old movie, watching the progression with a mixture of happiness and regret, sadness at being unable, for even a moment, to forget it is not your life, not your love.

Buzz arrived in Baldwin, Wyoming, in June 1941, the same day, coincidentally, that Germany invaded Russia. That is how Mother would from then on tell the story, Ivy laughed. She said Mother would remember it to friends and others who had not been there to see for themselves as "that day when Buzz and the Nazis changed our lives forever." Mother spoke it in conspiratorial tones, as if the two events were beyond coincidence and must have been somehow related. He had come out of nowhere—from prison, she suspected—though he claimed from Austin, Texas.

It could be said, by young ladies with no experience in this sort of thing—ladies like the then-seventeen-year-old Ivy—that Buzz exuded a certain style, a seductiveness having more to do with his baggy pants, stick-straight, greased black hair and anise breath than with any fiber of his moral character. Just his name was enough to incite mothers and older brothers into pulling their shades and locking their front doors. Buzz—there was something inherently deviant about it and there was much speculation on what sort of woman would name her child after a noise. Divorced, probably.

"When I fell in love with Buzz," Ivy said, "everyone thought Leona would be furious, but if she was she never told it to anyone, especially not to me. You didn't, did you, Mother?"

She shook her head. No, she didn't.

Buzz chose Ivy; and for awhile, the whole town held its breath, regarding Mother like a mule who'd just eaten a case of dynamite and would without a moment's notice up and explode all over everyone. She never did, and if she'd ever had a cross thought about Buzz in all those years she'd never said it publicly.

A few months later, in a moonlit ceremony attended by the whole town of Baldwin and some distant relatives from Landers, they were wed. The next day the Japanese bombed Pearl Harbor, and Mother would forever shake her head and wonder how bad things always know to come in threes.

"First Russia, then Buzz, and now this..." she would say.

Most of the men left that day, going straight from the wedding reception, which by dawn had barely peaked, to the enlistment office in Landers, where they would happily surrender their civilian status and enter the second great world war. Buzz went, too, leaving Ivy in white, a color that she had not yet outworn.

Nat loved more than love that day. She loved Ivy, loved Trina, loved Griff and who knew whom else. She loved the house. It was Ivy, and the house, that had captured her attention and admiration more than anything. More than Guy, more than Trina and all that she had left in Los Angeles. Although she was just a passing through, she took a vicarious comfort in knowing that no matter what these walls had seen—whether crib death or soldiers taken prematurely or just the monotony of life passing unnoticed—the house would wait forever for those who loved her to come home.

"Home," she spoke the word only phonetically, as she imagined it would sound coming from Susanna. It was a concept as foreign as quantum physics and the feminine mystique. She repeated the word, saying it softly this time, able to only mimic the hollow sound of this elementary, one-syllable word. "Home."

ten

After Gary disappeared into the house and Susanna ascended the stairs alone, Ivy recovered a photo album that chronicled hers and Mother's youth—with her pets, her parents, caught unaware picking her nose and bending over to show her panties, doing the things that adults find so offensive but that children simply cannot resist—and entertained her guests with stories of the family, some of which Mother remembered with a huff and some of which she claimed never actually happened at all.

Nat watched the others, and the passing of the afternoon, with a melancholic dread. Now rendered insignificant by the introduction of lives that did not parallel hers, that did not take into consideration her plan or her problems, the entire foundation upon which she had built her love fantasy seemed unsound. She was able to follow only the outlines of the others' background conversations; she nodded and smiled weakly when anyone looked her way, but to herself wondered over and over how she had come to be there, in that house, with those people, and when she would either get up the nerve or be asked to leave. Even in benign company such as the Goodes provided, Nat had lost her recently acquired ability to be—just be—and began again to fret about all sorts of terrible consequences that all began, innocently enough and like a child's game, with "What if...?"

Mother sat at a small, efficient desk in the corner and busied herself with paperwork that was likely meant only to keep her in the room so she could maintain her watch over Ivy and Griff, who, although separated by more than one generation, recognized within one another something to admire. He told how it was to travel and rarely see the same face twice, and Ivy told of spending her entire life in the same house, on the same street. Nat would have believed once that he was after only her money; knowing Ivy's condition, she might have kicked him out herself before he could insinuate himself into the fairy tale that was Ivy's life. But watching them giggling and making private jokes that to the others might as well have been spoken in pig Latin, she only envied them. What sort of love Griff could possibly believe he had crafted, Nat couldn't fathom. What sort of cruel prank of life had given to Ivy an empty, unwrapped gift of the stuff she longed for her entire life. But there they sat, thigh-to-thigh, whispering and laughing and falling in love.

She stole a sideways glance at Trina, who was growing bored with the reminiscing and the talk that did not invite her to contribute, and Nat wondered—no, worried—if she'd hurt Trina's feelings.

Would the wonders of love, she thought wistfully, never cease?

"Let's go," Trina said, reading her mind, and led her through the wide, swinging doors through which Gary had disappeared earlier.

He had changed out of his postal uniform and sat in the kitchen dressed in a crisp white tee and a pair of gray sweatpants, a lit cigarette dangling from the corner of his mouth. *Cleverly disguised,* Nat thought, *as a Regular Guy.* He sat on the counter and, like a sullen child who had been sent away to endure an undeserved punishment, banged the cupboard doors with the heels of his bare feet. A bucket of potatoes sat on the counter to his left; to his right was a smaller pail, inside which about a half-dozen peeled ones floated in a warm, opaque liquid.

"Uh-oh, Gary," Trina teased. "Caught smoking? You're gonna get grounded."

"Sshh," he said. "Not allowed in the house."

"No shit," Trina muttered.

"We got a woman who does the cooking usually," he told the girls as his forefinger braced the end of one large, misshapen potato and his thumb guided the paring knife over its rough, dirty surface. "She's out of town this week, visiting relatives."

"Visiting relatives," Trina repeated and then laughed.

"What?" Nat asked.

"That's what we used to say when someone was too messed up to come to work. They were 'visiting relatives.' You know, it was like a code."

"I wish I were visiting relatives," Gary said. "Like that."

"So, what's up with your aunt?" Trina asked with no shame. "Is she really a virgin?"

"Well, now, that's a story that just gets more interesting as time goes on," he said cryptically. "Stick around...you'll see."

"We don't plan on sticking around," Nat said. "We have to leave after dinner."

"Oh, don't think you're going to get out of here that

easily," Gary said. "Ivy doesn't get to make many new friends. She's going to ask you to stay the night. You'll see."

"I don't think your mother would be up for that," Trina observed.

"She won't deny Ivy," Gary said. "Ivy will invite you in front of Mother, so that you have to accept. That way, Mother can't take it back."

"Crafty..." Trina said admiringly.

"A lot of people think Auntie Ivy's a little off," Gary said. "But there's a lot going on up there, if you ask me."

"How come she's never remarried?" Nat asked, in an almost challenging tone.

"Long story," he said cryptically. "Maybe if you stay for dinner, you'll hear it." He smiled broadly, enjoying the teasing.

"How come you got stuck with the cooking?" Trina asked.

"I like it," Gary said, but added that he didn't like to clean, and that he'd become a sort of expert at the barbeque, although he thought he'd just broil inside that day. He continued in a nearly nonstop narrative of his life from his earliest memories on, not in chronological order nor in any particular pattern, telling that he had been a postman for eight years, that he'd had a promising high school football career that was cut short by a broken kneecap. A blow, he said, suffered not on the playing field but jumping off the roof of the house one night while trying to sneak out. It was Mother's opinion that Gary should make something more of his life, something befitting his lineage; and she'd maneuvered for years, finally getting him into the race for city council the year before. He lost, "of course," he added and then shrugged.

"I like things the way they are, anyways."

He said that all that talk about mailmen being the first to crack was a bunch of BS.

Gary was the first child of Leona and Martin Goode, and Ivy's only blood relative besides her sister. There had been a girl, a sister, who died in her sleep at only two years old. There were photos of her, Gary said, only in Mother's room. It was something she never talked about, and while the rest of the family eventually came to accept it one way or another—God's will, a weak heart—Mother could not.

Like Ivy, he had spent his entire life in the big house, first with Mother, Ivy, and his father—and, for a while, his sister—and then just the women. Soon Susanna came into the family. He had never had any children of his own. Had never sailed the Mediterranean. Had never robbed a bank or stalked big game. This he stated not with sadness or regret but just as fact.

Trina pulled open the refrigerator door and searched for something cold to drink.

"We got soft drinks in the back," Gary said, and she grabbed one for herself and one for Nat, who requested a diet.

"What kind do you want, Gary?" she asked, and he just shrugged.

"I don't care," he said. "You pick. So, I take it she told you all about Buzz?" he asked them, and they nodded. He smiled, as if remembering a private joke, and reached into the bucket of potatoes for another.

Nat didn't know anything about the war, but she enjoyed hearing about Buzz and the wedding night she believed would come with death. She needed to hear about it. She needed to keep them all thinking about the dead soldier, talking about him and remembering the things he used to do, as if their collective concentration could dig him up, revive him, and slip him onto the loveseat there between Ivy and Griff, providing that vital link between LA and North Dakota, between loss and love.

"Susanna has been deaf her whole life, didya know that?" Gary asked right out of the blue, like it was an amazing fact of science; Nat just shook her head.

"Yup," he said. "She's never heard the things you and me hear. Birds...voices...music. Things like that." His gaze wandered over the sink top and the cupboards then landed somewhere mid-air. "I wonder if she hears anything at all," he said thoughtfully.

"The ocean?" Trina suggested, and Nat nodded. It made sense.

"Maybe," he said doubtfully. He had never heard the ocean himself, and so he couldn't say.

Nat couldn't fathom how it was to never hear the words *I love you*—but wondered if it differed at all from hearing them falsely or under some pretense of relationship, and not out of love at all. On the other hand, she thought, it must be really something to never hear the one you adore call you a miserable fuck. Everything, it seemed, was a trade-off.

She was curious about what Gary was like when with his friends. Did he go to strip joints and pay a dollar to bury his face in some girl's boobs? Did he rat on people who tore used stamps off letters and taped them onto new ones? He seemed out of place in the kitchen—in the living room, too. It wasn't just his uniform or his laugh; nothing in the house looked as though it could belong to Gary. There was no mahogany pipe case or ceramic spaniel doorstop, and Nat wondered what his and Susanna's room looked like. Doilies or pictures of relatives Gary had never even known? A chenille bedspread or a shoetree bought by Mother for his thirty-seventh birthday?

Trina sliced off a chunk of potato and slipped it into her mouth and sucked it dry.

"I like your house," was all Nat could think to say.

To her, it seemed flawless and, like any gracious hostess, eager to welcome visitors—whether they were expected or not—with a mask of happiness, a determined resignation to the happy times they would spend together. But upon closer examination—beyond the dent in the door jam at the bottom of the stairs where, when she was five, Mother's skull was fractured after she was tossed one flight down by *her* mother, who was angry that the child had lost her hairbrush; past the bedroom door that never again shut right on its hinges after being broken off by Gary in a blind, childlike rage after Mother told him it was he who had driven his father away—Nat might see flaws, things a visitor, during their hasty stopover would never notice. She, like any outsider, might see only the marks on the kitchen wall that showed Ivy at five, eight, and twelve years; the trap door behind the pantry that led to a secret place where six-year-old Gary had kept a kitten hidden from his mother and fed it scraps, folded in a linen napkin and stuffed into his pocket, from the dinner table. These were the memories Nat wanted to know; but when Gary finished by telling that, because of the weeks spent stuffed into the dark, airless wall of the house, the kitten died and rats ate most of it, she wanted to shut her ears and run from the house. She wanted to not believe such betrayal.

The swinging doors to the dining room flung open unexpectedly; and Mother entered the kitchen, her eyes darting from Gary to Nat to Trina and then back again, sure she would eventually land upon some evidence of deceit. Suspecting that smoking was not allowed in the house, Trina quickly snatched the butt from between Gary's lips and flipped it into her mouth so it could not be seen. When Mother complained about the stale smell in the kitchen she just grinned and nodded, keeping Gary's secret. Nat wondered if there was anything the girl could not do.

Before exiting, Mother suggested to Nat and Trina, over her shoulder, that they might want to take advantage of the running water and soap to be found in the first room on the right at the top of the stairs.

"You'll find your bags by the front door," she said without turning around.

Nat left Gary and Trina in the kitchen and trudged up the steep staircase to a guestroom on the second floor to shower, change and contemplate a jump from the turret, which was just a few feet above her window. She bathed, wiped the grime and the stink from her face and body, and lay still in the hot bath water until it cooled and she started to shiver. From inside her room, she could hear nothing of the others' conversations downstairs. Birds sang outside her window and dogs barked in the distance; she could hear children playing somewhere down the street and the occasional roar of an engine as it sped away.

She dressed and sat on the small velvet-upholstered stool in front of a vanity that stood in the corner of the room. She studied her reflection as if she were gazing upon a face that was strangely familiar but fundamentally foreign. She dragged her short fingers through her unruly, wet hair and considered shaving it. She wondered what she'd look like with a shaved head, like Trina. She wondered what she'd look like with a tattoo.

"Home," she said to herself, not daring for a moment to believe she had arrived. "I want to go home," she said and was saddened to hear that simple statement come out sounding as incredible as "Let's go to the moon."

"So...why don't you get out of here?" Susanna's strange and discordant voice came from behind and startled her, and she turned to face Gary's wife—Gary's deaf wife—who had, apparently, been eavesdropping on Nat's conversation with herself.

"I'm sorry, I didn't mean to startle you," Susanna said as she came into the room, her hands, out of habit, speaking in cadence with her words.

"How did you...?" Nat started to ask, but was unsure of how to put it.

"I read lips," Susanna explained as she crossed the room and sat on the edge of the bed. "Ssshhh," she smiled and placed her finger to her lips. "It's a secret. Don't tell."

Nat grinned at remembering she had called Mother a bitch, and that Susanna had seen, and "heard," it.

"Nobody in the whole house knows you can read lips?" she asked incredulously. "How?"

"It's complicated," Susanna said, and pointed to Nat's cigarettes, which lay on the glass topped vanity. "Can I have one?"

Nat handed her a cigarette and lit it for her then watched as she walked toward the window, the one just below the turret, and opened it.

"Leona doesn't like smoking in the house," she said. "We all smoke, even Leona sometimes. Isn't that bullshit?"

Nat grinned. It was funny to hear Susanna cursing.

"I didn't think deaf girls swore," she said with a grin.

This, Susanna found hilarious, and to prove her wrong let go a string of expletives that even Nat, having been raised in a house of boys, was embarrassed by.

"Do you think deaf girls just sit quietly and knit chastity belts for themselves?"

Nat shook her head, embarrassed.

"People think if you are deaf," Susanna said slowly, "you must be good, do you know? Like you are special, in that way, always nice and sweet and demure. Of course, it's bullshit."

It was true. It was as if her inability to hear should

somehow shield her from the bad things those with all their senses—those like Nat, Trina and Griff—would no doubt eventually become despoiled by. Bigoted words, Muzak, profanity—those were the things her deafness would filter out, leaving only the beauty of a world that never talked back and never heard the F-word.

"You don't call her 'Mother?'" Nat asked.

Susanna laughed. "Ha! Would you?"

Nat shook her head vigorously.

"Gary doesn't know?" she asked again.

"No." Susanna sensed in Nat disapproval and added, "It's not as bad as you may think."

"Oh," Nat lied, "I don't think it's bad."

"I'm deaf," Susanna said with a grin, "not dumb. At first, it was like a game. No, not a game, a test," she admitted. "When I first meet people, I want to know what they think of me. Being deaf is a disability, but it's also very...liberating, you know? It gives you a chance to know what people really say about you when they don't think you're listening."

Nat remembered crouching in the backseat of the wagon, waiting for nearly an hour for Trina or Griff to spill a juicy detail of something about her they didn't like.

"I know what you mean."

"You hear some fucked-up things," Susanna said, and then, in a mocking voice, "'Oh, I don't like Susanna's hair that way' or 'That lipstick makes her look like shit.' I don't know how many times I've heard Leona tell someone that I'm smart but..."

"...deaf as a stone," Nat finished.

Susanna laughed. "Yeah. But I also hear her say sweet things, to me or about me, that she would never, in a million years, say if she thought I could hear them."

"Kind of risky," Nat observed.

"Oh, extremely!" Susanna said. "Oh, and the things I hear about other people! Jesus, I know everyone's secrets! The whole town's. If Leona knew, I think she'd have me shot."

Nat laughed.

"If you think about it, it's kind of a way of protecting myself, too." She paused. "I kept waiting for the right time to tell him, thinking 'It will come naturally'...but it never did. And now so much time has passed."

"So, you just lie?"

"I don't think of it as a lie," she replied. "It's my defense mechanism." She touched her chest with her petite, balled-up fist. "Don't you have a defense mechanism, Natalie?"

Nat smiled sadly. "I thought I did, but I don't feel very protected."

Susanna approached and sat on the edge of the bed beside her. "Oh, you are," she said. "You just don't see it."

They watched the sky grow crimson in the distance, and Nat knew it was getting late. The delicious aroma of home-cooked food wafted through the cavernous halls of the house, and she was suddenly very hungry.

Susanna inhaled deeply. "Gary is a wonderful cook."

"I'd better get downstairs," Nat said, and rose from the bed.

Susanna made her way toward the bedroom door and suddenly turned around. "Why? Why stay?" she said.

"What do you mean?" Nat replied, surprised.

"You want to go home," she replied. "You said you wanted to. Why don't you? Why don't you just go home?"

Nat just shrugged and replied, "Beats me."

"Don't stay too long," she said. "People in this house have a habit of doing things they don't really want to do."

The Goodes' formal dining room was as magnificent as any room in the house—high, beamed ceilings; dark, polished wood; and a crystal chandelier that hung low to the table gave the room a stately, privileged atmosphere none of the current visitors quite deserved. Trina fussed with her napkin and worried constantly about spills; Nat sat stiffly in her seat and watched Gary, who—needlessly, she knew—translated most of what was said for Susanna's benefit. Only Griff seemed at home. Sitting beside Ivy, he told clever, colorful stories about people he had met in his travels and fascinated her with descriptions of the rest of the United States, going into great detail so as to bring alive for her sites she would never see: Niagara Falls, the beaches of California, the Grand Canyon, the grandest, biggest, and best.

Mother, sitting at the head of the table, was silent during most of the meal, her only contribution to the conversations being an occasional sigh, shrug of the shoulders, or disapproving look. She ate very little, and seemed anxious for the meal, the night, to be over. Nobody but Nat appeared to notice her nervous habit of turning her knife over and over on the tablecloth.

"Look at the way she goes on with that young man," Mother said of Ivy, as if the pair were not even present. Directly to Ivy, she added, "I said you go on with that young man as if he were the son you never had."

Gary laughed with a mouthful of broiled chicken and playfully protested, "I thought I was the son you never had, Auntie Ivy."

"No, Gary," Mother said, "you are the son *I* never had."

The others looked at their plates, unable to comprehend the vocalization of such a cruel thought. Caught unaware by the confession of something she had probably not meant, and certainly not meant to share, Mother smiled a weak, crooked smile, and said to him, "Oh, you know I'm just teasing you."

Gary smiled back and said, "Sure, sure...I know you are."

"It's so nice having company," Ivy said excitedly.

"We often have company for dinner," Mother said, not looking up from her plate.

"Yes, that's true," she said sadly, as if she had been corrected. She picked at her food delicately, pushing the meat to one side, the vegetables to another, and then back again. "Gary," she said suddenly and brightly, "I *like* to think of you as the son I never had."

Nobody replied.

"I think I would have liked to have a son," she said to her plate. "Or a daughter."

"You have us," Mother reminded her. "You have family."

"Yes, I do..." she said, and then asked, of nobody in particular, "Do you think I could have married, and had children?"

Nat watched the others watching Mother, who was silent.

"I do," Griff said, leaning in close. "Why didn't you?"

"Yeah," Trina added. "How come you never married again? A looker like you must've had 'em lined up around the block in your day."

Ivy considered this question for a long moment. She knew the answer she was supposed to give, the one that had been told so often there were times she believed it herself. That once was enough. That Buzz was enough. But when she spoke, it was another, previously unheard-of reply.

"I don't know," she said. "I have wondered that myself at times."

"You know, sweetheart," Mother said to her, still

refusing eye contact with anyone at the table. "Because of Buzz."

"Do you think me beautiful?" she asked Griff.

"I do," he said again.

"I wonder why..." she began, and then set her fork down and placed her hands in her lap. "I didn't really," she said to Trina. "I never really had any suitors. I wonder why..."

The occupants at the table were silent. Only Leona continued to eat her dinner, not minding the contemplative mood that had descended upon the others, upon Ivy. Or perhaps ignoring it, Nat thought. Expertly oblivious, she thought, to what others were thinking, wanting, needing.

Knowing Griff, knowing what he was probably plotting at that very moment with the virgin Ivy in mind, Nat and Trina could only grin at one another.

It was nearly eight by the time dinner was finished and the dishes were cleared. Much later still in North Dakota, Nat thought as she gazed out the kitchen window into the blackness that must have gone on forever. Trina washed; she dried. It was not even a chore in such a place, at such a time. It was a treat—a simple, everyday task that consoled her in the same way she imagined a person battling insanity might find comfort in such mundane tasks as opening the mail, or folding laundry.

As Gary had predicted, Ivy insisted that Nat, Trina and Griff stay the night. They didn't know their way around, she said, and it was late. Repayment of such a debt as saving one's life, she stressed, could not be satisfied merely by one home-cooked meal. Mother smiled with tight lips and said yes, it would be fine to have guests for the night; but Nat could not help wondering if she were really considering how to do them in, and where to put the bodies.

As she dried the dishes, she wondered what would

happen in the morning. Trina had been strangely un-communicative about her plans—whether she would make her way back to Vegas, and then Barstow, or go all the way with Nat. What would become of Griff was anybody's call—he might be gone in the morning or might wake to find himself just another Goode man.

But she was too tired to contemplate anything be-yond the stairs up to her room, and by eleven everyone had said goodnight and gone to bed.

    *   *   *

Nat woke around one with the terrifying confusion of not knowing where she was. From the first floor came noises of the night—a ticking clock and P's nails on hardwood—that in Nat's hypersensitive state resounded like a steel wrecking ball against a brick building. She winced at the sounds from outside—twigs snapping un-der some unseen force, leaves brushing against one an-other, stray cats at the other end of the block howling demonically and setting off a chorus of dogs barking from behind fences all up and down the street—neigh-borhood sounds that varied from block to block, bed to bed.

Since early adolescence, she had been unable to sleep through the night. At home, she would always wake sometime before sunrise—by as little as a half an hour up to three—and would lie impatiently until one day finally succumbed to the next and the mystery of time was lost in the blue light that comes just before dawn. It never mattered how much sleep was lost, the effects of waking in the dark were always the same, instilling the fear that she was someplace she was not supposed to be.

She lay for some time, waiting for the night to pass; and just before two, when the moon was bright and high in the deep, black sky, Trina stole into the room. She couldn't sleep, she said. She was going crazy in that place—"It's got gingham curtains, Nat! For Chrissakes, gingham!" she said—and so they dressed, snuck out and unhitched Griff's motorcycle from the trailer behind the wagon.

Warmed by a shot of the Wild Turkey they took from Susanna's secret hiding place behind the grandfather clock, they pushed the bike for more than three blocks so as not to wake anyone in the house. First, Nat mounted the seat and dug her heels into the dirt. Next, Trina swung one leg over and flung herself onto the small seat directly behind. With one swift kick, the engine came alive beneath them, and like fugitives they disappeared into the night.

Guided by just instinct, piloted by just the low beam of the headlamp, they found their way out of the city limits and into the wide open of Wyoming only a few miles out of Baldwin. The bike sputtered under the load of both of them at once; like the low, pained growl of a laboring beast the engine moaned in protest. The seat sagged to the metal and almost all moving parts, coated with grease and sand that had hardened over the years like enamel, popped with even the slightest pressure from above. The rear footrests were stolen in '85, Griff had told them; and so Trina, knees locked and toes pointed like a novice ballerina, strained to keep her legs extended far above the ground that flew by beneath.

Nat worried about Trina's toes being broken against the low, jagged rocks she struggled to steer around; and she eventually pulled to the side of the trail and gave her the hiking boots to wear, pushing the sneakers Ivy had lent Trina into the waistband of her jeans beside the flashlight she had taken from the Goodes' kitchen. She drove the rest of the way that night in soiled tube socks.

Trina dragged the heels of the boots over the merciless surface of rocks and weeds, and Nat knew that in a few more miles the soles would be worn down completely, but she didn't care. They were just shoes.

Heading off for the horizon, for where they knew it must be under the biggest sky either of them had ever seen, Nat felt a sensation she would have never recognized as peace. Nothing to do out there, nobody waiting for her arrival and no words to practice on the way—it was just earth and sky and her and Trina. Not thinking of Central or Mountain Time, not even aware of the things she owned, was a pleasure that seemed to come from nothing. Like being on the rooftop in Vegas. Standing where there was no wind and feeling not what had passed nor fearing what would come—feeling just that moment. Her second so far this trip.

She shouted *I love this!* It seemed the right thing to do, but the words were sucked into the roar of the wind as she and Trina sped away into the night.

The air was cold. It hit her face like a sudden Arctic blast, like it probably felt in North Dakota, only that thought escaped her in that moment. The icy night air forced its way down the collar of her sweatshirt and encircled her torso in a whirling, freezing tornado, hardening her nipples, covering her entire body with goose bumps. She shivered with delight and with the cold.

Trina held on tightly from the rear, her legs straining through her thick denim jeans in an effort to clamp onto Nat's hips and not let go. The seat was small, was meant to accommodate only one at a time, and so she had to push her belly flat against Nat's lower back to keep from falling off. Nat felt the gentle contractions of Trina's legs as she rocked with the jerking, spastic tossing of the bike over the rocks and through the air. She remembered how it had felt to wake up in the suffocating heat that morning in Vegas; she thought of how everything was different now: the cold, the outdoors, the two of them—but the sensations were so familiar. Her fingers were nearly frozen, most sensation gone, and they maintained their grip by the instinct of survival alone.

The only part of her that was impervious to the cold was her neck, where Trina's breath blew hot over the wispy hairs there like the wind blew over a field of reeds. Trina's gasps were shallow and excited as Nat clumsily maneuvered the motorcycle over rocks the size of fists and potholes that could not be seen in the low light of the yellow moon. Occasionally, the tires' worn tread would find a dip in the road, throwing them forward or to the side, pushing Trina's hips into the small of Nat's back, so close she could count the number of buttons on her jeans. Trina would squeal in fright, and this Nat felt like a gust of desert wind. Hot, it tickled the outside of her ear, and she had to fight the urge to drive on until they could no longer remember from where they'd come.

There were things she was thinking—not things she had practiced or written down beforehand, but things that threatened to spill out without any warning at all—but the engine was too loud and any words she might have spoken would have disappeared. Music would have been nice. On another night she might have wished for a soundtrack to this unscripted moment, but this time she was content to listen just to the sound of their dark silhouette cutting a swath of black through the still, night air. She could hear it in her heart, in her mind—the air resisting at first, then parting to let them through. The sensation of Trina's hands, the light pull of gravity forcing her nearer still, all of this was set nicely to music by just the reverb of the bike's massive, roaring engine.

They rode for half an hour, until the vibrations that rose from the road underneath became no longer a nuisance but a gentle manipulation, a simple, repetitive stroking that hummed from one body into the other and then back again, fusing them to the bike, to one another. It was a sensation Nat had never known, had never even known could exist.

Her sense of direction was unerring; every turn she took, it seemed, took them deeper into the night. Her ultimate destination—Guy, Ruune, North Dakota—was tonight just an indiscriminate pairing of longitude and latitude; and in the cold night, in the warmth of their cupped bodies, Nat did not think about getting to the church on time. The path of least resistance led northward from Baldwin, and she wished they could drive straight on to the edge of the earth.

When it was so black that not even the bike's headlight could show the way, they stopped to sit in the dirt off the side of the trail. Still feeling the hum of the bike, her body still going through the motions, Nat stretched her legs out and wriggled her toes, spending all her energy to rid herself of that one sensation that lingered.

She pulled the sneakers from her waistband and tossed them onto the ground. One rolled out of sight, and only with the flashlight could they find it under some dead, dry brush. It would be fun to go exploring, she thought, with just the flashlight and their bare hands, finding their way through the plains on their hands and knees, looking under rocks for night creatures and discovering wild, prehistoric flowers where you wouldn't think anything at all could grow. Finding things they'd never see from the car or from the highway.

Trina lay back and watched the stars. Nat was amazed at the sight. You couldn't see them from LA, she told Trina as they lay shoulder to shoulder in the fine, cold dust. Too bright, she said. It was possible, she said, to live your whole life in the San Fernando Valley and never know what it's like to lie under a blanket of stars.

They looked for the Big Dipper but couldn't find it. Not the little one, either, and Trina told Nat she'd never seen them except in books anyway. It wasn't like looking at the clouds, finding shapes of zoo animals and women in rocking chairs. The skies were overflowing with tiny spheres of light, making it nearly impossible to distinguish one star from the next.

"Let's go for a walk," Nat said excitedly.

"You're crazy," Trina laughed. "It's too cold."

"Come on," Nat said and held her hand out.

Trina shook her head; she sat now on the floor of the plains, hugging her knees to her chest and breathing hot air into her hands. "I'm cold, let's make a fire."

She produced a pack of matches from her back pocket, and they set about collecting some dry weeds and sticks. They made a small mound in the center of the trail, so as not to risk sending an errant spark into the wild brush that grew around them on all sides, and Trina lit it.

The fire grew quickly, and in just a few moments warmed their faces and hands and cast a bright orange glow over everything within ten feet.

They forgot about Buzz and Ivy, and for a while Nat couldn't even remember Arizona's last name. Guy was a dream that belonged to someone else, like high school, like that day in the garden shed and everything else in between then and now. She told Trina a funny joke about a man named Art who hung on the wall, like the ones she'd enjoyed in the car all through Utah, and they laughed till they thought they'd wet their pants. Nat wished she'd brought a couple of beers; but even that wish lasted only as long as the next breeze, and then it, too, was gone on the wind.

But she could never go for very long without remembering who she was, and what she was about. So, while watching the stars, searching the sky for comets and meteors and other things not visible from LA, North Dakota came back to her with a thud. She squinted and searched the black overhead, knowing it was his sky, too, wondering if he might be watching that one star there and thinking of her and if he knew what she'd done so far would he be terribly disappointed. She wondered what she would really say once finding herself on his doorstep. She wished she were already there and back, wished she knew what was going to happen, and what would become of Trina. She wished she had a motorcycle, too, and she wondered if it was hard to live happily among the rocks and the dogs in Barstow.

"What are you thinking about, Nat?" Trina asked.

"Ruune," she replied immediately. "Going to Ruune." She laughed and rolled over onto her side to face Trina. "Have you ever noticed that?"

"What?"

"How that sounds...going to Ruune."

"Yeah...ruin."

"How come you never told me that?"

Trina looked at her sideways and shrugged. "I thought you got it."

"Going to ruin," Nat repeated, slowly. "How come I never noticed that before?"

"Don't you think about anything else, Nat?" Trina said, impatiently.

"Not recently."

After a short silence, Trina asked, "Can I ask you something...honestly?"

"Sure."

"What do you really expect to find up there, you know, in North Dakota."

She shrugged. "Love, I guess."

"Do you love him?"

"Don't I?" she asked aloud, as if to herself, and then,

"I did."

"If you're not sure, why are you going?"

Nat detested being asked that question. "Because that's the kind of thing people in love do, Trina!" she said.

Trina shrugged.

"What?" Nat asked defensively.

"Nothing. I mean, I don't know. I guess I've never been in love like that. Or, I should say, I guess I just don't think of love like that."

"Do you love Arizona?"

"Yeah," Trina replied. "But it's more than that, you know? To me, love itself doesn't really mean anything. It doesn't even really exist. In itself."

"Then how can you say you're in love?"

"Well, I'm not 'in love' with Arizona. I love him, but it's much more than that."

"How can there be more than love?" Nat asked honestly.

"We have a connection. You know? We're connected."

"Connected."

"Yeah."

"Like how? Like the kinds of things you like, like music and stuff—similar interests and things like that?"

"No," Trina laughed. "It's like a spiritual connection. I think you call it soul mates."

"Soul mates are meant to be together forever."

"Then it's not the same thing. You can love someone and not have a connection, like I love my mom but I'm not really connected to her. But you can't have a connection with someone without love, some kind of love. Not that romantic, wedding kind, not necessarily. But to me, love is the tip of the iceberg. And to you, it's the whole enchilada."

"I guess," Nat said, disinterestedly.

"Do you have anyone in your life that you're really connected to?"

"I guess I don't get it."

"Is there someone in your life, a friend or relative or even a boyfriend, that you could transcend love with?"

"How do you transcend love?"

"I guess we just see it differently, is all."

They were still, listening to the gentle wind blow through the dead brush.

"Ugh!" Trina said. "I'm thinking I'm tired..."

"Like a thousand days."

"Yeah." After a long, contemplative silence, Nat confessed, "I know I should be on the road..."

"You're just enjoying yourself, is all."

"I like that house, but I get a weird vibe there."

"Like you don't belong?" Trina replied.

"Sort of. Like, I feel like I think I belong, but nobody else does."

"Like there's something weird going on?"

"Yes!"

"Like it seems so normal on the outside, but on the inside it's just the opposite and kind of like something really, really bad is going to happen?"

"Yes!" Nat shouted. "Yes! Exactly!"

"No," Trina said and grinned. "I don't get that feeling at all."

"Bitch." Nat laughed and pushed her shoulder into Trina's.

"There's no weird vibe there, Nat," Trina said. "Unless it's coming from you."

"Is that your professional opinion?" Nat sniped.

Trina look at her with surprise, a little stung by her sudden, sharp tone. "Yes, as a professional weird vibe locator, that is my professional opinion."

"Have you noticed," Nat said, "when you ask Gary a question, he doesn't answer? Like if you ask him, do you want regular soda or diet, he says, 'You decide.'"

"So?"

"You ask him, do you want this piece of white meat, and he says 'If you're not going to eat it.'"

"So, he's flexible. What's wrong with that?"

"That's not it," Nat said, shaking her head. "I mean, he might be flexible, but it's more than that."

"Just because you have this overwhelming need to have everything be a certain way doesn't mean everyone else does. It doesn't mean that those of us who don't give a shit which way the wind blows have a 'weird vibe.'" Trina spread out her arms and legs and made dirt angels. "These work much better in the snow," she observed, trying to change the subject.

"He never says what he really wants," Nat continued.

"Maybe he doesn't care. Did you ever think of that?"

"Nobody in the house ever says what they're really thinking...that's what I think. Do you know what? Susanna..."

"What about Susanna?"

"Nothing. I just think it can't be easy to live with someone who never says what they think or want."

"Yeah, I can see that."

"It's not," Nat said. "Maybe you want to be a better wife, you know? Maybe you know you're being kind of bitchy, you know you could do a better job. But nobody's saying anything, and nobody's saying 'No, I want to do it this way,' or 'I'd rather have that for dinner.'

"Never knowing what the person sitting across from you is really thinking, always wondering when that shoe is going to drop and how many years will it be before they come home and say they're in love with someone else. It starts out small, with little things, like letting you take the last Pepsi, letting you decide which movie to rent.

"But sooner or later, you're sitting up at four a.m., listening to some tirade about what a controlling bitch you've been for the past ten years and having to answer for things that happened so long ago you can't even remember them. Why couldn't I have the right side of the bed, and whoever decided we wouldn't eat red meat anymore?'"

Eventually, Nat knew but Trina would never understand, people just see you walking down the street together and say things like 'He's so nice—how'd he end up with a girl like that?'"

Trina sat cross-legged across from Nat and pinched small pebbles between her thumb and forefinger as Nat slowly spun down. "Uh, are we still talking about Gary?"

"No," Nat said, picking up a large twig and stoking the fire. "I guess we're not."

A gust of live embers shot up from the flames and flew up into the sky, like supercharged fireflies, before spending their energy and falling back to earth, darkened, cold, and dead. "It wasn't me who cheated, Trina. It was Wes."

Trina smiled sadly at her and scooted along in the dirt to sit closer beside her. She slung her arm around Nat's shoulder and drew her in.

"I might have been better," Nat said, "if he'd have just said. You know?"

"Yeah," Trina said, and gave her a hug. "You're right. He should say."

The night had grown colder still, and the two girls huddled together on the trail, shoulder to shoulder under the stars. With no blanket, no journal in which they could scribble their true feelings, no tape recorder to play sweet music, they spent the next thirty minutes in absolute silence, the only backdrop to their time together being the strange, erratic sounds of wildlife that came from the black just beyond where the light of the fire could reach.

"God, love sucks!" Nat suddenly said, breaking not only the silence of the night, but a belief with which she'd always struggled. "What if he's not the right guy?" she asked Trina.

"Gonna be kind of hard to find another guy named Guy," Trina joked.

"I wish I were more like you," Nat said.

"How so?"

"You know...not take everything so seriously."

"Everything...meaning what?"

"Well, getting married, for example."

Trina nodded, extended her legs until they were straight and the fire warmed the bottoms of her feet. She tapped her toes together and placed her palms in the dirt behind her.

"You think I don't take getting married to Arizona seriously? Why do you think that?"

"Well, I mean..." Nat replied. "It's like this secret. You haven't even told anyone."

Trying to seem casual, Trina replied, "It's nobody's business. And you know what? It's like, ever since, you've had a great big bug up your ass about the whole thing."

"Trina, I didn't mean..." Nat started, but stopped, because at that moment she truly did not know what she meant, but she was sure it would sound bad to Trina.

"No, I get it, Nat. So, you think that getting married is somehow less important to someone like me than it is to someone like you. My taking vows with someone I care about, someone I'm connected to, must look to you about as inconsequential as some random fuck."

"Well, let's face it, Trina, it's not a real marriage, is it?"

Trina was speechless. Nearly. "Not real? What's not real about it?"

"Well, I mean...come on. Why did you marry him in the first place? You're gay, for Chrissakes."

"So you keep telling me."

"You aren't going to have his kids. You aren't going to devote your life to making him happy. I mean, why did you get married, anyway? I mean, is it some kind of legal thing, or what?"

"No, Nat," Trina said, pulling a cigarette from her jacket pocket and lighting the end. Sucking hard on the tip, she inhaled deeply. "It's a love thing...but I guess you weren't listening. I guess you wouldn't understand that."

"Are you saying I don't know anything about love?"

"No, Nat." Trina shook her head rapidly, tapping the ashes from the tip of her cigarette into a small pile beside her thigh. "I'm saying you don't know anything about anything. You have this idea of how things should be, and you don't see anything that doesn't fit."

"I see things," Nat said defensively.

"You see that I'm gay, and you think Arizona is just some pity thing to me. You see Madeline as a man living as a woman, and you figure he must be fucked up and miserable, or some pathetic junkie..."

"She was!" Nat protested.

"...You see Ivy, a woman who's been kept a virtual prisoner in her house nearly her entire life, and you think that makes her the goddamned poster child for unrequited love!"

Nat got up and tossed more dead weeds on the fire, and it popped and crackled, sending a spray of embers over their heads. "This isn't exactly what I expected when we came out here," she said with disappointment.

"Well, God knows it's all about what you expected.

Look at you. Look at where you are. Where are you, Nat?"

"What are you talking about?"

"Well, I mean we've all heard about this great plan you've got. Well, shouldn't you be there by now? Shouldn't you be getting on with your life? What are you doing here, with me? I mean, if this is such a great plan, if what you're doing is so fucking meaningful, and if you really believe it's your destiny, that you're in love, then why aren't you getting on with it? *Why are you still here, Nat?*"

It was a good question, but one she resented being asked by Trina, by someone whose life didn't appear to be the result of any particular plan, but more the outcome of a series of stupid choices and bad luck.

"You're hardly one to criticize," she said.

"Why? Because my life is such shit? Because I have no call to say what's good and what's not?"

"You said it, not me."

"Ugh! Bitch!" Trina said, and stood up, slapping the twigs and dirt off her legs and ass. "Ever since we met you've looked down on me. You think I'm just this poor, pitiful thing who couldn't do any better than a man in prison. Oh, yeah, I'm just this fucked-up dyke living out there in the desert with some stupid dog with a stupid name who doesn't even have a car—well, I have a car, I told you that!—and who can't fucking function without some guardian angel like you to come down and take pity on me."

Nat watched with wide eyes as Trina stormed around the fire, circling like some mad dog. Her arms flailed and she spit as she talked. She seemed on the verge of tears—Nat knew they were there but would not be given up to her.

"Well, you know what, Nat?" Trina yelled, pointing her finger directly at Nat. "Fuck you. I don't care what you think. I don't need your pity, *or* your ride, *or* your clothes...or your shame, *or* your guilt..."

She was right. Since the moment Nat spotted her on the side of the road, soaking wet and looking like a lost child, it was poor Trina this, and poor Trina that. Poor Trina has to hitchhike to see her man in prison. Poor Trina is marrying someone she'll never get to know as a husband. Poor Trina has some shitty-ass job and lives in some shitty-ass desert town. Poor Trina is following me through the desert because she has no place else to go. Poor Trina doesn't even have a chance.

"...*or* your friendship," Trina spit out and turned her back.

It was true. She didn't need anything Nat had to offer, especially her friendship, which Nat was saddened to realize was not especially true after all.

"I don't pity you, Trina," she said, truthfully. "I don't think I'm better than you."

"Fuck you, you don't," Trina replied. "Would it surprise you to know, Natalie, that I wanted to be a doctor? Would it surprise you to know that I had a 4.0 grade-point average and a full scholarship the year I graduated from Barstow Hills High School? And would it further surprise you to know that I did quite well in my first semester?"

It did. It surprised the shit out of Nat to think of this girl who rose from the rocks, who seemed so lost, so poor and out of place when they'd met, at one time, in one place, kicking all that academic ass.

What did not surprise her was that she never became a doctor. One fall day, Trina had been walking to class with a girlfriend, talking about what to do that night and how she was going to ace the two finals that were scheduled that day. A few doors down from her first class, she suddenly stopped. Turning on her heel, she spun around and left the building and never returned.

She'd told her parents, Arizona, and others that she was ready to move on. She'd experienced college, she said, and decided that it wasn't for her, that she was ready for something else.

It was the right thing to do, she'd been told by friends who'd never made it that far in the first place. It was the most courageous thing they'd ever known. She received a failing grade in all her classes that semester, but at least she'd come away with a really good story to tell.

Nat stood up angrily, stomping her stocking feet on the dirt. Trina stood less than three feet away, her hands balled up into tight fists, which were planted firmly on her hips. She defiantly stood her ground as Nat approached, like some ninja master about to execute some secret but deadly girl move to break Nat's nose. Nat knew the risk as she stepped closer but accepted it willingly. Her muscles tensed with each step forward. Locking her gaze onto Trina's glaring eyes, she reached with her right hand and didn't see even a hint of a flinch in Trina, who would not stand down.

Not thinking of Guy, in the specific, or guys in general, not imagining how cold it must have been in North Dakota that night, not picturing herself in a wedding gown or doing any of the other things she thought were the reason she was on the road to Ruune in the first place. Nat's fist opened. She cupped her hand and swiftly but tenderly palmed the nape of Trina's neck and drew her in. With the stars above and no liquor to dull the senses this time, she touched her lips to Trina's and kissed her.

Overhead, the sky, alight with the energy of a billion faraway stars, twinkled like a giant astral Christmas tree.

There were no fireworks, as Nat had imagined would accompany such an anticipated event as her first girl kiss, no music in the background. This was a girl who knew her story, her license plate number, knew she had been married and knew she couldn't hold her liquor. No anonymity, and last names had been revealed. It was the best.

Nat felt Trina's arms wrap around her waist and draw her closer. The fire raged beside them and warmed their bodies, but it was their hands that sweat and their faces that felt damp with perspiration. It was soft. Sweet. Exactly how one who had never actually kissed a girl would think a girl would kiss.

Nat cupped Trina's face in her hands and turned her head slowly, so that Trina could feel Nat's warm breath on her ears. She came closer, to whisper something to her, as if there were a danger, even under the great expanse of the night Wyoming sky, that her secret would be overheard. It was warm close to Trina's face.

Their breathing was rhythmic but not in sync, and this provided another layer of experience Nat was thrilled to discover.

"I love you," she suddenly said, exhilarated at being able to think, to say, such a thing and not have it come from fear or fantasy. This time the thought was said not into the wind, not silently like Susanna would hear it when Gary spoke. It was said not inside of herself, but to Trina's face. "I love you," she repeated.

Next, Trina's small, balled-up fist slammed into her chest and pushed her back, a sensation of pure shock, like when that fishtailing MG popped the first fantasy, way back there on the highway.

With love came so many surprises, and Nat took this one as she had taken all the others, like laying her hand on a lit stove and saying *yep, that's hot allright.*

"I'm not a fantasy, Nat!" Trina spit out. "I'm not some experiment for you while you figure out how to get yourself over the next thousand miles, and I'm not just another nostalgic piece of ass that you can tell your husband about one day while you're laying in bed and confessing all the bad things you did for love."

Trina picked up the flashlight from where it lay in the dirt and slapped it with her hands, but the batteries had gone dead and it was dark. She flung it into the weeds. "How can you be so insensitive?"

"What? What did I say?"

"It's time to go back," Trina said firmly, and Nat knew she was not just talking about Baldwin, Wyoming.

Nat looked over the horizon toward where she thought the interstate was hidden behind some jagged black rocks that rose from the earth like giant stalagmites. She had told her things. Trina had extracted things from her that night that she had wanted, but never meant, to say. Her words sounded fucked-up spoken out loud, like Susanna's had that first moment Nat had heard her speak. Like they were forced, mimicking, with no real understanding of their meaning or connection to one another. Everything had been twisted around, and her thoughts had been corrupted by this...this...girl, and it was getting hard to keep a linear thought.

There were reasons she didn't have girlfriends; there were reasons she avoided relationships. There was a reason she traveled alone, and now she could recall each and every one of them in painful, gory detail.

If she had caught a flight from LAX, like everyone said she should have done, none of this would have happened. That was her first thought. Her second came swiftly on the heels of the first.

"Are you coming all the way with me?"

"Why does it have to be all or nothing with you, Nat?" Trina said as she struggled to lift the bike from where it lay among the weeds on its side.

This infuriated Nat. Trina might as well have asked her why do you breathe, Nat? Why does your heart work the way it does, one beat after another like that?

"Because that's the way it is!" she replied. "That's what love it—it's all or nothing."

It was a belief she had held her entire life. It was the tenet that kept her from forgiving her parents, from letting go of a boyfriend who tried to kill himself, for Chrissakes. From really giving a shit about how her early marriage would turn out, and from letting anyone else who came along after have a fair shot. It was imbedded in her DNA; it was the strand that kept the mixture of chemicals they call a brain in working order. It was what set her out on the road to Ruune in the first place, and when Nat said this to herself, she had to finally laugh at the irony.

"Love is what it is," Trina replied cryptically. "Maybe it's ten percent." She cupped her hands and gathered some dirt to put out the fire. "Maybe it's ninety-nine percent, but only those who are in it are equipped to say if it's enough. Or not.

"Me, I don't think I've ever been in for more than fifty percent," she confessed as she extinguished the last of the fire by kicking the dirt onto what still burned. They were plunged into the moonlit darkness under which they had arrived. "For me, fifty percent is pretty fucking good."

It did sound good, Nat thought. It sounded good at that moment.

"What about Ivy? All or nothing," Nat said. "It's possible."

"Nat," Trina sighed, "Gary told me something when we were alone in the kitchen..."

Nat was immediately sure it was something she would not want to hear; otherwise, it would have not have been broken to her in that manner, at that time.

"I wasn't sure I should even tell you," Trina added.

"Then don't," Nat said simply, and meant it. "Don't

tell me."

"But I think you should know."

"Is this, like, some kind of intervention?" Nat asked tiredly. "Or are you just fucking with me?" Trina ignored her last comment and drew in a long breath, seeming to brace herself to hear what she herself was about to speak. "It's about Buzz..." she said.

This was the biggest secret Gary could tell, Trina said, and to reveal it was the worst thing he could do. He made Trina swear to God she would never tell anyone, not even after driving away—even then, Gary had told her, she should just try and forget the whole thing.

Like a child, Nat held her hands to her ears and turned her back on Trina. This was a secret she did not wish to share.

"Allright, then," Trina said. "Ask him. Ask him yourself."

She was right about one thing: it was time to go. No telling how long they'd been out there, but it looked as if it might be nearly dawn. Nat didn't want to be caught out of the house when the others woke up; she wanted to crawl back under the covers and imagine that the entire night was nothing more than another one of those occasional, illicit dreams—the kind that are initially lovely to enjoy but from which it is usually a relief to eventually wake.

They mounted the bike, revved the engine, and sped back toward town. Trina held on just as tightly as she had on the drive out but with no more familiarity, no more tender a touch, than she'd shown before IT happened. With Trina's shoes stuck in Nat's waistband and the spent flashlight lying hidden someplace where they couldn't find it, they headed back to Baldwin, where they would spend who knew how many more hours before Trina went back to her husband and Nat would have to face the culmination of her trip alone.

eleven

The others were sound asleep when Nat and Trina returned; there would be no evidence of their secret journey. They hitched the bike onto the trailer and snuck up to their separate rooms without saying goodnight.

Nat slept deeply for an hour but soon was awake for good, trembling in the darkness like a child who waits breathlessly for the sound of Santa's heavy footsteps. She listened for signs of life from within Gary and Susanna's room and writhed silently in the dark, neither sedated nor annoyed by the constant rhythm of her own heavy heartbeat.

The truth would come, she knew, with the light, but that knowledge provided little assurance. Like her needing to bolt from the bed and make a run for the phone, here, too, was the maddening realization that everything she had ever wanted of life was waiting on the other side of that door, if only she could make that goddamned sun do as it was supposed to.

At five, Nat leapt from underneath the covers and

stole silently downstairs and found Gary, already shaved and showered. He had been up since four, anxious to get out of the house and wishing perhaps it were a fishing trip he was taking; hunting, maybe, something men in other houses did.

"Trina told me something last night," she said, eyeing his face for the slightest hint of deceit. "Is it true?"

"Well, shit," he said good-naturedly, "she coulda told you just about anything last night. How do I know if it's true?" He grinned.

"She said you told her something about Buzz," Nat replied, steely-eyed.

Gary exhaled. "Oooh. I guess girlfriends really do share," he said.

"Not entirely," Nat said. "She didn't tell me what it was. She said to ask you."

He set his coffee down and told her to go upstairs and get dressed. He had an errand to run that morning, and she might as well join him.

There was no time for eggs or toast—the others, Gary's wife and Mother, his aunt Ivy, would wake soon; and he wanted to get out while they still slept. Excuses would come later; there would be questions and suspicions once it was discovered they were gone, and Gary seemed not to want to tempt either fate or Mother by hanging around any longer than absolutely necessary.

This was the biggest secret he could tell, he said, using the exact phrase Trina had recited just hours earlier. It was the worst thing he could do, and Nat must swear to God that it would never go beyond them.

"The only reason I'm telling you," he said, "is 'cause, after today, y'all'll be gone."

This told Nat little, but the teasing puzzle was a small price to pay for a dream fulfilled. The Easter Bunny, good fairies, dead Buzz—they were secrets she would happily take to her grave.

The sun had just begun to rise by the time she climbed into the passenger side of Gary's truck. The seat was cold and hard, and it bounced maniacally even on the smoothest patches of road.

Over the horizon, a sliver of baby blue was beginning to seep upwards into the rest of the sky. The cold was bitter and still; it blanketed the tiny town of Baldwin like a sheet of ice. Nat crouched over and huddled against her own knees; she cupped her hands over the dash, where an anemic breath of warm air blew from the vent.

Was Buzz really buried in his uniform? she wanted to know. Had Ivy really visited the grave every Saturday for fifty-some years and did she leave flowers and if so, what kind? Nat was full of questions, but Gary was too secretive. He just grinned and shrugged his shoulders and only once did he say anything about what she could expect to hear, and that was just

"You'll see..."

In another twenty minutes the sun was up. Not that it mattered; not that Nat needed to see where she was going. She could have found the way alone, on her knees. Using desire like a divining rod she would have found that dead bastard and danced on his grave and said thank you, Buzz, thank you, sweet Jesus, for keeping my faith alive.

When Gary was not teasing her with vague hints about where they were going, he described what it was like to live with the "Goode girls"—and that was how he said it, as if it were written in quotes.

Fairy tales aside, there was more to the women than the pictures on the wall revealed; and Gary liked to joke that he'd married a deaf girl so she'd never hear his family history. Their surname was an irony only he appreciated, he said.

Gary's grandfather, Charles Eichmann, was a Dutch

immigrant who came to Wyoming from the East shortly after he arrived in America. There wasn't anything special about his hardships, Gary said.

"Pretty much your standard immigrant sob story. You know how it goes, one sack of belongings and—what?—ten cents in his pocket, something like that."

Seeing for himself no future in produce sold off the street, Charles spent everything he had on a train ticket that would take him as far as Wyoming, although his ultimate destination was farther west. There were pictures of him back at the house—his face stark, barren in black-and-white—but photos don't usually tell the whole story.

Once Charles got to Wyoming, he worked as a ranch hand for William Harding McMahon, the man who originally own Mother's and Ivy's home and as much surrounding land as a person could see.

"McMahon was a gambler," Gary said. "A heavy gambler. Stories go that he would sit for hours, watching a fly stuck in some spider's web, and then he'd bet you on which part of the bug that fucker would eat first."

"They don't eat 'em first," Nat said dryly. "They wrap 'em first."

"That's why he always won." Gary laughed. "Of course, few of those bets were on the up and up, but that didn't stop him from collecting on each and every one. Put more men out of their homes than I don't know what..."

"Seems kind of like a jerk."

"That's putting it mildly." Gary's grandfather had been one of the most unfortunate victims, having lost about two months' wages betting on what color the walls in his room would be underneath the sheets of paint that were starting to bubble in the corner.

After losing almost everything, he made plans to return to the East, having had his fill of the Wild, Wild West. Without even enough money for a train ticket, though, he plotted to win back just enough to get him the hell out of Wyoming.

Gary flicked his cigarette butt out the narrow space where the window was cracked open. The spent filter caught on the wind and flew backwards into the sky, where it disappeared in the vaporous exhaust of the truck.

"So, they made one more bet?" Nat said.

"One more was all it took," Gary replied.

"Bugs this time?" Nat laughed. "Leaves on a tree? What?"

"Whores."

Nat's eyes opened wide, and she straightened in her seat. It was like one of those prairie legends that old men tell you when you're standing in the middle of some garage sale, buying some crappy copper lamp that they swore had been owned by Jesse James himself.

The legend was that there was a cute little whore in town, a young seventeen-year-old natural blonde for whom the male population of the western United States had developed a deepening affection. McMahon was her number-one client; and Charles, being a devoutly religious man, professed not to know of her "in that way." One night while sitting around drinking, McMahon started spouting off about all the women he'd had and how he knew them inside and out.

"If you know what I mean," Gary laughed.

Spotting an opportunity to wreak some monetary revenge, Charles wagered that this whore was not a natural blonde.

"Are you telling me that they bet on the color of her pubic hair?" Nat asked incredulously.

McMahon, having righteously screwed this girl on several occasions, believed he'd set his sights on an easy mark and overbet his hand in a big way. He wagered that if her bush were blond, Charles Eichmann would agree to stay on in his employ for two more years—no wages, only room and board. If her bush was not blond, McMahon said, he would deed the ranch and all in it to Charles on the spot.

"He bet the whole ranch?"

"As the saying goes," Gary laughed. "So, McMahon sends one of his guys to get her, right? Offers her one hundred dollars to come up to the house and drop her drawers."

"So what happened...what color was it?"

Gary spit out the window. "Oh, she was a natural blonde."

"So, your grandfather lost."

"Yes, and no..."

Nat's eyes narrowed and she said, after much thought, "What's the catch? She dyed it?"

"Not exactly," Gary teased. "See, they sent for this girl to drop her panties, like I said. McMahon and my grandfather were waiting at the house. She came in, looking just as sweet and innocent as could be in a pretty little white dress. You'd never have guessed she was a whore. After collecting her hundred dollars up front, she set those two men down, one each in a big comfy chair, and then without so much as a how-do-you-do lifted her dress and dropped her drawers."

"And?"

"And goddamned if that sneaky whore hadn't gone and shaved her bush off completely!"

"So, who won the bet?"

"Well, it wasn't blond, was it?"

Instead of being angry at having been tricked, the story went that McMahon was delighted at having been outsmarted by young Charles and, true to his word, deeded the ranch and all surrounding land, all that to this day made up Baldwin, to Charles Eichmann, who promptly married the woman who had made him what he was.

"You know the saying," Gary laughed. "Behind every good man..."

"Your grandmother was a prostitute?" Nat gasped in disbelief.

"That's about the sum of it."

The rest of their family history, Gary said, was not nearly so colorful. Charles' and his naturally blonde wife had two daughters, Leona and Ivy. Leona was only nineteen when she married Gary's father, a rich local businessman named John Goode, who was forty-eight. A year later, Gary was born, two years later came the baby girl. Shortly after her death, John died of a massive stroke while in the company of a forty-three-year-old executive secretary named Muriel. The last anyone had seen of Muriel, Gary said with amusement, she was boarding a plane to Florida.

After John passed away, it was just Ivy, Gary, and Mother in the house which would forever be known, Gary pointed out, as the "Goode Home," and this pissed off Leona more than everything put together.

After his father's death, Gary said, was when things went from bad to worse. It was like a curse, Gary said. "That house is a family curse." He found it surprising that Nat felt so welcome there, was shocked she could think of it as home.

"I don't think your mother likes me," Nat said.

"Don't take it personally," Gary replied. "I don't think she likes me, either. Oh, I know she loves me, in her own way."

"Which way is that?" Nat snorted.

"Only way she knows how, I guess," he replied. "You can't ask someone to give more than they got, Natalie. It just don't work that way. Being part of a family is hard," he said. "You'd think it should be easy, like second nature. You know, everyone loving one another and accepting and all. It's not always like that. It's a lot of work."

Unlike Ivy, it wasn't sweet honor that kept Leona's bedroom door locked for so many years. It was hate. Mother had loved her husband deeply, Gary said, and then added, with emphasis, "at one time." His betrayal—first by the discovery of his infidelity and then by his death—was a blow from which she would never recover.

She came to resent all men, including her son, who was in her eyes merely an extension of her dead, unfaithful husband. She would take great care, he theorized, in exacting her revenge upon their shiftless gender, through her domineering, controlling ways raising a man who would be the antithesis of the potent traits upon which they prided themselves the most. Receptive, not controlling. Loving, sensitive, kind. Things she believed would make him an anomaly, such distasteful traits that not even a mother could love.

Mother's only regret, Gary sometimes imagined, was that Charles had left her with only one son and not six.

They drove on and listened to a little portable radio that dangled from the rearview mirror. There was a talk show that truckers called on CB, and Nat was amazed to learn how many others were already up and on their way to wherever it was they were going. Perhaps they were just passing through Wyoming, heading north or south on the way to someplace else.

She wondered what it would feel like to suddenly stand on the grave. Would the significance of such a place be obvious or would it exist unnoticed, like the invisible equator in the middle of the sea?

It had been an hour since they left Baldwin, and Nat

wondered if she was missed back at the house. Trina would be up by now. She might be playing with the dog, running through the backyard and feeling the ice crystals that coated the grass give way under her feet. She wanted to talk to her, wanted to know if she could forgive the bad things that had happened between them the night before.

They passed a small rectangular sign off the side of the road. NATIONAL CEMETERY, 2 mi.

"Here we go," Gary said with a loud sigh. He checked his watch and squinted at the sun. "They should be up by now," he said ominously.

They exited off the main highway and drove eastward on a narrow dirt road pockmarked with large rocks and deep holes. Shredded rubber littered the shoulder, where weeds were crusted with dirt and oil spray from passing cars and flowers died their first year.

"I can't believe that Ivy has never...well, never..." Nat remarked. "I can't believe that a love like that could actually exist. I mean, I always hoped, wished..."

"Is that what you think Ivy is about?" Gary asked. "That she can't bear to be with anyone but Buzz?" He laughed. "What, like they're going to be reunited in heaven, or something like that?"

"Well," Nat whimpered. "Sort of..."

"You women are too much." He laughed. "Ivy's never gotten together with anyone else because Mother won't allow it. Plain as that."

"Won't allow it?"

"You have to understand something about Leona," Gary said. "She loves us, I mean, she feels love for all of us. She just doesn't know the right way to go about it."

"How do you mean?"

"Oh, I know what people say about her, how she treats me, and Susanna. But she loves us both. She loves Ivy more, I think," he said wistfully. "Don't think for a minute that Leona would ever let Ivy go through the pain of a cheating husband, 'cause she wouldn't. It would never happen, not on Leona's watch."

"How...how...?"

"Jesus, Nat, Leona owns the whole friggin' town! Nobody says 'boo' around here unless she tell them to. Word was put out long ago that Ivy is hands-off. That's why Mother keeps such close tabs on her."

"Why?'

"'Cause she loves her!" he said as if to say, Why else?

"What about Griff? She doesn't seem too concerned about them spending time together."

"Griff?" Gary guffawed. "What the hell reason is there to worry about a young man like Griff?"

"Yeah, well..." Nat muttered. "You'd be surprised. I don't know him very well," she cautioned.

"Oh, he seems a nice enough guy," Gary said. "Where did you say he was headed for again?" Nat only shrugged.

"Mother thinks he amuses Ivy," Gary said.

Nat smiled to herself and wished Trina were there to hear this. "If he gets her alone, he will..."

She peered out the window and felt her heart leap in her chest at the sight that lay out there. To the right was a dark, jagged horizon made up of row after row of scattered, dissimilar tombstones, some ornate likenesses of angels in flight, some simple concrete slabs upon which a name and a date—maybe "Beloved wife and mother," something like that—had been chiseled.

Did it matter, she wondered, that Ivy's virginity was held more tightly by Leona than Ivy? Would Ivy have given herself up to another, if she'd had the chance? Knowing people, their histories, made it harder to maintain a pure perspective, she thought. Best to keep driving, look at the houses from the street and just imagine what sort of fantastic, uncomplicated lives were being led behind closed doors.

Bare, wintry trees stood over the dead like frozen scarecrows, their brittle limbs intertwined in a clinging, arthritic chokehold. Others slouched and bent close to the ground, where their twigs, like bony fingers, scratched in the dirt and brushed their own fallen leaves off the graves. There were no mourners; it was still early in the year, and the ground was sheathed in a slippery film that rendered anything beyond the outer pathway impassable. The closest one could come would be to stand tiptoe on the perimeter and search for the familiar marks that would pinpoint the location of their loved ones—sixteen deep and four to the right—but it was unlikely that anything could be seen from that distance, and so most would wait for spring.

Interspersed among the civilian dead was evidence of local heroism—aged and splintered white wooden crosses, each placed at the crest of a small mound and honoring some dead patriot who lay beneath. It was this sight that empowered Nat and baited the anticipation of her one dead dream's resurrection.

The truck labored on, traversing through what seemed like miles of corpses, and Nat settled into her seat and waited for Gary to lead her to The One.

"It doesn't seem like there would be that many people out here to bury," she said of the unending rows of tombstones.

"Not just Baldwin," Gary said. "They come from all over..."

Nat cringed.

"...just dying to get in." he laughed, and she smiled weakly.

"What was the wedding like?" she asked.

"Huge," Gary said.

Mother had arranged a big ceremony at the church

and then a potluck at the house, cooked by all the neighbor ladies and some school friends of Ivy's whose husbands drove them in from as far away as Cheyenne. They danced all night—some neighbors and a man who used to work for the family moved all the furniture onto the front lawn so everyone from town could come in. There was dancing, drinking, something for everyone; and then, in the morning when folks started saying goodnight, good luck and happiness to you, the army came for Buzz. Ivy was left sitting on the porch, holding a flower Buzz had more than likely picked off the ground. He placed it behind her ear, kissed her goodbye, said he'd be back before she knew it, and then he was gone.

"Ivy always said that being married was nice while it lasted. Said she'd recommend it to her friends." Gary laughed.

Months went by without any word from Buzz. Then, some time later, a strange man came to the house and said Buzz had been killed in North Africa. There was never any telegram, no official notice, but to see it in writing wouldn't have changed anything for Ivy. She went in one afternoon from wearing white to black; her life had always been as simple.

"Auntie Ivy told my mother she'd never marry again, and my mother said to her that's just fine. And that's how it's always been."

Devotion worthy of a God spent on a man named Buzz. You had to love it.

"This is it," Gary said suddenly and braked hard. The radials kicked up a cloud of thin desert dust that billowed over the hood and the windshield like a demon fog; and when it cleared, Nat looked out into the middle of nowhere.

Somewhere behind—maybe miles, for she had lost all track of time and distance—was the cemetery they never did stop at. Ahead, there was nothing except a pickup on blocks and a faded Airstream trailer that leaned into the wind.

Nat, frozen to the seat of Gary's truck, did not want to get out. She didn't want Gary to get out, either, and with a silent wish implored him to turn the truck around and drive away. She dreaded that she'd been tricked again, and she prayed it wasn't one of those blessings in disguise that always seemed to bite you in the ass just when you least expected it.

Gary shut off the engine and hesitated; they listened to all life drain from the motor, the dying clicks and pings that signaled the end of a long trip. Soon there was just Nat's heavy breathing. She waited to hear some crude remark from Gary about a little piece on the side. She would have given anything for a peek at a girl like the one who took her own father. One for Gary, right now. That's what she wanted to see.

"Some shithole, huh?" He nudged her shoulder and smiled.

Like the giant, hollow casing of some mutant bug, the silver trailer huddled close to the dirt, its back to the wind and its head totally obscured from sight. The morning sun was absorbed in its faded, oxidized finish; not even a glint of light reflected back into their eyes. Nat stared, unblinking, at the torn canvas awning that flapped like a loose scab above the doorway. Who, or what, hid behind the frayed curtains and peered out at these unwelcome visitors, she was afraid to know.

Two lawn chairs—not green-and-white, not any color she could see—anchored with bricks, were stuck in the dirt out front where a porch should have been. Cactus grew from rusted-out coffee cans and a garden gnome—pitted with sand and bleached white except for a faded green patch on its pointed hat—lay on its stomach near the front door, its pointed, chipped nose buried at least half an inch in the dirt.

The dog is missing, she thought. Bony or diseased or walking on three legs, cowering in the dust out front, snarling its thin, bloodless lips and crackling its spine as it shuffled back and forth and begged to be let in for leftover sloppy joes.

"Where am I?" Nat asked, more rhetorically than specifically asking directions.

"Lander's that way," Gary said, reaching past her and popping open the glovebox. He removed a small black notebook and, from it, a sealed plain white envelope. On the face was written in black ink April. "Wait here."

"Who's April?" Nat asked, but Gary ignored her. He pushed his left shoulder against the door; and it burst open violently, caught on the tail wind that blew past the truck, and rocked it from side to side. It was a cold, freezing wind, warmed not at all by the sun; and in just the moment it took Gary to slide out and push the door shut again, it was enough to chill Nat to the bone.

"*Who's April?*" she hollered again, but Gary didn't hear.

She watched him move away from the safety of the truck and toward this strange sight that lay in the desert like a time bomb, and she was suddenly overcome by the need to scream out *Come back, you idiot!* Even through the windshield she could hear the gravel crunching underneath his boots, like walking over graves and crushing bones into dust.

The noise gradually faded as Gary abandoned Nat and approached the spindly chicken wire that haphazardly cordoned off the trailer from the rest of the natural world. Using just the toe of his boot, he pushed the gate open and stepped inside. He held the white envelope loosely between thumb and forefinger, his other hand dug deeply in his pocket for warmth. He made one cursory pass of the area in front, marching between the chicken wire fencing and the narrow slat windows that gaped like knife wounds.

Nat heard the word then, enunciated perfectly and not distorted by buildings or cars passing or the screams of children playing in the street. She heard the one syllable, the ultimate desecration; and although she prayed that it was a trick of the wind, there was no mistaking that word when Gary opened his mouth and screamed it a second time.

"Buzz!"

There really was no going home. There was no kiss to return to. No going forward or back. There was nobody waiting for her—at the house, in California, Nevada, or North Dakota. There was nothing but that wind and the cold and that fucking garden gnome, entombed in the sand.

"Buzz, get out here! I ain't got all day!"

Nat leaned into the windshield, out of the shade that the roof of the truck provided. The sun was bright but cold, but she made no effort to move back again into the shadows.

Presently, Buzz came out of the tiny Airstream, accompanied by a woman who, she would learn later, was his wife, a woman who, Nat knew with heavy heart, was not a virgin.

The next few moments seemed to take as long as the whole trip so far. Gary handed Buzz the envelope and they had a smoke. Nat tried to read their lips but they kept turned away; the only time she got a look at Buzz's face at all was when the old bastard turned his back to the wind to light his cigarette. He didn't look the same as in the pictures Ivy had shown them. Not just older, not just less hair. There was no resemblance at all between the young proud bridegroom on the wall at home and this desert rat who spent his days hiding from the wind, from Leona and her wrath.

The woman tended to some dry plants that tried to grow in the cold sun. She poked her finger into some dirt but didn't bother to water any of them. She spotted Nat and waved; and before she could even get her hand up and her fingers to work, the old woman closed the front of her nappy sweater and stepped back inside where it was warm, where nobody could see.

The way back was hard. There were vows of secrecy and promises extracted from Nat to never breathe a word of what she had seen. At first, there was little in the way of explanation, other than to say that, obviously, Buzz had not died in North Africa.

"Buyer's remorse?" Gary pondered. "Or maybe he knew this cupcake before auntie Ivy came along. Hard to imagine, isn't it? That she was once somebody's cupcake." He laughed, but Nat tasted vomit. "He just disappeared, is all. After we got the news about his death, it took about two days to figure out where he was, which was right back there where we left him. The two of them have been living there all this time. Can you believe that? You just can't make shit like this up."

Soon, it was common knowledge in town that the bastard had abandoned Ivy, and what was supposed to have been a couple of days away to get over this condition turned into a couple of weeks, and then a couple of months; and before anyone knew what had happened, the weird story of Buzz and Ivy became another local legend, like Paul Bunyan or Sasquatch. Everyone knew it. Folks passed it down to their kids, and told it for entertainment at Thanksgiving. Maybe, Gary said, someone might write a folk song about the bastard one day, but as long as Ivy walked the streets it was still spoken of only behind other people's doors, Mother made sure of that. Everyone except Ivy knew about Buzz and his girlfriend, but nobody would tell. Lack of heart, lack of nerve—it could have been either, as Mother had long ago made it her mission to ensure that Ivy would never know the burn she had suffered at the hands of her first and only love.

"She pays him off," Gary said simply. "Pays him to stay there and keep his mouth shut. Shit, that fucker's probably richer than you and me put together!"

They passed the cemetery on the way out, this time on the left where Nat could not see it so easily, and for this small favor she was grateful. They didn't stop at anyone's tomb. No reason to anymore. The path northward stopped abruptly at Buzz's door. The trip was over. The plan was no more.

She sat powerless in the front seat of the truck. Her choice was clear—live with it or completely erase the memory. She wanted to kill Gary, could have easily wrestled control of the truck away from him and driven him off into the wilderness, where with her bare hands she could have killed the man. What delight he had expected to share with her was a mystery, what pleasure he could have gleaned from such a nasty secret as Buzz would never be solved. It was all Nat could manage to keep herself from hurtling toward the driver's side of the truck and wrapping her fingers around that fucking postman's neck.

So, her initial instincts had been right—love was nothing more than a trick of the light, like faces on the wall at the Goode home, eyes that seem to follow you from room to room but in reality never move at all. Her grandparents had probably fought like alley cats, she thought morosely. Her grandpa had probably known a lover in his youth, had avoided coming home to dinner so that nobody would see the lipstick on his shirt and neck. Nat's father probably hated mango, and maybe Chrissie killed her children herself.

It was impossible now to know what was real and

what was not. It was hard to care one way or the other. Even the smell of fresh balm and the mentholated vapors would do little to lure Nat back to where she was just days before. The comfort of hope, the constancy of dreams—these and more were left in the desert like the foam coffee cups and shredded napkins that lay alongside the road. The trip had already taken such a heavy toll, and there were still two and a half states left to go. She would never forgive them—any of them.

Especially one of them.

It was better that both Trina and Griff were gone by the time Nat arrived back at the house. More than the boundary of any state, to suddenly see the real face of love—not distorted by music or fantasies or the promises of another but its true, human face—marked the end of the trip for everyone; and Nat's dismal humiliation at discovering she was wrong not only about Ivy but about everything could have been worsened by only one thing, and that is to have faced it in front of Trina, who must have known all along.

Nat returned to that grand house empty-handed, a defeat made even more unpalatable by the finality with which her dream was finally laid to rest. It didn't help knowing that the others knew the truth as well; her misery did not love company. Rather, it longed for a dark hole into which to burrow deep and pull the dirt up around her eyes and her ears so that in time she might forget the Goode secret. Maybe, someday, she could forget it—them—all.

The truck pulled into the driveway around eight, and although the sun was up and the low clouds that had drifted down from the foothills were dispersing, the air was still damp and the ground still wet. The stiff grass crunched under Nat's feet as she slipped out of the truck and made her way across the massive front lawn, toward where Ivy and Susanna were sitting on the porch.

"Good morning," Susanna said to her then blew a kiss to Gary, who kissed the top of his wife's head as he pulled open the screen door and slipped inside. "What mischief have you two been up to?"

Nat smiled weakly and took a seat beside Susanna, who poured her a hot cup of lemongrass tea.

"Nothing, just a drive."

"You're the only one left," Susanna whispered to Nat and then, with a nod, indicated the inside of the house. "I don't think I've ever seen Leona so...so...I don't know what. I don't know what she is." She laughed and smiled with such pleasure that Nat had to laugh, too.

Ivy, whose gaze had been lazily taking in the sights of the neighborhood—the trees, houses, and other familiar landmarks—suddenly noticed Natalie. She smiled broadly and took her hand, squeezing it affectionately.

"Natalie," she said, "have you ever noticed how beautiful the morning is?"

Susanna smirked, and Nat smiled at Ivy. In her heart, she felt dead and cold, inanimate as the stone statues that lined the road to Buzz's house. Watching Ivy, knowing what had probably happened to her in the night, Nat saw new breath rise from within her old, tired body. Nat jealously saw within Ivy's blue eyes the prize she had coveted for so long, yet had never even come close to achieving: Possibility.

Dressed only in a thin cotton nightgown, rocking slowly back and forth, Ivy smiled to herself and waved at the birds that lit on the lawn. She wore a silly, contented expression and could have appeared, to those ignorant of the complexities of love, completely insane.

The screen door flew open behind them, and Mother stepped out onto the porch, following by a snickering Gary, who, whenever Mother looked his way, tried to look as shocked as she. Her lips were drawn tightly across her face, and her eyes wore a stern expression that was directed primarily at Nat. She held the cordless phone in one hand and shook it as she spoke.

"I should be calling the police," she said harshly.

Susanna looked down at her cup of tea, hiding her grin; and Nat just shrugged.

"Go ahead, then," Ivy said.

"I should," Mother said again, softer this time. She stroked Ivy's long, gray hair with her free hand and cupped her head in her palm.

"Do you know what he did, your friend?" she said.

"I have a pretty good idea," Nat replied.

"It's not the money, or the jewelry," Mother said, and Ivy suddenly sighed, as if just having woken from a lovely, deep sleep.

"Oh, they're only things, Leona," Ivy said.

Gary's eyebrows raised in shock. It was the first time in ages that anyone had ever heard Ivy call Mother by her given name.

Ivy turned toward Nat and said softly, "They're just things."

Nat nodded.

"They're not what you take with you," she said, and leaned back in her rocker.

"How did this happen?" Leona said, more to herself than anyone else.

"If I knew that," Ivy said, "I think I would have done it sooner."

Everyone laughed, in the way that one finds humor in some sweet, sad event that you know to have fundamentally changed a person. Ivy had spent her entire adult life, in Trina's words, as a "poster child for love." Unknowingly, Leona had all those years ago put her up onto an impossible pedestal for everyone to admire, and aspire to. Her life, her love, had been false. And all the while she waited for it to come back to her, the real thing had passed her window probably a million times, unnoticed, unnamed, and unsuccessful.

"You just can't plan these things," Ivy said, and Nat nodded, her eyes wet with tears.

Nat left then, just an hour or so behind Trina and in the opposite direction. Eventually, their paths would extend like long, crooked veins over the map of the United States, and in time, they would forget one another entirely and the time they had passed together on the highway.

Her life, left to its own devices, would surely put an end to all this nonsense.

twelve

"I can't believe you didn't go all the way," the sympathetic voice on the other end of the line whispered.

"How could I?" Nat said. "After what happened?"

"How could you not?" the voice replied. "I mean, you were so close."

In the long, drawn-out pause that came next, Nat heard soft breathing, quiet sounds of papers rustling, the phone being shifted from one ear to the other, hands doing other things. She put the teakettle on the stove and turned the knob, igniting a burst of blue flame underneath.

"No. I wasn't even close," she said softly, ashamedly, like a confession.

"It was brave of you to go."

"Huh," Nat snorted. "It's worse when you patronize me."

"I'm not," the voice pleaded. "Not many people would even attempt what you did, Natalie."

"There's a reason for that." She leaned back against

the kitchen counter, watching the spout of the kettle for rising vapors. "God! I'm such an ass!" she shouted into the phone.

"Don't!" the other voice begged, as if talking a jumper off a precarious ledge.

"It's like...like a bad dream. Like it never happened," Nat said.

"How is that?"

"He never knew I was coming, what I was going through. Nobody knew where I was. It was like I was just...gone. Like I just disappeared for—what, almost a week? Who knew? Who noticed?"

The kettle began to whistle and steam rose from the spout. Nat turned off the stove, wrapped a dishtowel around the handle and gripped it tightly. As the boiling water ran over the tea bag and filled the cup, the scent of orange pekoe, the warmth of the rising steam against her face, provided a small, temporary comfort, the only kind she had been able to attain since returning to Los Angeles.

"Don't discount what happened," the voice warned.

"What?"

"The worst thing you can do is put it behind you."

"That's exactly what I'm going to do. I'm starting over."

"I know you lost your job."

"That's what happens when you don't show up for two weeks. You know, they kind of frown on that kind of thing," she said sarcastically.

"So, what are you going to start over?"

"Everything. Me. My life. I'm tired of being me."

"Don't say that."

"I hate me."

They were silent.

"I even hate that I hate me. Ugh, I hate self-pity."

The voice on the other end of the phone laughed softly. "At least you still have your sense of humor."

"My mother used to say," Nat said, "when I was feeling sorry for myself, 'Get over it. Some people wake up and have no legs. What have you got to complain about?'"

Another laugh. "She's right. You've got legs."

"That's a comfort."

"Natalie, I don't think you're through."

"Oh, I'm through," Nat said. "I'm through with it all. Love. Soul mates. Happily ever after. Ugh, what shit I've been carrying around."

"I don't think you're done."

"I am."

There came another long pause, and the voice on the other end of the line finally said hesitantly, carefully. "Then why do we keep going over it?"

"Look," Nat said angrily, "you don't have to talk to me, you know."

"It's not that."

"Then what? I'm just talking, you know? I went through this...this...thing!"

"Went?"

"Yes. Went. What is that supposed to mean?"

"I think you're still going through it," the voice soothed.

"Only the aftermath," Nat said.

"No. How there can be an aftermath when nothing has really happened?"

"You're saying I'm not done," Nat said defensively.

"That's what I said."

Nat sipped her tea and watched the lights in the basin below begin to flicker on. Dusk had passed quickly, and the night LA sky, the sky that showed no stars, began to spread from east to west like thick gray goo toward the Pacific, where what light remained of the day, a brilliant pink-and-orange blend, was swallowed in a matter of minutes. She moved about her apartment, the phone cradled between her shoulder and her ear, and paced in the darkening ambient light of what was to be another torturous evening going over the events again and again and again.

"Do you feel like you're done?" the voice asked.

Nat couldn't answer, not truthfully. She couldn't admit to herself, much less to another, that she was undone, that she had not fulfilled the plan, that she had let herself, and her dream, down. She couldn't fathom having to admit she had blown it a second time. She had no idea where to start again and, even if she had, didn't feel she had the strength to do it, anyway.

"Were you in love?" the voice asked.

Nat sighed heavily. "I don't know," she replied. "But I think I felt a...connection."

"I think so, too."

"I have to go," Nat said quickly.

"All right. We'll talk again."

"I'll call tomorrow," Nat said.

"Not tomorrow," the voice said. "I won't be working tomorrow. Call on Friday."

"Okay," Nat said.

"One more thing," the voice interjected before she could hang up.

"Yes?"

"There's a reason you feel the way you do, Natalie. I believe it strongly."

"Yes."

"It's unresolved. It's not just loss. Do you know what I mean?"

"It's like..." Nat began. "Oh, never mind."

"Yes? You aren't mad that it didn't work out?"

"No," Nat agreed.

"You still don't know if it would have worked out."

"Yes."

"Because..."

"...I didn't go all the way."

"Then go all the way."

"So, how do you know all this? What makes you so smart?" Nat said.

"I'm psychic," the voice said. "It's my job."

"I'll talk to you Friday," Nat replied.

"Don't forget to ask for me by name."

"I won't."

Nat hung up and contemplated, with what little sense of humor remained, the abject humiliation of having nobody to call, no shoulder on which to cry without paying $2.95 per minute, ten-minute minimum. Phone sex lines were cheaper than psychics, she thought, but there was just no depth there.

It had been a little over two weeks since she had returned home, empty-handed, disillusioned, and exhausted. Her unzipped, unpacked bag sat by the front door, loaded with smelly, sweaty clothes that reeked of P. On top were postcards of Madeline's she'd accidentally taken while trying to hide them that morning in the bar. Inside one of the interior pockets was a photo, the only photo, of her and Guy, taken just two days before he tried to commit suicide. She couldn't bring herself to unpack the bag, to put away the pictures and postcards.

"They're just things," Ivy would say, if she were there.

Nothing of Trina in there. No remembrances, photos, letters. Not a barrette, or a scarf, or anything that would remind Nat of what it felt like to be, for at least a few days, best friends with a girl.

After returning to LA, she had holed up in her apartment and refused to take calls or visitors. Guy called a few times and left curious messages on her machine that spoke of needing to talk to her, needing to know if she was all right. He'd thought they had a connection, he said. But his calls would not be returned, either.

By not returning to work after her two weeks of vacation expired and not answering the messages left by Human Resources, she was considered by her employer to have abandoned her job. An official letter of dismissal soon arrived by overnight mail.

She had saved enough money over the years to take a wild, exotic vacation. Or to continue to hide out in her apartment for approximately ninety days without worry of being put out on the street. She watched a lot of television, and was proud to have resisted the maudlin urge to go through old photo albums, reminiscing about things she was sure hadn't happened the way they were remembered anyway.

She curled up on the couch with her tea and watched the lights below. It was early in the evening, people were just getting out of work, and she watched with wonder the ribbons of white and red lights that dissected the LA basin in all directions, a wonderful and beautiful consequence of the worst freeway traffic in all the country. Her apartment was completely dark and still; she walked through it again, in her mind, wondering which turn was the wrong one, which exit the one she oughtn't have taken. The answers weren't there, and it did not occur to her that she was, again, asking the wrong questions.

She called her mother for the first time in two years, not knowing what she expected, or wanted, from the woman. It seemed a ridiculous thing to do. But honoring the desire, she picked up the phone and called. Although the conversation was of no real substance—and, in fact, Barbara didn't even know Nat had been out of town—she was moved to feel the resuscitation of the kind of comfort a girl can get only from her mom.

After leaving Baldwin and the Goode family, she felt

badly beaten but had fully intended to finish the task, to make good on Guy. The first day, she'd made a decent start, driving at least five or six hours beyond the boundary of South Dakota without even a subconscious desire to stop and turn around.

But it was lonely in the car. It was quiet, and cold. Nat drove over plains of frost and ice and then through mountains that were capped in great swirling mounds of fresh powder. At the start, so many days (weeks?) earlier, she'd honestly believed that getting there would be half the fun; but as she drove northward, her dreams of Guy, of love, her entire sense of self imploding, she began to suspect that half of her fun had been squandered when she wasn't looking.

There was no landscape to keep her mind occupied, no people to wave to and no license plates from which she could collect letters of the alphabet or spell out names of presidents. She missed Trina, and Griff, and even P. There were no lovely fantasies to contemplate. No giddy anticipation of the look on his face when he opened his front door, and she lost the ache to phone him and ask him to wait just a few more days, a few more hours, till she could get there in one piece.

By the time she reached Sheridan she was engulfed in a bleak grayness that wet the car as she passed through low clouds and fog that made it difficult to see in any direction. The yellow and white lines she had been using as a guide stretched ahead for maybe twenty feet and then disappeared into a vaporous, opaque haze. She slowed and peered out the windshield, seeing not man or animal for hours at a time, trying to imagine if there was ever a time she had felt so small and...pointless. Trees, propped upright by no visible means of support, stood like the skeletal remains of some primitive sacrifice; like human skulls skewered on sharp sticks, they clustered in snow banks on both sides of the highway.

Once mighty and strong but now lifeless, left for dead where they had been slain, left as a warning for others of what fate was sure to await them down the road.

Later that night, she stopped at a small motel off the main highway. She saw the soda machine before she ever saw the sign that in burned-out cursive spelled At Daze End. There were six rooms, free-standing bungalows that measured maybe six feet by eight constructed of smelly, wet wood splintered with age that trembled from the wind rushing down the mountains. Dry, brittle weeds grew high on the sides of the clearing where the motel was situated, and beyond the waist-high brush trees grew tall and dense. Even bare in winter, their twisted, gnarled branches blocked the view in all directions. Only directly overhead could there be seen a small patch of sky—and a lovely canopy of stars—the only view afforded from the dirt clearing where Nat parked.

She lay down, still clothed, and covered herself with a nappy blue blanket that smelled like detergent, rubbing her stocking feet together and wrestling in vain to wrap the edges of the blanket around her frozen toes. The temperature dropped quickly as she lay listening to the wind. It swirled in the clearing like a giant twister; and she imagined that at any moment it would lift her from her bed and hurl her across three, maybe four, county lines, where it would roughly deposit her in a dumpster behind some ratty apartment building or twenty-four-hour liquor store. The gusts rocked the bungalow from side to side and howled like the soundtrack of old film noir about terrible family secrets and murdered first wives. A frigid breeze found the cracks in the window glass and the spaces under the door.

Her breathing was shallow and weak; in her growing anxiety, she practiced breathing techniques she'd read about in books on yoga, and positive visualization, but it was no use. She was nearing stage two: complete wretchedness.

After an hour of ignoring the warnings that came on both the wind and in her short, desperate gasps, Nat finally let herself fall into a fitful, unsatisfying sleep, taunted by dreams of love, hope, dead birds and other thoughts unsolicited. She slept lightly, nervously, tormented by such complexities, and at two awoke from a nightmare in which Trina appeared like a vision at the foot of her bed and whispered to her "Don't..."

She awoke for good at four and went outside to where a pay phone was planted in the center of the circular drive. The cold gravel stung her bare feet as she picked out a rough, clumsy path from the door of the bungalow to a phone that would not accept incoming calls. Rather than moving in a direct, linear fashion, Nat swerved from side to side, avoiding empty plastic cups, broken glass, and other things tossed from the big rigs as they barreled through this dense stretch of road. It would not be light for another hour, and in the time it would take for the sun to reach the tops of the trees that surrounded her on all sides, she might change her mind and back again at least eight times.

The wind rattled the phone booth doors and created a swirling vacuum when they were shut. Up there, she dreamed, where she would find him, the sun might be bright and there would be no new snow. She would be tempted to tell him where she'd been but not what she'd done or seen. He might want to know why it was so noisy on the phone and where was she calling from and there would come endless questions and excuses. She remembered what Madeline had said, prophetically, on the roof of The Star Struck Room.

"Even a good excuse is nothing but."

The only thing that even mildly surprised Nat was that, despite everything, the car was still pointing north and she hadn't yet taken refuge in some tiny town off the map where she could waitress and learn to get along with strangers.

This she longed to tell to Guy—this, and the story of Trina, and Griff and Ivy and Leona and Madeline and so much more, but her hands were frozen stiff and it was painful to bend her fingers around the receiver. Frustrated, confused, hungry and cold, she slammed it into the cradle and then picked it up again. After finally mustering the strength to punch the buttons, she had to laugh at the cruel irony of no dial tone on the other end.

The next morning, she loaded the car and found a nearby town to gas up and get a bite to eat. She went about her business efficiently, finding strength in her new strategy: a lack of strategy. It was absurdly simple, she decided, deceptively obvious.

Pointed north again, Nat was glad to see the weather had cleared in the early hours of the morning. The sun was bright, it would be warm soon, and the road this day would not seem so treacherous. She settled back into her seat, put on a favorite CD, and tapped her fingers lightly against the steering wheel as she checked her reflection in the mirror.

Two miles later, with no warning and for no apparent reason, she suddenly braked hard and brought the car to a skidding halt on the shoulder. With nobody else in sight, ahead or behind, she gripped the steering wheel tightly in her hands and jerked hard to the left as she accelerated, executing a perfect U-turn that, when completed, left her headed for all points south.

That was the last Nat had seen of South Dakota. Wyoming came and went uneventfully, as did Utah, Nevada, and most of eastern California. Only when safely within the boundary of Los Angeles County did she exhale completely and feel comfortable enough to take her eyes off the rearview mirror.

Two weeks and a seven hundred and eighty-five-dollar phone bill later, Nat still hadn't come to grips with what had happened. Why she had turned around, why she hadn't called, why she so recklessly threw away her second-best chance for love without even considering the pros and cons was a mystery to her, as well as to Lisa, her own personal, part-time psychic.

And Lisa was right—the whole goddamned mess, though over, was unresolved.

Thursdays, Lisa's only day off, were always spent wishing for Friday. The other six days of the week were always spent the same way, in some weird recurring dream during which Nat would tell Lisa what had happened and berate herself for the choices she had made... or not. She was hooked on the phone calls, the anonymous, non-judgmental, and encouraging voice on the other end of the line. But what had started as a way for Nat to profess confusion and helplessness was turning into something else. Between the lines, she was hearing a dare, a challenge, like one of those infomercials whose host screams at an eager, fanatical audience, "I *dare* you to fail!"

A week later, at ten a.m., at the predetermined time Nat was to have called the 976 psychic hotline and ask for Lisa, she was already on the road again. No plan this time, no notes, no highlighted maps beside her. She carried on this trip nothing but the glorious, terrifying, and liberating realization that she had everything to lose.

Alone in the car, she took to heart something Madeline had told her in Vegas: "Sometimes," she had said, "on the brink of losing it all is where you have to be when the real thing comes along."

*   *   *

The second attempt, not like déjà vu at all, not based on memory or fantasy or even the lure of that elusive, intangible sensation one likes to think of as love, this trip was specific, purposeful, and revealed a capacity for intent that Nat had never known she possessed.

Time on the road passed quickly. In the time since she set out the first time, the rain had stopped and a warm spell had started to descend upon the western United States, the warm, quick gusts of wind a welcome contrast to the frigid rains and intemperate climate she had suffered her first time out.

The wagon sped north, away from LA, the path this time unambiguous, uninterrupted and focused. Nat played her favorite music on the stereo and sang along to the songs she knew. To those she didn't, she hummed and tapped her fingers on the steering wheel. Six months' worth of living expenses in her wallet—the result of a moving sale during which she emptied her apartment and sold all of her belongings except for the car—only a few night's changes of clothes in the seat behind her, Nat had made her decision in, literally, a moment. And, within just a few days, was on the road, forever leaving behind the life that had never felt right, had never quite fit. On the passenger side floor sat a small brown cardboard box. Inside, wrapped in tissue paper, was her only souvenir of what had previously been.

She would remember this decision in total clarity; she would revel in its retelling at dinner parties, at initial introductions to strangers, at any moment when one might ask, "So, how did you two get together, anyway?" She would excite, frighten, and inspire others with the story of how one day she was Nat, the un-Fresh girl from the San Fernando Valley, and the next she was someone other. Someone else entirely.

"I did not find myself behind the wheel of my car," she would say with a wide smile. "I put myself there."

She stopped only for the essentials: for a Coke, a pee, a meal. Once, in a grassy rest area that shouldered the interstate, she pulled over and sat behind the wheel, laughing and pounding the dash with her fists and screaming, "Oh, my God! I must be crazy! I'm doing it! I can't believe I'm doing it!"

There were long stretches of highway when her mind would wander, and she would remember the circumstances of her life—her childhood and family—with such clarity that she could only sit in wonder at with what stupidity she had, until now, lived her life. She would call her father, she vowed. She would see her mother. Her happiness no longer so precarious, no longer hinged upon the thousand possible outcomes of whatever plans she might have been afraid to make, no longer at the mercy of what someone else might or might not do or say in return. Nat had changed. The fear that was fundamentally Nat, the essence of Nat, was gone; and left in its wake was that fantastic, lyrical mantra that she never tired of chanting: "I've got everything to lose. I've got everything to lose."

Not counting the minutes, the miles, she was taken by surprise at the sudden appearance of her final destination. She pulled the wagon into the parking lot, sending a billowing cloud of dust and dirt swirling around the car like a tiny but ferocious tornado. She shut the engine off and listened to the sounds of coming home: the hissing, clicking and pings that came from the undercarriage, and from beneath the hood. She checked her reflection in the rearview mirror and remembered how foreign and unnatural she had looked in the vanity at the Goodes. Not much older now, doubtful any wiser, she nevertheless saw in her eyes and expression something new. Something fresh. She reached down to the passenger side floor for the cardboard box, opened her door, and stepped out into the hot sun.

Striding toward the door, not stopping to call or knock or announce herself, she stepped in and was nearly knocked over by the impact from a smell, an aroma that she never in a million years thought she would miss.

"Well, fuck me!" a familiar voice shouted out. "Am I dreaming? Am I awake? Pinch me, goddamnit, I think I'm seeing a ghost!"

From the dimly lit interior of the room appeared the statuesque, shapely Madeline, skipping toward Nat with arms outstretched and bosom bouncing in cadence with the clickety-clack of her high heels on the hardwood dance floor.

"Hello, you," Nat said and gasped for breath as Madeline reached her thick arms around her and lifted her up off the ground. Toes dangling at least six inches above the floor, she flopped to the left and right, back and forth like a favorite rag doll just discovered in the most unlikely of places.

"Hello, yourself!" Madeline said, and planted a big wet kiss on Nat's lips. "Would you believe you were missed?"

"I would," she said, grinning like a pirate. "Where is she?"

"Well, I'm sure I have no idea who you're talking about," Madeline replied coyly.

"I know she's here," Nat said.

"How do you know that?"

Nat shrugged, and hugged Madeline tightly. "A girl just knows," she whispered into her ear.

"Uh, heads up...she's...changed a bit," Madeline warned Nat.

"So have I," Nat said confidently.

"Hmm, we'll see." With a nod she indicated the back of the bar, down the hallway toward the storeroom.

Nat maneuvered the darkened interior with ease;

keeping a straight, steady line she walked confidently to where she would find Trina. Her heartbeat quickening in her chest, her breath shallow, she gripped the cardboard box in her right hand and with her left pushed open the door to the storeroom to find the only girl she'd ever really known.

Her back was turned, bent over as she counted boxes of liquor and jotted their totals on a clipboard she held close to her chest. She didn't hear Nat come in, which pleased Nat, who stood silently, watching her, taking in the sight of her.

Her hair had grown out to a cute, bushy shag—the tattoo of the tiger was completely obscured now. The color had been dyed to its original jet-black. Her skin was tan, her arms were toned, and Nat pictured her basking in the summer sun on the rooftop during the day, lifting kegs of beer, or maybe tending bar, at night. She had put on more weight, and it suited her.

Nat cleared her throat and stood rigidly, barely able to contain her excitement when Trina turned around and their eyes met.

"Oh, Lord," Trina said with a gasp. "I can't believe it!" She covered her mouth with her fingers, dropped her clipboard and spread her arms. Nat stepped forward to hug her but was stopped short by Trina's full, round belly, which showed that she was carrying more than a few extra pounds.

"Oh, my God," Nat whispered and laid her palm on Trina. "You're going to be a mother."

"I am," Trina said, her hand resting on Nat's. She laughed. "Pretty scary, huh?"

"Not at all."

Trina moved her hand to the small of her back and carefully lowered herself onto a carton of pale ale. "I never thought I'd see you again, Nat."

"Ditto."

"Well...what are you doing here?" she asked, and craned her neck to look past Nat toward the door. "Is he here with you? Is Guy here?"

"No," she said and shook her head. "No guys here." She set the cardboard box on the carton beside Trina and said, "I brought you something."

"Presents!" Trina squealed and took the box into her hands. She touched the ribbon that it was wrapped with, tracing the lines of the soft fabric with her fingertips, as if the box itself were the loveliest of gifts she could ever hope to receive.

"Open it."

She did, and inside found a small wooden likeness of Abraham Lincoln's head. On the bottom was carved "Laramie, Wyo."

Trina laughed. "Not so giant, is it? I would consider that false advertising."

"Well, I couldn't fit the real thing in my car," Nat said.

"You got this for me? Just for me?" Trina asked.

"Yeah, for you."

There was a short, awkward silence, but Nat let it pass in its own time, and then said, nodding toward Trina's belly, "So, what's up with that?"

She laughed and shook her head. "Well, this is a long story."

"How far along are you?"

"Six months."

Nat was visibly surprised. "So, you were...when I...we...?"

"Yeah," Trina replied, nodding her head with humility.

"Why didn't you tell me?"

Trina just shrugged.

"This is why you got married," Nat said, finally getting an answer to a question that before had nagged her incessantly.

Trina nodded.

"It's not...?"

"Arizona's? No."

Trina said the father was nonexistent; he was a mutual friend of hers and Arizona's who, one night while crashing at Trina's place, had too much to drink and helped himself to the hostess. He was long gone and, considering he'd had no particular fondness for the Nevada penal system, with which Trina had threatened him, she doubted she would ever see him again.

"It was Arizona's idea to get married," she said. "I didn't see the need, but he didn't want me raising a baby without a proper name. He's old-fashioned that way, I guess." She smiled, rubbed her belly and cocked her head. "Whaddya think of the name 'Utah'?"

Nat's eyes filled with tears. Not just sadness for Trina and what had happened to her; but for missing all that before, for being such an ass and being so blind and for being so caught up in the chase of someone—something—else that she missed this thing, this huge thing, that was happening to her best friend.

"I'm so sorry..." she said.

"Yeah, I didn't think it was much of a name either," Trina replied.

"Seriously!" Nat protested.

"Don't be," Trina said. "I'm not. I'm doing good. Hey! You...you look good."

"I feel good," Nat replied.

"So...Nat, what are you doing here? I know you didn't just stop in for a beer."

Nat heard the jingling of a bell, or of small pieces of metal, and she knew it was P. She called his name; and he bounded into the room behind her, jumping up on the backs of her thighs and burying his nose between her legs. She laughed.

"Did you teach him that?" she asked Trina.

Trina laughed and nodded. "Damn straight..."

"What am I doing here?" Nat asked aloud. "That's a good question," Nat replied. There were a million things to tell her, a thousand ways to arrange the words and feelings. Just like that first time in the car when Trina asked about her and Guy. How to begin? How to tell it right? How not, this time, to fuck it up?

"Trina, what I said that night, the night we took the bike out..."

"Nat..."

"No," Nat said, "wait. I know you think I just got carried away that night, and confused about everything. I know you think I was a jerk. I know you think I didn't mean...that I'm not......"

"Good with girls," Trina grinned.

"Yeah," Nat laughed. "Trina, I..."

"It's okay, Nat," she said as she stood. Nat reached out and grabbed her forearms and helped her into an upright position. They stood toe to toe, Trina's delicate belly buffering the empty space between them, standing close enough Nat could feel the life inside of Trina against her own body. "You don't have to explain," Trina said. "I know. I know."

They hugged. Warmly, tightly, like old friends who had been lost to one another for decades. They held on tight and with wet eyes looked at one another and smiled.

"What do I need some guy...some man, for?" Nat joked.

"Yeah," Trina said.

They kissed tenderly; and when they broke, Nat exhaled deeply, feeling the breath completely drain from her body. Home, she thought. On this day, in this room, with this girl, she was home.

"We're going to have a baby!" Nat whispered excitedly and cupped Trina's belly with both hands.

Trina rolled her eyes and laughed. "Yeah, we sure as hell are."

"Let's have a Coke and a toast," Nat said as she took Trina's hand and led her out of the storeroom. Trina picked up the tiny Abe Lincoln head in her hand and followed.

"I've only got one question," Nat said as she reached inside the door and turned out the light.

"What's that?" Trina asked.

"Does this make you the girl?

small dogs press

Keep current on upcoming titles from
Small Dogs Press by visiting us
at http://www.smalldogspress.com.

Small Dogs Press, PO Box 4127, Seal Beach CA 90740.
info@smalldogspress.com